Susan Delle Cave lives in South-West London and her first novel was published about four years ago. She writes about the human condition and aims to encourage readers to reflect more deeply about the world we live in.

Before becoming a writer, she taught English and Modern Languages in a range of secondary schools.

Her interests include archaeology, the theatre and all types of music.

I dedicate *Being James Newhouse* to my nine grandchildren: Isabella, James, Jessica, Jasmine, Anthony, Susanna, Carlo, Francesco and Vincenzo.

And to my great granddaughter, Liliana.

Hoping they will, each in their own way, carry forward my love of the written word.

Susan Delle Cave

BEING JAMES NEWHOUSE

AUSTIN MACAULEY PUBLISHERS
LONDON * CAMBRIDGE * NEW YORK * SHARJAH

Copyright © Susan Delle Cave 2025

The right of Susan Delle Cave to be identified as author of this work has been asserted by the author in accordance with sections 77 and 78 of the Copyright, Designs and Patents Act 1988.

All rights reserved. No part of this publication may be reproduced, stored in a retrieval system, or transmitted in any form or by any means, electronic, mechanical, photocopying, recording, or otherwise, without the prior permission of the publishers.

Any person who commits any unauthorised act in relation to this publication may be liable to criminal prosecution and civil claims for damages.

This is a work of fiction. Names, characters, businesses, places, events, locales, and incidents are either the products of the author's imagination or used in a fictitious manner. Any resemblance to actual persons, living or dead, or actual events is purely coincidental.

A CIP catalogue record for this title is available from the British Library.

ISBN 9781035888252 (Paperback)
ISBN 9781035888269 (ePub e-book)

www.austinmacauley.com

First Published 2025
Austin Macauley Publishers Ltd®
1 Canada Square
Canary Wharf
London
E14 5AA

A special thank you goes to Tommaso, Francesca, and Isabella, who patiently sort things out when they go wrong and enable me to complete all the online tasks for publication.

Table of Contents

Author's Note	11
Prologue	12
Part 1: The Speckled Ectrum	15
Chapter 1: Margaret	17
Chapter 2: 'With the Beatles'	24
Chapter 3: Somewhere Near Penzance	29
Chapter 4: Arthek and Marazion	34
Chapter 5: In the Mouth of the Cave	39
Chapter 6: A Short Story Competition	45
Chapter 7: Big Brother	50
Chapter 8: The Trip That Wasn't	54
Chapter 9: Moon Struck	58
Chapter 10: Harriet	64
Chapter 11: Narnia	69
Chapter 12: Harriet's Visit	75
Chapter 13: Home Truths	80
Chapter 14: Getting Active	86
Chapter 15: The Holidays	91
Chapter 16: Alexander Pope	95

Part 2: Eight Years Later…   **101**

Chapter 17: Patched; Fixed   *103*

Chapter 18: James's New Chapter   *108*

Chapter 19: In the Abercorn Arms   *113*

Chapter 20: Light on Water   *118*

Chapter 21: The Choir   *124*

Chapter 22: The Tourist   *128*

Chapter 23: The Replacement Child   *133*

Chapter 24: James and Dolly; James and Harriet   *139*

Chapter 25: November Pain   *145*

Chapter 26: Ed   *150*

Chapter 27: The Return of Dionysus   *157*

Chapter 28: The Wedding Web   *162*

Chapter 29: Big Unavoidable Once in a Lifetime Event   *167*

Chapter 30: Immacolata   *172*

Chapter 31: Dilemma   *177*

Chapter 32: Aftermath   *182*

Chapter 33: Preamble   *188*

Chapter 34: The Whole Truth…   *193*

Chapter 35: DNA   *199*

Chapter 36: "Mirror, Mirror…"   *205*

Chapter 37: Comparisons   *210*

Chapter 38: Lorenzo De Martino   *215*

Chapter 39: A Brief Heart to Heart… With Himself   *220*

Chapter 40: The Unburdening   *223*

Epilogue   *228*

Author's Note

My first choice of title for this novel, the last in the *Casa Stella* trilogy, was in fact, *The Speckled Ectrum*…

Echoes of biologist David Attenborough perhaps. With a hint of wordsmith Roald Dahl? The image of a rare and exotic bird, or merely a childish play on words?

In truth, a title that in an unguarded moment, had simply flung itself at me.

Of course, it was never to be. Awkward, nonsensical and non-existent. And on a practical note, would defy the talents of the most gifted translator.

However, it simply refused to go away. It felt perfect not only for what I had set out to convey but also connected to a late and deeply personal discovery I made during the writing of this novel. I thus felt compelled to include it.

Without apology then, I transferred the words *The Speckled Ectrum*, to head Part One of what has since become…*Being James Newhouse*.

Prologue

Spiralling...

I watched the pair of little white legs above me. From behind, from the side. On the move. Backs of knees bend and stretch. One two, one two. Ever ascending. Long grey ribbed socks, one pulled up a bit higher; school shoes, shiny black, which clattered. Up and up, round and round, up and round again. How many steps, did they say? 500, 550...? Like the other boys, I had long stopped counting.

It had been fine at first. As an idea. Climbing to the top of a tall and ancient structure. How exciting, how many times had I played out a world of knights, dragons and castles in my bedroom or in my head! Now, in the open air. Away from the clammy claustrophobia of school...Our parents having paid extra for the travel and visit. Therefore something good, something of value. We could learn while having fun, they said.

The first ten steps, not much of a problem at all!

I wanted to scream out but lacked the voice, lacked the courage. I wanted to tell them that I needed to wind myself back down that vicious coil. Yet how could I? An army of identical white legs in grey socks, firmly anchored in sturdy shoes was marching right behind me, each little body connected to those legs and shoes, taking up practically all the available space...and air.

Never will I forget the smell or touch of that day's ancient stone. A memory, wedged in my brain (and nostrils) forever. Lurking well beneath the surface of my skin, my fingertips. The ancient smell of cold damp mossy fungus. I cried out in silence for a return to the lessons of the sterile classroom; history was after all my favourite subject then. The invading Romans, the Angles, Saxons and Jutes, the Vikings. The Ancient Greeks and Egyptians. All set out in books. Safe. You can't get better than that.

I hated this 'open-air' experience of the past. The evil staircase curling its way ever higher. Targeting me in particular, closing in on me, its rounded sides becoming ever narrower. Like being born, but dying instead.

Teachers' echoey voices funnelling down from above or could it be from below? Head in a spin, I'd lost my bearings, my sense of where the adults were…and how far up I might be. Was I there at all? Was I even me? Did voices mean it was nearly at an end? That we were almost at the top, properly able to open our lungs. Oh, please God, please, release me from this torture. No reply. Except for those same adult voices threading through their same instructions. Keep moving, don't slow down. Keep to that rhythm. Think of who is behind you. Keep sight of who is in front. With me barely able to breathe, dying perhaps, and nobody knew. Way beyond the teachers' or the other boys' sensitivities, their inability to think to ask, let alone empathise. Out of reach. With me wearing a chest as tight as stretched rubber, palms sickly wet, fingers skimming the next cold cobble step or furry bit of wall for anchorage. Round and round. Up and up. Don't look up beyond the child in front, don't look down.

Still not there. Still to be squeezed out, like paste in a tube, out of the vertical tomb.

The others clearly ecstatic with anticipation. Their childish chatter, their wows and oohs, their breathless, nervous laughter. Hungry for the promised views. Now mountaineers as well as history detectives. Hungry for more adventure…

Next time, next time…I will know what to do. If not able to get out of it, make up an excuse to go last, providing if necessary, an escape route.

This is how I have learnt to deal with life when it hounds me. From all the bad stuff. A mounting pile of cowardice. It has made me cunning…a cunning directed at me alone, which brings temporary relief and comfort…but never manages to help with anything unknown or unanticipated. Never cures me. It has left me hating myself for hurting, for being useless. My real self…condemned to anonymity.

Did anyone else ever feel like me…fearful of life itself, not just sky-high, narrow staircases, which could from then on be avoided…instead leaving me clinging on, and only just, to the same shameful secret? A crouching secret, yet one also bursting to escape its cage. Could there really exist someone else like me, locked in a separate brain and body, living the same sordid experience?

A fantastical notion. All signs wailing the words that I was the only one.

Back to that day. Not yet released from that day's nightmare, conscious that I still had to make my way down the spiralling steps. That would surely be much easier…strangely, I can't remember that bit at all. Only that I think I was closest to the last descending teacher.

I learned nothing about castles…or cathedrals that day, not even remembering which structure it actually was. Not remembering a single detail of what we had to try to make out from the battlements. The all-important view. Needing air but unwilling to stand too close to the edge, yet another congenital fear…Just a passive, wistful curiosity drawing me far away, to the waves of migrating birds in a clear blue distance. As they made their escape to kinder climes…to freedom.

Only years later did my brain allow the name of the place to return to me.

Part 1
The Speckled Ectrum

Chapter 1
Margaret

Margaret caught on the edge of the precarious web of her mid-30s looked down onto the street from her bedroom on the first floor. Vaguely relieved that it had stopped raining. Failing to appreciate, precisely because she hadn't bothered to notice, the delicate constellations of tiny wet rain diamonds clinging to the windowpane…

Staring out, amid the garish yellow light produced by a line of lampposts, while her attention flickered to the swish of a few passing cars.

Then back in the moment, she reapplied her lipstick, with its absurd name of 'cherries in the snow', followed by a dabbing of cheeks, forehead and chin with some pale beige powder from something she called a compact, complete with little round mirror that once again needed polishing. Always leaving the brushing of hair until last. A tiny mindless yet necessary ritual she performed each evening, coinciding with her husband's expected arrival at the railway station, followed by the fifteen-minute walk to his home. The quilted housecoat, with its three-quarter length sleeves, which she had worn for most of the day, now discarded from view, as was an apron hanging from a hook behind the scullery door.

Now exposing a grey skirt and pale blue twinset.

Time, in those days, chopped itself into neat little segments within the wider boundaries of day and night, 9 to 5, weekdays and weekends, with Sundays different again, as everything shut its doors for an unquestioned 'day of rest', when for just a few hours, only the pubs and churches were open. No merging or blurring of the edges, little room (or desire apparently) for flexibility. Certainly not for their type of people. Men with their Monday to Friday work outside of the home…and if married, their wives remaining on the inside to wave goodbye, greet them on their return and see to the family's daily domestic needs.

Looking after any children, which usually meant two or three per nuclear family. Middle-class women lacking autonomy and yet at the same time propped on top of a mental and social pedestal.

A myriad of books on housekeeping to glorify them. A wealth of dedicated magazines, littering homes (as did an avalanche of sewing and knitting patterns), the magazines bearing such titles as Woman, Woman's Own, Woman and Home, My Weekly and whose contents taught a vast and loyal readership how to run their homes even more efficiently, how better to economise, cook, bake, knit, embroider, darn and sew. How to apply eye shadow, the latest shades of blue and green. Little scope then to make even minor changes to the status quo. Perhaps nobody thought to, not least the women themselves. People merely looking straight ahead. Following a system that seemed to work for them. An antidote to the chaos and slowly fading memory of wartime devastation, yet not without its own set of unspoken sacrifices. All in the cause for a stable present and future, the creation of a new, war-free and healthy generation, who were already benefitting from the daily spoonful of foul-tasting cod liver oil and the contents of little bottles of orange juice.

Margaret, likewise part of the system, entrenched in her own role of wife and mother, had long 'decided' that it was her duty to be first up. So from Monday to Friday, she tiptoed her way downstairs at six o'clock each morning to check the house was ready for everyone and for their lives on the outside. That she hadn't forgotten anything. Then wake them all up at pre-established times, which allowed for a smooth flow in and out of the only bathroom, all of which would guarantee a punctual arrival…at school or the workplace. She would prepare breakfast for them: cereal or toast and marmalade, a pot of tea, which squatted under a rust-coloured, hand-knitted cosy…and after piling the clutter of used bowls and cutlery into the sink, would briskly walk James to his school. (By now, their elder child Harriet able to make her own way to hers by bus). Followed by some light shopping and equally light household chores.

Clearing away, flower arranging, lining a drawer or two, (feather) dusting, putting underwear into soak. Each weekday identical to the next, Margaret, like many others, having abandoned the ancient convention of washing on a Monday, ironing on a Tuesday and so on, as immortalised in a range of children's rhymes. For company, only the wireless voices of 'the Archers' breaking through the silence. She remembering to lay out Raymond's suit, tie, socks and underwear the night before, as she did with her children's school uniforms. Checking for previously missed stains or creases, removing bits of fluff and making doubly sure pleats still looked sharp.

Saturdays and Sundays, she would concede herself a much-needed lie-in, sometimes up to sixty minutes. Later in the day, only when convenient of course, she would take a long soak in the bathtub, into which she either crumbled a couple of rock-hard scented tablets or poured a slowly vanishing trail of brightly coloured bath salts, whichever she chose for the occasion.

The understated comfort of habit, duty, punctuality. Stiff upper lip. Everything and everyone in its, his or her correct place. She, like many of the women of her 'kind' not seeming to question whether there might exist a different way of using or arranging her time, a different way of thinking, which might allow for a modicum, at least, of self-expression, of escape from such a humdrum, albeit pain-free existence. To follow one's dreams. Safety in numbers.

Margaret was unusual, however, in that she had never learnt to cook properly, and always skipped those magazine pages devoted to recipes. Food and the digestive process had always disgusted her. She was fortunate in that her husband did not aspire to a gourmet diet and that he earned enough money to pay a local woman to come round and produce an array of nourishing meals for the family four times a week. Also for a charlady to handle the heavier housework, anything which involved mangles and ladders, scrubbing brushes and heavy buckets of water, coal bunkers or messy spring-cleaning which in the Newhouse household took place continuously through each of the four seasons. Neither did her husband ever make a fuss about it, accepting that she was, in every other way a loyal, diligent wife and mother.

On Saturdays, regardless of the weather, Raymond liked to spend a few hours working by himself in the garden. Margaret would attempt to rustle up something straightforward for lunch: a ham salad, or leftover shepherd's pie, or lamb chops with mashed potato. Followed by tinned peaches and cream or stewed apple with custard. Fridays spelt fish and chips. Teatime was a much easier affair, with no actual cooking involved. On a Sunday, they would usually eat at Raymond's sister's house. The much-anticipated roast dinner.

She bizarrely, clinging to the notion that she came from a line of French aristocracy…a family of barons or baronets. No one in the family took the claim seriously, in spite of her regal ways, or became sufficiently interested to find out more, establishing, finally, if there was indeed any truth to the story. With her own parents having died when she was a young girl and no other (known) living relatives. 'Reduced' to middle-class serfdom or should that be wife and mother status?

Her children, still too young to care about family history. Which child looks back into their own past? Their thoughts ever projecting forward.

That all comes later…

Although Margaret had given up speaking about it, she felt it important to maintain her own imagined standards of such a noble bloodline. For her to continue to play the part at all times, to present a perfect image of herself to those around her. Especially in the 'lesser' things, things that only left a vague impression: posture (very straight back at all times whether standing or seated.) A respectable if not royal way when sitting, especially as regards the arrangement of her legs. Always sporting a vague, semi-fixed smile (so never allowing her mouth to droop at the corners), and a certain way of moving across a room, deliberate but never less than graceful and dignified. The way she articulated vowels and clearly pronounced key consonants, whenever in conversation.

Hands under control. Legs, hence feet, never apart. Trying as hard as possible…because this was the most difficult…not to speak badly about anyone, to keep buried any pain, bitterness or hostility she might feel. Perhaps they had taught her this as a child, 'part and parcel' of such a heritage, and then mixed it up with a generous dose of Christian conduct. Perhaps, she had merely invented such niceties along the way, believing that to be what people would expect from someone of her (secret) social position? Nobody really knew, never took it upon themselves to consider. It also fitted quite neatly into the 1950s zeitgeist…

If she was disappointed with her family's lack of response, she never showed it, dealing with it just as she did with everything else. Keeping all emotions…including those heart-wrenching moments…packed away in her head or the pages of notebooks and fancy little boxes.

There was an unexpected couple of knocks on the bedroom door, followed by a male voice, "Peggy, are you decent? May I come in?"

So bizarre and awkward that he was back so soon. It had never happened before, never home before 6 pm.

For some reason, it was usual then for women called Margaret to have the nickname, Peggy.

She loathed the name Peggy. Why did he use it? What did it have to do with her? Someone of her standing. Surely, he should realise even though she had never actually told him. Once or twice in the past, he had sunk even lower…he had referred to her as Peg. Peg? It rhymed with egg, eggs, which gave off a bad smell. She never ate them. Peg leg, stump, dark gaping mouths revealing the remains of decaying teeth…a stick of broken off splintery wood, rising out of the sludge…Peg, which rhymed with 'beg' and with 'keg' of beer. Eggy Peggy.

The image of her father once again floated into view; her father, who she was certain, had always called her his 'petite Marguerite', each syllable articulated with just a hint of silky French accent…surely not an illusion. He really had been there at her side.

She smoothed the bedcovers for the umpteenth time that day, each time in fact she entered the room…pink candlewick tightly spread over each of the closely positioned twin beds…calling out as she did so, "Yes, dear, I'm decent, and I'm coming now." Unlocking the door, she realised that he was already making his way back downstairs.

As always, the evening meal taking place in relative silence; Raymond tired, more often than not, but seemingly satisfied with his day at work. The children having learnt, that now was not the time for idle chatter.

Harriet would continue the latest account of her own day in the classroom, once she and her brother were back upstairs. Possessing a talent for making even the most mundane of days sound important or exciting. Today she had chosen to mimic a new teacher, a Mr Whitehead, which left her younger brother James (as always) in fits of laughter, as she strode around her bedroom with outrageously tousled hair, fake spectacles, sticking out her top teeth as far as they would go, so that they protruded from her mouth. Splattering out the words, "Now which one of you knows the Latin word for aeroplane? Hahaha." "Which two Ancient Greek heroes share the name with a scouring powder your mothers use in the kitchen and bathroom? Hahaha."

The poor diminished teacher, oblivious to the fact that his efforts that day to be jokey and popular had not borne fruit and that his appearance and now reputation, things he could now do little about, would always go before him.

Once her brother had run out of complimentary giggles and his sides had stopped splitting, Harriet shooed him out of her sacred space, suddenly declaring that she still had lots of important homework to finish and that he was in the way. Shoo, shoo.

James left on his own once more.

Somewhere between the evening meal and his established time for bed…a kind of indoor 'twilight'…James liked to install himself on the stairs, about halfway down, just below the bend. He felt strangely comfortable there, in this open and yet undisturbed place. Unbeknown to the rest of his family, he could hear and sometimes glimpse that other world, a world that, as he grew, fascinated him more and more (quite different from his sister's), a world of adults…a secret world of whispers, half-finished phrases and words or comments he didn't know the meaning of. A world, which he tried to make sense of by putting together…often meagre…scraps of evidence, with every likelihood, getting the wrong idea of what he thought they had been saying.

In the summer months, he could also carry out such reconnaissance activity during daylight hours. There was an outside lavatory, or privy, that no one had thought to dismantle, situated, 'conveniently' for James, very close to the kitchen itself. As far as he knew, no one in the family used it for its original purpose. Warm weather spelt open windows, and if he stood on top of the black lavatory seat, he could peer, practically unnoticed, into the kitchen, getting a very good view of any comings and goings. Even better at weekends, when both his parents were present. He had become the latest spy recruit from 'The Man from U.N.C.L.E'. …morphing now into James Newhouse Kuryakin.

What did he think of his parents thus far?

Well, if put on the spot, he would have to admit that he preferred his father. He was a man. This meant having a proper life: a job in the City. With a sister in the ample shape of Aunty Hilda, with whom Raymond enjoyed lively discussions on the current state of the world.

He had outside interests, gardening, in particular; was partial to cricket, and sang in the church choir. He could also drive a car.

His mother didn't appear to have a life at all. Or any relatives. All she did was float and hover around the place, mostly out of the way, popping up only when needed. Even what she did do was invisible. This made him feel a bit sad but for the most part, grateful that he had been born male. Assuming then that this was the fate of nearly all women.

Therefore, James encountered that 'other' world, whether clinging on to the bannisters, or from his outside lavatory perch, places no one else noticed, where no one else would think of occupying. It marked the time of day when children his age were already out of sight. There would soon be the 'called up' reminders to brush their teeth, say their prayers and climb into the covers…and that, in his case, his mother would soon be popping her head round the door to say goodnight and switch off the light. That special space between day and night, light and dark…appearance and reality. From his own halfway position on the staircase. 'Undercover' in an unused toilet, which in spring and summer doubled as a lookout tower.

Once in bed, the secrecy continued, with James reading an adventure book, under the covers now, while pretending to sleep, with the help of a little torch.

Chapter 2
'With the Beatles'

James, from an early age, had never liked people very much, in spite of a somewhat morbid interest in their 'day-to-day' behaviour and habits, in what made them tick. Contradicting the sometimes misleading truism that 'man is by nature a social creature'.

However, he didn't really dislike people either. Having to accept that they were there, of course, but at the same time, sensing that they had little to do with him or his place in the world. To avoid when possible, once the school day (or 'spying' session) ended. Beyond the necessary people to feed and clothe him. To educate him. Provide him with 'a roof over his head', which was one of his father's favourite expressions. To walk him to and from school, until reaching the day, when they suddenly announced that it was high time for him to start going by himself.

He wouldn't have thought about it in quite those terms back then, but little by little as he manoeuvred his way through early adolescence, this notion of being 'unconnected' was becoming ever clearer. In an almost mystical way, he believed himself anonymous, close to invisible even. Never one to draw attention to himself. No one had made him like this. It was no one's fault or doing. He bore no grudges. It was simply fact. And he had even, gradually, found a way of getting used to this unusual state of affairs, learning to live alongside it…even revelling in it on the odd occasion.

Separate, when life wasn't being awful, felt like superior. Close to all-knowing.

In later years, he sometimes found himself thinking back to his early life and in particular to his schooldays. How in spite of any awkwardness vis-a-vis others, it appeared that he had always had friends to play with, had generally gone along with the wishes of his parents and teachers, and on the surface, at least, had followed most of life's good advice. He was hardly rebellious in the normal sense. There were very few bouts of erupting anger. Not your stereotypical outsider or black sheep. Never shunned. Only the most perceptive onlooker able to detect that something might be amiss, or at least different about him. Something about the strained expression, perhaps, unusual on such a young face?

Perceptive onlookers naturally in short supply…

He fixed his thoughts way back to a particular Christmas. A memory, which often returned to him, having turned out to be his favourite Christmas ever. Something no one else could have understood. Nothing whatsoever to do with Santa Claus or pulling festive crackers. The only one, as far as he could remember, that had left a profound impression upon him. At about 7 pm on that evening of the 25th December, he had found himself in the front room of his home, with just one frugally dressed pine tree for company, after the rest of his family had, fortunately, more or less forgotten about him. Perhaps assuming he had dozed off after such a long day, and that he was in his room.

In that darkened living room, he placed a brand new Beatles LP onto the turntable of the family gramophone, and within minutes, it had become his most precious possession to date. That Holy Night he had listened to its 14 songs as they escaped from within the cumbersome lump of furniture, which squatted along the opposite wall. A magic wand had tapped his parents' and sister's shoulders, causing them to leave him alone. Allowing him to breathe in the scent of wax polish and pine needles, which came in wafts, and stare into the monochrome record sleeve. At those four half-shaded heads, suspended as if in outer space, three at the top and one bottom right, listening to the sounds of John, George, Paul, and Ringo.

Their music had suddenly become his music. His…even though he shared it with countless other teenagers. With those who had already encountered it. However, he felt from deep within that The Beatles had written and recorded each song for him alone…because they knew something of that 'other world'. Their music stroked his soul. Whatever that meant, but he liked the sound of it. No need to find out what…if anything…lay below the surface. Lyrics and melody consorting in liquid form. Songs about love and the pain it caused, something huge he hadn't yet experienced…but that didn't concern him. The songs simply flowing into him…he needing nothing more. The very best Christmas of his young life. Spent alone in a room with pop music and a tree.

Those solitary hours took him light years away from current circumstances: school, which seemed never-ending, and then the farcical world of his parents and sister, who that night, together with some neighbours were sitting and chatting, watching the TV, and playing board games, just a room away. Normal people doing normal Christmassy things.

The 'espionage' sessions continued, on and off, for at least another year or two. It had reached a stage when it was no longer enough to look and listen, but James felt he now needed to keep a record. Have something tangible to work on, return to and think about. Admittedly not for the majority of his findings. That would have been tedious, both to write up and revisit. He simply dismissed a lot of what he saw and heard. No, James' notebook contained what he considered matters of significance: the colourful phrases he didn't quite understand, proverbs, swear words (all of which he deemed had to do with God or sex), quasi-philosophical sayings, half-heard statements or bits of cryptic conversation, something said by someone that appeared out of character. Extending to things that he found original or witty…a very rare event…which he might use one day, though wouldn't have known quite where or with whom. All with dates, places and names attached.

No one was exempt. He chose to listen in on anything and anyone. The neighbour's dog, the man who brought the post, the milkman, the man who picked up the laundry, the charlady. Even the rag and bone man, whose alien lifestyle he found particularly fascinating, assuming that he dwelt in some kind of robbers' cave. The familiar band of local shopkeepers. His parents, and more and more, his sister, who was now trying to hide the fact that she was on the lookout for a boyfriend. His aunt and uncle on a Sunday, whose conversations, when compared to his parents, he found much more stimulating, due to their vast circle of friends, which in turn broadened their own horizons. It was hard work, which he had to squeeze into an already tight schedule of school and chores at home. It was now much more than a hobby. It was a necessity…the secrecy serving to increase the pleasure.

Most of the time he remained unnoticed, as did the accompanying notebook. Something that he had 'borrowed' one afternoon from the school's stationery cupboard when a teacher had sent him there to fetch a pile of copies of *Great Expectations*. Surprisingly, teachers' lives weren't of much interest, because he instinctively knew they couldn't really be themselves at school (or so he imagined) as they had to keep up appearances, in order to maintain their individual worth, their intellectual credibility to the rest of the school community. Professionalism. Everyone, however, students included, able to guess who 'ruled the roost' in the staffroom, the ones who lay claim to the best chairs, a certain place at the central table, and not necessarily those who'd been there the longest or were considered the most inspiring. A seething hierarchical hotbed.

James, the boy, amused himself experimenting with cryptic codes so that if the notebook were ever found, it wouldn't mean anything much to the finder. The pages deliberately interspersed with sketches, poems and sayings, which everyone already knew he collected.

He then took on his most ambitious task to date, which was at a party held at his family home. Having forgotten the reason why his parents had chosen to host such an event…the only party ever held there to his knowledge. He did remember, however, having to be on hand to welcome guests in the hallway see to their coats and handbags, indicate the location of the vast bowl of punch set out on a sideboard, and take round trays of vol-au-vents. It opened his eyes even wider to a different type of people, some, strange though it seemed, nothing like his parents at all. Harriet was in her element, as she charmed and chatted her way through the evening, by now looking and feeling very grown up. Even James having to acknowledge a glint of inner pride at this, her 'coming out'.

From the woman in the purple dress, "…I don't agree at all. We should be grateful for religion. I'm saying that as a staunch agnostic. Think of the state of the art world without Christianity for example. No 'Pieta', no 'Last Supper', no Sistine Chapel, no Transfiguration, or St Paul's Cathedral, come to that. I could go on and on (she really could) and just think, of the thousands of tiny villages, dotted all over England. Imagine those same places without their pretty, little churches, fixed at the centre of each tiny community. Their stained glass windows offer up a vast picture book of biblical stories for the illiterate, their Norman and Gothic style architecture. Sacred places which witness the high points of human existence…birth, marriage and death. On the basis of art and architecture alone, we have to appreciate what religion has given us…the inspiration…"

"…yes, but art isn't the reason we have religion, is it? Art and architecture are just a byproduct. For the few who have found a way of outgrowing the appeal of an established religion, there's no going back…unless people feel the need to replace it with something else…" Interjection from the man with a lazy eye.

All of a sudden, a male voice rang out, a voice theatrically loaded, "Here ladies, come, come and get a sprig of bright yellow mimosa. Find somewhere to keep it safe for the rest of the evening. Pin it to your frocks, fix it in your hair. What do your husbands know? It takes a foreigner to show these Englishmen of yours how to appreciate the pinnacle of God's creation…woman. Where would we be without them…? Come, come, yes don't be scared…it's a token of appreciation, a celebration of the female…"

The words booming from the wide grin of a balding man, complete with short, black cloak, and what turned out to be a strong continental accent…James later finding out he was Italian…had definitely stopped the guests in their tracks, both male and female. A few of the women, including Harriet, tentatively lining up to collect one of the flower sprays, with their floppy, feathery leaves and tiny puffball flowers. To see what it all meant. (It so happened to be the 8th of March). Then little by little, others gaining in confidence now, themselves joining the queue.

James later caught sight of his mother in the corner of the room seemingly without her own sprig of yellow mimosa. If he hadn't known better, he would have guessed she'd been dabbing a stray tear or two from running too far down her cheek. She was with his aunt and two other women that he didn't recognise, and yet, strangely removed from them and their whispery conversation. They then suddenly stood up, each going their separate ways. His mother returning to her evening duties…refilling glasses, checking that everyone had someone to speak to and had enough food on their plates…as though nothing had happened.

Chapter 3
Somewhere Near Penzance

For a few summers in a row, the Newhouses took to spending a fortnight in a quiet seaside town, somewhere near Penzance, turning up at the same hotel as soon as the school holidays began. No one seemed to remember why the family had opted for that far-flung limb of the British Isles, admittedly a richly intriguing part of the country…Raymond Newhouse driving them there and back in his reliable black Wolseley, which spent most of its 'other' life in the garage attached to the house.

For an unsuspecting James, Cornwall would turn out to be a place of existential significance.

Each of the 14 days ran along the same lines: with three meals always taken in the hotel restaurant, as well as tea in the dining room between 4 pm and 5 pm. Most mornings and late afternoons, the family would make their way down to the nearby beach, which spread itself over a mile or so along the shore, in the form of sand dunes, its upper levels covered in bold tufts of long windswept grass. The sand's tiny grains made up of countless trillions of pulverised, prehistoric sea shells, so the holiday brochures claimed. The beach therefore delivering up a satisfyingly wild-looking appearance.

On fine days, James spent most of the time jumping in and over the never-ending wavy lines of lacy surf. He also enjoyed creating sandcastles and engineering a maze of water channels; he played beach ball with his father (and sometimes even with Harriet) on the wet sand, just as the tide was receding, or explored nearby rock pools for little crabs and any other trapped marine finds. Harriet likewise kept herself busy, swimming or just roaming along their stretch of beach. Sometimes even stopping to chat to people, some of whom she recognised from the hotel.

Margaret, dwarfed by a wide straw hat, never appeared to want to join in with any of this, but instead sat welded to a rented deckchair, as she leafed her way through pages of daily newspaper and a pile of magazines. Sometimes staring out through her large sunglasses, past the other holidaymakers dotted here and there, at that last bit of English Channel before it became ocean. Her knitting she left in her hotel room to prevent the sand from ruining it.

For James and Harriet, wet days normally spelled table tennis in the games room, or playing board games, which children could borrow from the hotel owners, who lectured them on treating them 'with utmost care', always deploying the same words and cautionary tones. After the evening meal, they would then read until bedtime. A healthy mixture of comics, magazines, non-fiction and storybooks. Or sometimes do crosswords or write their postcards…if only to get that particular chore out of the way and so put a stop to their mother's grating reminders.

There was also what was to become the annual pilgrimage over to St Michael's Mount. A massive lump of grey granite, which stuck up out of the sea, doubling as a tidal island, and which even boasted its own medieval castle. The Mount, of course, reachable by foot only at low tide with the causeway taking about 15 or 20 minutes to cross. Seemingly much longer for a child with a head spinning from the need for pirates, shipwrecks or similar high drama. James having already devoured the likes of Treasure Island, Moby Dick, and the very English Swallows and Amazons.

During what must have been about their fourth Cornish visit (and about halfway through that particular holiday), he happened to witness a somewhat embarrassing scene unfolding in the hotel lobby, which held him transfixed. A new family had arrived a day or two beforehand…James having already noticed the girl…The receptionist had apparently called them all to the front desk. It looked and sounded as though an argument was on the point of erupting; something about hotel guests locked inside their room for over three hours. It turned out that an exasperated Mr and Mrs Douglas Blanchflower had banged on their door and shouted for help, but unfortunately, there had been no one around (not even someone they could see passing by outside), no fellow guests nor staff to rescue them. Their cries that afternoon all the while going unnoticed.

The Blanchflowers turned out to be an elderly married couple, whose creased and crumpled faces betrayed who they once might have been. Faces now even more ravaged by their shared mood of bellicose intransigence.

James realised that he had seen them before, as they were perennial visitors to this establishment and therefore always treated with utmost care by each member of the hotel staff. The 'VIPs' having adopted, however, the rather unwise habit of leaving the key to their room in the lock on the outside. Incidentally, James learning that the key had also gone missing.

It emerged, through process of elimination (and a good dose of prejudice against young boys) that the most likely culprit just had to be the 'new' girl's brother…who, surely like most of that gender and age group, had a somewhat shifty and wayward look about him.

The hotel manager then arrived on the scene, smoothing down his hair and pulling the features of his face into professional mode, all the while doing his best to lead the noisy throng swiftly away into a more private area, from where James, if he concentrated hard, was still able to follow proceedings.

"I told you. It wasn't me. I know nothing about it," protested the boy, aged about 12, going quite red in the face and almost crying out of sheer frustration. "Why pick on me? Just because our room is next door. It could have been anyone, even someone who works here. It's a stupid thing to do anyway, who in their right mind would leave the key in the door…?"

Perhaps, not the wisest of comments at this delicate time, James being acutely aware of the hole that the boy appeared to be digging for himself.

"Are you really telling me, son, that it wasn't you then? If you just own up and say sorry now, explain that it was just a silly joke, I'm sure Mr and Mrs Blanchflower will, in time, come to forgive you. Come on, boy, if it was you, be brave and take it on the chin, let's just clear the matter up now…" cajoled his father.

"No, I won't!" persisted the boy, whose name turned out to be William. "How can I say sorry for something I haven't done, something I know nothing about? The key was in the door the last time I saw it. Why would I want to steal it? Why does everyone always blame me? It's just not fair…"

William's father and the hotel manager now exchanging meaningful glances, one which begged support, and one which revealed hesitation. As far as the father was concerned, he wanted to know what evidence there was that it had been his son, and yet neither did he wish to appear weak, weak in front of a mere boy, predictably running rings round him. Yes, William did occasionally tell lies, didn't everyone? Children and adults alike. However not to the extent, that he could describe his son as a pathological teller of untruths. Surely, William would have known that if it had been a joke gone wrong, now would be the time to confess and apologise, just to 'bring the matter to a close'. They were on holiday after all. He had had his fun. The Blanchflowers were, by the expression on their faces, holding out for a severe penalty, for justice. They were the victims. Using their advanced years and reminders of loyal hotel patronage to best effect. The manager was now under extreme pressure…

It was the girl who had once again caught James's attention, William's older sister. Silent, and so different from her sibling in stance and manner. From her intensely sparkling eyes, he could tell that she was enjoying every minute of this 'family fiasco'…as her head switched back and forth from face to face to face, whichever happened to be doing the talking. Displaying an exaggerated wide-eyed innocence, and yet never bothering to put a good word in regarding her brother's character or even create an alibi for him…

Just then, James's mother appeared on the scene, beckoning him furiously from just below the little mezzanine landing, to follow her, at once, to the restaurant area. What bad timing! So annoying! He probably would never get to know the outcome now…

Somehow, and of course, it was only a hunch, he felt certain that William had been telling the truth and that it was possible his sister knew much more about the unfortunate incident than she was letting on…and it wasn't just because boys naturally defended one another.

All through the meal, James continued processing all that he had just witnessed, hoping that William's family would eventually join the other guests for the 7 to 8 pm sitting. That the expressions on their faces might reveal a clue or two as to what was going to happen next. Yet, sadly, they didn't make an appearance, not even the ancient Blanchflower couple, who were probably eating off trays inside their room. Did it mean that William's family had been 'sent packing', back to where they came from? Did the manager finally succeed in getting a written or at least verbal confession from him? What punishment, other than banishment from the premises, would he have to face? James only had his imagination to help him work it all out. He decided to keep all this from his own family; it was his discovery, his intrigue to unravel.

No one could have been more surprised than James then, when the following morning, both William's family and Mr and Mrs Blanchflower were back in the dining room, albeit on tables positioned on diagonally opposite sides of the rectangular room. Everything back as it was, as though James had dreamed it all up during a long, warm summer night's sleep.

He watched William and his sister on the beach that morning with even greater attention than normal. The boy obviously spending much of his time having fun in the sea, the girl preferring to walk along the wet sands, every so often stooping down to pick something up, and then popping it into the large plastic bucket she was carrying. She would then take him by surprise, by putting down the bucket and producing a sudden chain of cartwheels, almost as though she knew she had an audience, but after, continued walking as though it had never happened. He thought he saw her look across at him a couple of times…but couldn't be sure. Perhaps that was what he wanted to happen…but he couldn't be sure of that either.

If that were the case, his luck was in later that afternoon. As James and his family were taking tea, she brushed past him on her way out of the tearoom, deftly tossing a little note into his lap without the rest of his family noticing. He dreaded to think what his sister Harriet would have made of it…she would have teased him mercilessly for the rest of their stay.

Making excuses to leave the table, he practically ran out of the room unable to wait a moment longer to discover what it said.

The girl had noticed him then. What could this possibly mean? Where might it lead?

Chapter 4
Arthek and Marazion

The note's words informing him: I will be in the games room. M.

Not stopping to ask himself why, James's only thought was to make his way there as soon as he could, once getting permission from his mother, of course. Unaware, that he could have pretended to ignore the note or at least, keep the girl waiting. He had half an hour…which didn't leave enough time to work out, what he was going to say or what exactly she might be expecting of him. He found her sitting at a little round table, pretending to read an oversized, tatty-looking book, he remembered seeing there the year before, and most likely the one before that. She looked up at him, clutched his arm and took him round the corner of the room, even though there was no one else around…where there happened to be a couple of armchairs.

"Where are you from?" She demanded.

"London," he managed to reply, grateful that he had kept his answer vague.

"I love this place," she suddenly declared. "So different from home. I feel that I must have spent time here once, in another life. I sensed it even though I didn't exactly recognise anything…We first came here…a few years ago, but never during the summer."

"What's your name?" James asked, thinking that it was surely his turn to ask a question now, but frustratingly unable to produce something that matched her words or delivery. He had turned into a lump of clay and couldn't even remember if he had ever spoken to a girl before, well, not counting his sister of course. There again, this one didn't seem to match up to anything he thought he already knew about…girls. Feeling unsure as to what it was she wanted from him. If she even liked him. She didn't seem to care what his name was.

"Oh, I suppose I will have to tell you then. It's Dorcas, I know, simply ghastly, but it does have a nice meaning. It means 'gazelle'. I thought we could give ourselves new names actually, while we are here. You're usually called James, aren't you? I heard your mother use it. So, if you have any brilliant ideas, just let me hear them. I was thinking I might take the name Marazion, after the little town close by. What do you think?"

"Wwell, yyes, it's beautiful. (He wanted to add, 'like you', but was far too afraid.) Why don't you choose a Cornish-sounding name for me too…?"

She smiled impassively at this request, not giving him any outward sign, as to whether she would bother or even be willing, to take up the idea.

"I will see you on the beach tomorrow then. I've discovered a little cave. We will be safe there. It's very dark inside. There's a huge pebble…"

At which point, she jumped up, leaving James (or whichever local name she might choose for him) in a frozen daze. "Safe there…?" What did she mean? Safe from what or whom? Why had he let her do all the talking? She was obviously around his own age, maybe a bit older, he calculated. He knew hundreds of clever words. Why was it that he just couldn't think of anything clever to say now, when he really needed to…?

He could at least find a Cornish name for himself! He would go and speak to George, the young man in reception, and ask him if he knew any. If she disapproved or tried to change it, well, this time, he would stand his ground.

Marazion burrowed her way into his thoughts for the rest of the evening, even though as far as he was aware, he hadn't in effect invited her in.

Having noticed that she went barefoot, whenever she could, in and outside of the hotel. There was something mysterious about her, beyond the simply unconventional, beyond the fact she didn't appear to like footwear. He smelled a whiff of danger, horribly seductive, but James had already left that secure place within his family setup. There could be no return now. He had taken that first giant leap. Even though nothing had happened. Just a few words passing between them. James fixed on the epithet 'esoteric', one of his recent favourites. He wanted to solve the mystery; he wanted to ride the danger and pass the test. Somehow aware it might take him to…unknown places, that it might cause him pain.

Her image awaited him, once again, on waking the following morning. The thick brown hair, tied back from her face, the wide brown eyes, her dimpled smile. The battered straw hat, the habitual jeans or shorts and t-shirt, when not in the sea…

It seemed as though many hours had passed after breakfast, when his father Raymond did eventually pipe up with, "Everyone ready to go down to the beach, then?"

They all left their room, Margaret having dutifully prepared everything they might need in advance, all packed into a couple of enormous beach bags. After about five minutes of their alighting on what was now 'their' patch of decimated shell sand, Dorcas alias Marazion appeared out of nowhere, swiftly introducing herself to James's parents, and asking in an unexpected, even old-fashioned way (in reverse…she being the girl), if it would be alright that she could 'borrow' James for a little while. Not bothering to consult with the boy in question (or even acknowledge his sister). To which his parents could only agree. It seemed rather odd, but what possible harm could come to him? Four pairs of eyes fixed upon her, with a particularly bemused, yet unusually silent Harriet, left open-mouthed. (What was so special about him? Why waste time with her gangly younger brother?)

"What a nice girl and what charming manners!" Margaret finally gushed, as the girl led her son away.

"Well, that's sorted," said Marazion, as the two walked across the sands. "I don't suppose we shall be hearing from any of them for at least an hour or two, and every so often we can reappear from a distance, so they know everything's alright."

The words…why shouldn't it be? Now invading his head. "I have a Cornish name too. I've chosen Arthek."

"Oh, that's beautiful," she replied. "Perfect. It reminds me of Camelot and the Arthurian legends. Ok, so from now on, in our Cornish bodies and Cornish lives and whenever we are together, we are Marazion and Arthek."

They spent their shared time that morning fooling around in the sea. Laughing, while paddling, splashing each other, trying (unsuccessfully) to share an abandoned Li-lo, pretending to drown each other or slapping bits of loose seaweed onto each other's backs. Lots of fun, but nothing other than what 'normal' people did on summer holidays spent by the coast. No mention of the cave. He didn't mind though. He simply craved her company. To look at her, never trying to make it obvious, and therefore his admiration all the more obvious! She had freed her hair from the hat and out of its habitual ponytail, and it spread down her back, past her shoulders, made straight and even longer by its wetness. Sometimes strands of hair got caught up under her armpits and each time, fascinated, he watched her remove it. He decided that once in the water, she turned into a slithery mermaid as she cavorted in and out of the waves. Fearless. At ease.

Marazion didn't go on that day to show him the cave she had mentioned on the previous evening. Arthek, in spite of mounting curiosity and anticipation, was far too proud to remind her to take him there. It had in any case turned out to be a wonderful day.

During the hours and days that followed, James growing gnawingly conscious that his holiday was almost at an end, plucked up the courage to ask her if they could write to each other. Contorting all the while inside as the words rolled clumsily off his tongue. Full of passion on the inside and yet unable to make it sound natural, let alone an attractive proposition.

"Oh no, I don't think so," came the sniffy reply, as blunt as it was swift. "I have a pen pal already. It was fun at first. Now, I make up stuff in my letters, and she probably does too, just for the sake of clinging on to past friendship. Whereas, it's all meaningless. We both know it's over. We've said everything we had to say, well, anything that counted."

"Yeah, I see what you mean, but isn't it a bit sad for it to end just because you've run out of conversation? A bit heartless? There will be more to say as you both get older and do more in life. You must have liked her…at the beginning at least? Won't you miss her?"

"Haha, no, not at all! I have found you! I've also come up with a brilliant idea, much better than exchanging letters…no more Dear so and so, I hope this letter finds you well. As for me, I am fine…" adopting a contemptuous Joyce Grenfell-type accent.

"Tomorrow, we will go to the little cave I was telling you about, it's not far. In the meantime, try and remember those times when something scary or strange has happened to you, something that you haven't wanted to tell anyone about…Or a secret you are just bursting to share with someone, but can't or I don't know, something very bad you have done, and even got away with. A burning desire that seems to be getting closer…"

James, his head now spinning with nausea as if hit by a rounder's bat. He knew by now that she wouldn't reveal any more, nothing he could prise out of the unassailable shell, which shielded her. He was feeling hot and bothered, a potent mix of deliriously happy, deeply sad and yet angry too at her words. She was always 'streets ahead' of him, speaking and acting in ways previously unimagined. He sometimes felt he did have, in a subconscious way, an inkling of all that she meant and it scared him. There again, he could have been completely wrong.

Needless to say, James's parents wanted to know what she and their son had been doing, who she was, confirm her age, discover what kind of family she had, where they came from, hitherto unable to detect a regional accent…James was in the main unable to return a proper answer. He told them instead about the fun they had swimming, 'like playing with another boy, really' and that she had a pen pal. *Boys*, his mother and sister must have thought, *never can rely on them to ask the obvious, find out all the important things*! They also concluded, after a short discussion, that Dorcas was a strange-sounding name, one they had never come across, but James could then at last feed their curiosity, by stating that it had also been her grandmother's name.

Unsurprisingly, that night, he again did what Marazion wanted. He wracked his brain for what she needed to know. Perhaps it would double as an opportunity for her to come clean regarding the 'locked room' incident at the hotel. At least for this 'task' she had given him some preparation time. He made sure he wasn't going to be the only one spilling out childhood misdemeanours or future dreams, she might want to humiliate him over. On this, he would once again stand firm.

However, what exactly was he going to tell her? He had no idea. Not being his way of dealing with life. He learning as he went, and then moving on. Never until now revisiting past scrapes or worse…

Chapter 5
In the Mouth of the Cave

James's family was generally accepting of their son's holiday friendship with Dorcas. She appeared affable and considerate whenever in their company, taking the time to ask about how they were, what plans they had for the day and how much she would miss them, as their time in Cornwall was drawing to a close. Moreover, she always brought their son back safely at the given time.

James aware that she stage-managed everything to perfection. Aware that she showed great flair in her dealings with others.

The two finally made their way to the cave, their bodies appearing to draw closer together, the further away they walked. It took longer than Arthek had envisaged, not even convinced that there would be a cave at all.

It turned out he was wrong.

"This is the 'truth pebble'," she announced on arrival, wasting no time in picking up the bulky white-grey stone with its mottled and veiny beauty, surprisingly able to lift it using both hands. "I found it outside the entrance a few days ago and just knew it belonged to us. As we take it in turns to speak, we can clasp it close to our hearts, as a reminder to stay truthful. In this way, don't you see, our lives will be connected forever? Jointly purified. Much more than penpals or blood brothers. Our two lives indivisible; sealed. We will never tell anyone anything of what we hear today. No one else in the whole world will ever know, and even in the years to come, should one of us forget and leak something out, then it would mean nothing to the listener…anonymous acts and rantings from someone else's childhood, told as if third-hand…probably half-remembered if not totally made up."

She had thought everything through. He had learnt…in a split second…that there could now never be any kind of future contact between them. Outside of this time and place. A bittersweet experience then, but still the very best so far that life had had to offer, perhaps even greater than his first encounter with The Beatles. Unplanned, momentous and subtle. Not something James could fully appreciate then, he being too young, his naïve tongue tasting only its sadness.

Nevertheless, a new potency had surged inside him, bordering on the mystical…

The two would be making their farewells moments after sharing a unique intimacy. There was no way back for him, even though he knew that he could have run out of the cave at any moment, declaring that it was all nonsense. Back to the safety of his parents' cosy patch of sand. He could have called her crazy, saying that he wanted nothing to do with her wild plan. That all he had really wanted was to touch her cascading hair, and take her lovely hands into his…hanging feebly onto a quickly constructed dream that he would one day search the whole of Buckinghamshire until he found her again.

Something, however, much deeper and stronger, held him rooted to the spot. Something, which fed into yet another need of his. He looked down at the cold, unfriendly pebble, gathering his most recent thoughts and wondering how he would express them when it came for his time to open up. Perhaps the ordeal would somehow take care of itself…it would have to.

They both sat down and at an agreed centre of the cave, Arthek went first, of his own accord, picking up the 'truth stone' in both hands, as their made-up ritual dictated. Starting at the beginning, taking things chronologically. Marazion staring back at him.

He spoke, courageously, on the subject of fear, of his fears in particular, that went a long way back in time, his terror whenever feeling trapped in narrow spaces, believing he could no longer breathe…referring to the winding stone staircase of a long-ago school trip. He told her that it didn't stop there; there was also the fear he carried with him of feeling exposed and vulnerable whenever high up in the open air. Even more terrifying in a way, because he also experienced an overwhelming urge to throw himself down. Wanting to take off and fly. Not so much an act of suicide, as an irrational yet powerful need to become part of the view, the landscape, especially if it was beautiful, as it lay stretched out below as if lying in wait for him. Both beckoning and taunting him.

He spoke of nocturnal dreams, starkly real, which involved him falling, repeatedly, into the same familiar stretch of the River Thames. He somehow slipping silently between the arched bridge's short white stone columns, as if something were drawing him down. Followed by a cold, deafening thud or splash…finding himself 'landed' on the floor beside his bed.

It was thanks to Marazion's 'crazy idea' that he was now putting these pieces together and seeing that there really did seem to be some kind of link or pattern emerging, in spite of the fact that he wasn't yet in a position to properly grasp it. Had he just been born that way? Had he, as a highly sensitive child, just realised that we were all far more vulnerable than most of us imagined? That danger was always there, all around us, even under the protective blanket of family, peacetime and economic growth.

On the other hand, perhaps he had simply suffered an early childhood trauma, which might explain his 'condition', one that no one had since been willing to mention to him.

However, it also felt like a fear of life itself, which could on occasion leave him exhausted, debilitated and yet he knew he wasn't weak, well, not in the usual way we think about weakness; he had always found ways to talk or joke his way out of awkward or dangerous situations. His school friends, as far as he knew, had never referred to him as cowardly or stupid. Except neither had they any idea that every day presented a new challenge for him, every day another towering wall to scale. Made even more wretched by the tireless need to cover it up. Again, he wondered if it really did have to do with his fear of open heights and tight spaces…or if they were merely a byproduct of something much deeper…

To such an extent, for just a few seconds, as ridiculous as it may sound, he couldn't remember who he was. It felt like dropping off the planet and becoming part of the wider universe. A little like dying.

He had never put all this together until now, neither aloud nor in his head. Each event had therefore remained un-joined from the next. They were unsettling findings, but at the same time liberating, as he was beginning to feel a kind of release. Probably because he would never be seeing Marazion again, once he had climbed back into the car. Homeward bound. By now, beyond worrying that he might lose face…she could make of his stream of nonsensical or vacuous words whatever she wanted…

Marazion listened, serious-faced and attentive throughout and yet said nothing. Giving nothing away.

It was now her turn. "I found out recently, quite by chance in fact, that I am…adopted. You are now the first person I have told. It should have been a massive shock, but then again, it strangely didn't come as a total surprise. I never did feel that I really belonged to that family. Thoughts about it won't leave me alone though. They don't know…yet…that I know. One day, my 'borrowed' father…yes, that's how I think of him now…had left some papers on his desk, and I, bored as usual, had for some reason just picked them up. Never expecting to read the bombshell news, which I did, over and over. Making sure that I had got it right. However…and I've always been this way…I don't think I ever loved them the way other children seem to love their own parents. I even kind of understand why they haven't told me the truth; perhaps they are planning to, when they think the moment is right…I can't say I feel any lasting anger towards them."

She then read his mind, interrupting the flow with the following:

"If you are wondering about my brother, no, he is their real child, I remember my…'mother'…being pregnant."

Then continuing:

"No, it's not so much the shock now. It's that it begs many questions…where are my natural parents? Who are they? Well, especially my mother. Where do I come from? Why could she not take care of me? Here, each year in Cornwall, I feel that this is my true place…here are my roots, where I belong…but then again, perhaps I've made it all up, like in a book. I've read hundreds of stories about all sorts of things. That has to leave some kind of mark, doesn't it? On my imagination, on my soul, only in part quenching a thirst about wondering, who I really am. Yes, that's it. The need to find out who I am, and yet I felt that way long before I discovered…the truth of my family situation."

Arthek likewise listened attentively, head bowed and said nothing. Deeply engaged by now, trying hard to understand the situation from her perspective. Unaware if it showed up on his face. Beyond worrying. His turn again. They were to have up to three 'goes' each.

"Strangely, that's similar to what I'm about to say. Well, it is and it isn't…from quite an early age I've been, well, kind of spying on people, people in my own family…it sounds a bit creepy, doesn't it? I don't do it much now; I've just sort of outgrown it, I suppose. I can't remember even how it started, maybe by chance or probably like you, out of boredom. I think it's when I would sit halfway up the staircase…it had become my favourite spot in the house, not being hidden exactly, but just a place, where no one bothered to look…it was then I began to hear and see things. Real things. Then of course, later, watching 'The Man From Uncle' on the TV, well, that kind of fed into it too. Oh and of course, James Bond films at the cinema. As harmless as it might sound to some people, just a silly childish game really, you run the risk of discovering things you never wanted to know, or aren't ready for, or sometimes things that you can't fully understand, but that are…intriguing."

A long pause.

"Once, when I was a bit younger, my mother sent me to give my father a message at the church, and I found him slobbering all over this woman, one who sings in the choir with him. I froze to the spot, just praying that he hadn't seen me. Can you imagine…it was like me taking on my father's guilt? I know that had nothing to do with the spying, but it still shows what you might stumble upon when a child's world gets mixed up with the adult world. Things you are just not ready for…the two worlds running separately."

"But that's not what I wanted to say, just an example. The thing is I happened to find out, but only a piece at a time, that there was another child once, a boy, who would be my older brother. That makes me…a replacement child. A substitute. I don't even know if that's a bad thing. It means that I probably wouldn't have been born at all if something bad hadn't happened to him. It makes me feel guilty, being the son they kept, but also unwanted, like a booby prize. He never lived with us. I don't even know if he is alive or dead…no one speaks about it at home. I guess he died…"

Another long pause.

"And so I can't talk about it either. Some things began to get clearer though. It explains now why every month or couple of weeks, my father used to disappear, mysteriously, for a few hours, and return to 'report back' to my mother, always in whispers, the atmosphere becoming tense. Though come to think of it, it hasn't happened in years, but I can't remember exactly when it stopped…"

"When I was really young, you know at an age when it's impossible to properly remember things, maybe three or four, I am almost certain my mother would burst into tears whenever she took me to the doctor's for jabs or check-ups. I remember him, on each occasion, kindly allowing us to leave by the back door so that she wouldn't have to face other people in the waiting room as she wiped her red eyes…Maybe that has something to do with it…"

"I can go for months at a time, maybe a whole year, not thinking about it at all…but then it somehow creeps back…and then, I'm not even sure if I do want to learn the truth…"

When the two had finished the business of the day…they began their long silent walk back to the Newhouse deckchairs. The cave experience had drained them both, but at least, in his eyes, the girl was now restored to human status. However, Arthek never got to hold her hand or stroke her hair. Marazion merely complaining that she couldn't go for a swim that day; how sometimes she hated being a girl!

Chapter 6
A Short Story Competition

Once while still at school, James decided to enter a short story competition. With no expectations of winning or commendation, he just got on with it, doing it for himself, almost enjoying this new adventure. Surprised as to how many ideas hot flushed their way into his young head, once he opened his mind and allowed them in. Much of it turning, as if by magic, to inky words on the page. His spying activities now about to pay off! Quite different from the dull homework his teachers set him, or the tedious essays he had to write in class. If only temporarily, it had set him free from something. He wouldn't have been able to explain from what, or why. The project taking him about three or four weeks to complete.

The set theme was Family Life…and after much redrafting of the structure and a good few spelling corrections, it went like this…

The Brilliant Idea.

One day, Miss Josephine Squelch, a warm-hearted member of a large and unusual family, came up with a brilliant idea. For quite a few years, she had not liked the way they had come to exchange gifts at Christmas, with everyone getting exactly what they wanted from everyone else, resulting in NO surprises, NO fun…it had all become ridiculous. This state of affairs had of course evolved for the best of reasons…in short, to avoid the disappointment of loved ones.

Wearing a stick-out yellow dress covered in polka dots, chosen for the occasion, she set out her ideas during a family lunch, on an unexpectedly warm Sunday in October. The others, maintaining deadpan expressions, and more than a bit disgruntled (mainly because they hadn't thought of it) huffily agreed to 'give it a try' in any case. It involved writing everyone's name, separately, on little pieces of paper, which were then carefully folded and put into a hat. Each family member, in turn, had to pull one out, keeping eyes tightly shut and then secretly read the name on it. Provided no one had picked his or her own name, a new present-giving experience would be underway.

So that Christmas everyone only needed to buy (find or make) a gift for that one person. Josephine also came up with three simple rules, which she hoped the family would choose to follow:

Absolute secrecy regarding names and gifts during the days and weeks leading up to the 25th December.

Carefully matching present with person. Character, age, situation, interests.

Spending no more than a modest amount.

Who were the Squelches exactly?

Here follows a short description of some of the more interesting family members…

Starting with Uncle Lionel, someone who liked to entertain people with his stories of life 'on the road', it mattering to no one whether or not they were actually true. He had a way of passing off the incredible as real and certainly possessed a unique way of thinking. Most of the time, and no one ever did find out how he made his money, he rode around on his beloved motorcycle, an old Ducati. As for his latest yarn, he told the eager listeners, how on a recent very cold evening, when he was on his way home, two angry officers signalled him to pull over onto the hard shoulder, as they jumped out of an even angrier police car. Raising their fists and blowing their whistles, while repeatedly accusing him of using the roads in 'a reckless and hazardous manner'.

Because of how his brain worked, wired up a bit different from that of other people, so he claimed, he still could not understand why the red-faced pair had prevented him from riding his cherished bike with a ten-foot (possibly exaggerating here) Christmas tree tucked under one perfectly healthy left arm. Where was their sense of festive spirit? For carrying a tree, which, to his horror, he had to abandon by the side of the road. The very one that had singled him out with its wavy branches.

However, an even more worrying incident, involving Lionel and his 'superbike' had to be on the day he finally agreed to give his long-suffering wife, Aunt Honoria (Norrie for short) a lift into town. It was only when he arrived at her favourite high street shop that he discovered to his horror that she was no longer clinging on to him…she had in fact, as he found out later, slipped off the back just outside their home, fifteen minutes beforehand!

Then there was a Myrtle Hartlebury, nee Squelch, Lionel's sister, whose prime aim in life was to make sure everything shone. All the usual things like cutlery and glassware, windows, taps and brass doorknobs…but best of all her husband's big and bulbous white head. Probably in honour of the brilliant brain, encased within. Aubrey, whose vocation in life was to serve his fellow man as an expert on every subject under the sun. Happily handing out, at any time of day or night (and free of charge), detailed information on all matters, ranging from the state of the local drains to alien life in outer space. Always with solemn authority!

Their daughter, the very studious and bespectacled Deidre Hartlebury, spent most of her free time in her bedroom, which doubled as a site of archaeological interest. Rather than hide her messiness from the world…or even pretend she was about to start a clear up…she actively invited all sorts of people in…announcing that she liked it 'that way', it now symbolising how she wanted others to perceive her. She had, in effect, recently discovered the word 'Bohemian', loved all that it signified, especially delighting in each (bourgeois?) visitor's shocked facial expression, as they entered. Lesser people in the main, 'un-arty', lacking depth and originality. Her long-suffering parents ever making light of the situation…putting it down to a mere fad, a 'passing phase'…

By way of compensation, they had a very tidy son called Nigel, who willingly gave memorable impersonations of people from Liverpool, Northern Ireland and Scotland, which all sounded very much the same.

There was also a Vivian Squelch, Josephine's cousin, and his extraordinary capacity for locking himself out of the house (or car)…so many other things on which to concentrate. It was quite common, therefore, to see him scaling the wall of his property or prising open a side window at any time of day or evening. Neighbours no longer 'batting' an eyelid. It was doubtless his preferred way of entering, they concluded, whereas they, like most others, would simply and boringly, turn a key in a lock. His twin sister Bertha, who everyone agreed was the sweetest person ever, except that she could never manage to hold onto a secret, no matter how hard she tried, unless it involved staying quiet about the new frocks, shoes and handbags she appeared to acquire with great regularity.

Best of all were the terribly ancient…born way back in the 1890s…Herbert and Queenie Squelch, who looked down upon their family's goings-on from a very high, almost royal perch. Herbert with his excruciating to listen to coughing bouts caused by smoking (he suffered from chronic bronchitis); Queenie with her tiny glittery blue eyes, which could pierce concrete. Both with an aversion to American culture…

Five Christmases have by now come and gone, and a variety of gifts exchanged. The potion for rapid hair growth, a second-hand copy of the highway code, an American flag, a weighty key ring, the pack of feather dusters, to name a few of the less brutal.

However, like many successful enterprises, it already incubated the spores of its own destruction. It helped explain why Communism was doomed to fail, as a viable political system, and why true Christianity has penetrated so few hearts in nearly 2000 years.

Yes, it was another brilliant idea that fell into the hands of a collection of human beings, and things began to go downhill from the outset.

Although this family had agreed to put Josephine's idea into practice, the majority wanted to continue with their traditional present-giving as well. Josephine felt thwarted, but not wholly surprised.

It was also not long before an insidious curiosity took root, admittedly in some minds more than others, as regards who was buying what for whom.

Were there any tiny pieces of paper carelessly left behind? Could comments made (or not made) throw further light on the situation? The apparently thoughtless, just loud enough to be heard, 'Oh no, I haven't got him again, have I?' leaving behind a wealth of information to the 'casual' listener, whose mind and heart were in truth ticking over at an alarming rate.

On the other hand, could such comments have been a deliberate attempt to divert the scent? Sherlock Holmes and Hercule Poirot would have been genuinely impressed with this family's ability, regarding tactics and thoroughness when it came to sifting through meagre evidence. Knowledge is power, after all!

It came out, long after each event of course, that generous amounts of money had been made available for 'name swaps' to take place, husbands and wives breaking their temporary vows of secrecy…Even worse, a (last-minute) laziness had set in, usually among the male contingent, causing them to bribe other family members to find gifts on their behalf. Ludicrous amounts of money spent, well above the agreed threshold, as some had left it too late.

Things definitely came to a head last Christmas, however. Boundary lines crossed when someone bought a 'calico bubble eye' fish. For those who haven't yet encountered it, it just happens to be the ugliest, most 'misformed' fish God ever created. Nigel bought it in the full knowledge that even though Josephine would hate it, she would never have the heart to flush it down the lavatory.

Time for a new tirade of threats. Next Christmas promises tarantulas, piranhas or even worse. Revenge has escaped and she is baying for blood. There are also those who've been biding their time, emotions hitherto suppressed, just waiting for an opportunity to avenge themselves…the family daggers, clearly drawn.

That simple idea, originally put forward, to give meaningful low-cost Christmas gifts in an atmosphere of fun and wonder, has by now deteriorated into a hotbed of vice, corruption and revenge…and it's become…the absolute highlight of every Squelch/ Hartlebury Christmas.

What would you like for Christmas this year?

The end.

James was quietly pleased with his work. The culmination of his years spent reading, imagining, but mainly spying on his fellow man. As well as coming up with an amusing little story, he had also managed to create an eccentric family, deciding that it was similar to one, that he would have liked to call his own.

Chapter 7
Big Brother

Something that James hadn't considered regarding his 'condition', and wouldn't for many years, was the possibility that being that way could also signify something beautiful. Of course, it was his secret, his discovery and therefore he never planned to talk about it. He didn't think there existed words to describe it. He had however always sixth-sensed that human life meant something infinitely precious, but one day, this reality would suddenly rise up and slap him in the face. Revealing a truth, which transcended all former, merely accepted platitudes. More simply put, an instant burning realisation that we had an unasked-for life on planet Earth, which lasted only a short while…that was it, with nothing beforehand, nothing following on…

So the possibility that his 'weakness' was not weakness at all…just something of a different kind. It much later opening up a glorious red wound of intensity, which connected him to the workings of the cosmos. Difficult a concept to share, no one ever appearing to 'suffer' the same fears, stirrings and longings. Difficult, therefore, impossible almost, to discern what to do for the best with such a sacred gift. That one vast, and yet fast-moving opportunity. Learning all the while from mistakes, one's own and those of others. The universal and colossal mistakes from history. A frantic race. Simply must stay safe. No time to lose…

Not wanting to depart from life until you had lived it out in the best way possible.

By whose rules though, whose measurements?

Unfortunately, none of this fully encompassed or began to explain his own sense of detachment. The anomalous indifference towards his fellow human beings, or at least those he had so far encountered. It just seemed easier to show the world, that as well as being part of a respectable family, he belonged to a loose group of friends and thus came across as 'normal'. He knew he didn't really need any of it though, he was on the inside, treading his own path. In rational terms, knowing that their lives were just as precious, equally significant…yet at the same time, it was a 'truth' strangely unfelt, impact-free. Precisely because he had always felt so removed from them.

More and more spiralling thoughts.

Of course, James was also evolving into a different person now, as he withdrew in fits and starts from boyhood ways. That surreal encounter with Dorcas, alias Marazion, having pushed him even further into a future that he both longed for and viscerally feared. Knowing now though, rare as it was, that he was not the only one. She and he had recognised it in each other straight away. With little need for words or explanations. James sometimes doubted that she or 'it' had been 'real' at all. His parents continuing to speak of her, confirmation that she had indeed existed and…that he was still (relatively) sane.

Sometimes wondering if she had made any progress regarding her own family origins…but even more crucially…wondering what would have happened next if he'd been brave enough to stroke her hair or kiss her neck while in the cave.

As far as James's 'hidden away' older brother was concerned, thoughts of his possible existence continued to inhabit his brain. Where was he? What was his name? James did try on a few occasions to broach the matter with first his father and then his mother but found that each time, the words he needed stubbornly refused to form in his mouth. That he knew there was no way to speak of him, without bringing unforgivable hurt and disruption into the well-ordered household. However, questions if only in his head, continued to formulate themselves. He had to find out more. The significance of his own existence depended on it.

He hadn't wanted to, but running out of ideas had eventually decided to turn to his sister Harriet. Choosing a 'good' time to make his ambush.

"Don't say anything about this to Mum and Dad but do you know anything about us having a brother?"

A few long seconds later: "What do you mean? Who have you been talking to?"

"Not to anyone. You know, me just putting things together…things I've heard, things that don't make much sense…"

After letting out a prolonged sigh, all the while deeply probing his eyes with her own, she made the momentous (and probably foolish, she thought afterwards) decision to impart, finally, bits of the 'big secret' that she too had long carried with her.

"Look, I don't know much about the whole business myself, but of course, I'm older than you…and just remember certain things…actually more sensing than knowing perhaps…as they try to keep it from me too! It's only Dad who ever went to see him…"

"So where is he then? Why did they send him away? Why didn't they want him, treating him as though he was some kind of…reject?"

"Look, I'll tell you what I know, which I promise isn't much, but you mustn't say anything. They'd kill me. Promise me! For them, by staying quiet, it's like it never really happened, I suppose. All before your time."

James solemnly giving her his very best three-fingered, boy scout promise.

"You know where we used to live, where we always show you in the car. That place not far from those war prefabs they took ages to pull down, well in that house when I was 3, nearly 4 I think, Mum gave birth to a little boy. I vaguely remember Aunty taking me out for the day until it was all over. Apparently, I bought the baby a toy duck with some money she had given me…They called the little boy Peter…He only lived with us for a few days. At the time, I just thought he was ill and had to spend a while in hospital. I remember them telling me, the day he went in, to kiss his head, and they lowered him down for me, so I could reach properly…I have no memory of his face at all, and like all babies, he was covered in a big white shawl…but he had this amazing white hair…not the usual blond."

"Well I never saw him again, and don't even know now if I ever asked about him, but he never came home. I think, much later, that Dad got in touch with our MP about it. He was always at his desk in the evening asking for quiet, writing important-looking letters, and then there were those visits he made every couple of weeks or maybe once a month…to go and see him. I somehow knew or guessed without anyone telling me. It's just so strange…I don't remember Mum ever going with him. But no one spoke about it, not even outside the family, or never at least when I was there…I don't even think there are any photographs…"

James so caught up in her account had for a minute or two forgotten where he was (and once again almost who he was) and that his sister was actually talking about their brother, their flesh and blood, his 'would be' older brother, and not simply about some tragic boy in a storybook or newspaper article.

"And so, what happened in the end, did he die? How do you cope with all this, the sort of knowing and not knowing?"

"Well, no one ever said it in front of me, but I think he has to be dead now. Dad stopped making those trips a good while back…" Harriet suddenly remembering she was running late. Sorry, but she really had to go now.

"Just remember, James, to keep your promise! If anything else springs to mind, I'll tell you. You are old enough now. It's only fair you should know too," words which she used to cover her own shame at having shared what she knew.

As with any important investigation new off the ground, James, of course, needed to know more; his overworked mind flooding with the more graphic scenes from Harriet's account and even more questions. Some parts of it he would have (unknowingly then) witnessed already from his 'twilight' position on the stairs. He needed some time to himself, to digest everything she had told him, work out and record dates, times, places and fix his own life within them; it was all so strange and muddled! Cruel as well. Trying to picture how he himself fitted into the whole picture. He, the normal healthy replacement child. The rest could wait…

Chapter 8
The Trip That Wasn't

His own life hurtled on despite the inner turmoil. That's just how it was. Not able to come up with anything more about Peter, he once again let the matter drop.

Around this time, when he was about 13, he got a 'last-minute' opportunity to go on a skiing trip with the school. It had been organised for the boys in the year above, but when a few pulled out, he felt a sudden urge to put his name down for one of the newly vacant spaces. It was a trip to Engelberg in central Switzerland and was to last ten days at the start of the Easter holidays. His parents, surprised by his request...their son never having been a 'joiner' or any kind of team player...duly prepared the deposit money, which he took to school the following day. The name of James Newhouse, now added to the list.

Had he given the matter the usual deep analysis, he would almost certainly have changed his mind and 'missed the boat'...or in this case...the train, the boat and then another train that would be taking him and the other boys there. James still too young to consider that it might be possible to overturn such a decision once made. Therefore, a done deal. It would mark his first trip abroad, and skiing aside, that in itself, already felt like an exciting prospect. With teachers rather than parents in charge instead. An adventure, that would take him into unknown territory, literally and metaphorically. He learned a new word that week: couchette.

Not knowing yet which other 'second years' would be going with him...or even if he would recognise anyone from the year above. Significant steps into the unknown.

His mother busied herself with purchasing all the correct clothing from the sports department of a big store a short bus ride away...anorak, ski pants, special socks (which gave off a strange oily smell.) All he had to do, in the days leading up to their departure, was attend some extra-curricular classes at the end of the school day, which involved muscle-strengthening exercises. Not quite understanding why he needed to do them, as they never made his arms and legs feel any different, any stronger. There just hadn't been time.

Each boy was allowed a small fixed amount, looked after by the teachers, of Swiss francs for the buying of souvenirs. He found out that they would be staying in a German-speaking canton of Switzerland, and so was interested to discover what the local people sounded like in a language that he had only begun to learn a couple of terms beforehand. Surely not the same as his teacher, who was from the West Country with (in his humble opinion) a very dubious German accent. His accompanying teachers were a mix of those he quite liked, a couple he didn't really know and one that everyone detested. The latter to avoid at all costs!

Then everything went wrong. It was not to be. The adventure mat wrenched from under his feet. He caught chicken pox a couple of days before the departure. 'How strange he hasn't had it already. Most children…' flowed the stream of predictably unhelpful comments from bemused teachers and members of the family. Meaning of course that there was no way he could be part of the trip. Confined to the family home, his highly anticipated Easter break…the skiing trip ruined. Two and a half weeks of feeling itchy and alone, covered in smelly calamine lotion, his biggest, most unsightly spots having erupted on an otherwise fresh adolescent face. He looked up the word for chicken pox in his bilingual dictionary: die Windpocken (wind pox)…sounding even sillier in German than in English, but cleverer too in his opinion, as it taught people that it was an airborne disease. The way he interpreted the world, a noun that came with a 'free gift'.

During his time at home, he eventually came to accept his situation, deciding there was no plausible alternative. Trying to persuade himself that he'd never particularly wanted to learn to ski in any case…it all sounded a bit too far away, a bit too energetic…and that at best, his up to now, had only been a lukewarm relationship with the German language. He drowned his spotty sorrows in a pile of library books.

What he hadn't envisaged and so wasn't ready for, was the change in his three returning friends, who had followed his example and taken up those last remaining places. How it had somehow transformed each of them in both subtle and more obvious ways. One of them in particular departing as a gangly boy, only to return looking and sounding like a man. In ten days! Had it been the alpine air, the food, or the skiing? Perhaps all three combined, if not also a little in denial about the impact of hormones.

Oh, and how they continued to talk about it. Rare in itself, conversation topics normally undeveloped, passing quite rapidly. Returning again and again to the (twice-daily) funicular railway, the swinging and fast-moving ski lift, the breath-taking and blinding combination of sun and snow when they were out on the slopes…the weather was never like that in England. Impersonating the ski instructors' clipped accents, but also agreeing that considering they were foreign, their spoken English was truly impressive. Impossible to think that they too might one day speak German with the same level of competence. Sharing their excitement with the unfortunate and still a little spotty James, with one proudly declaring (and as a reminder to the others) that he had been part of the first group of pupils to graduate from the nursery slopes, despite being the youngest.

James sensed that it was he himself who had given them the silent blessing, to go on and on about the ski trip making it appear like an act of generosity on their part, just so that he didn't feel excluded. Comparing and showing off their tanned faces and tanned hands, and where the skin became white again from just above their sleeves. They had grown up, gone forward and overtaken him in some strange, almost mystical way. It felt to James, therefore, that it was no longer a matter of missing out on a few rudimentary skiing lessons, but something far more important: a 'coming of age' experience; something that couldn't be recouped, from which he had been cruelly excluded. Something he had merely read about in books. Something he had never anticipated as regards the trip, well beyond learning to ski a little.

As balmy days dragged forward, in the lead-up to exam season, complete with the anticipated and accompanying bouts of hay fever, the skiing stories finally faded. However, James still had to grapple with one remaining feature of the school trip that he had missed…the best thing of all…girls! For the friends, girls hadn't really existed before Engelberg, which incidentally translates as 'angel mountain'. However, in Switzerland, they had finally made their appearance (coming from at least two other English schools) and staying at the same hotel. Now here forever. His friends saw girls at least three times a day, mainly at mealtimes. They also saw them during two of the evenings when little disco-like parties…heavily supervised, of course…were laid on for them.

It was an older girl called Jane, who had unwittingly bewitched them, with her long dark brown hair and beautiful light eyes. Like Olivia Hussey in

Zeffirelli's Romeo and Juliet. Each boy planning, alone and within the group, ways they might speak to her. Dreaming of her at night…feeling both awkward and unworthy of her attention, helpless and yet completely smitten. Each boy, secretly hoping beyond hope, that he might be the one she chose as she looked down from her high balcony. Or in their case, from the top of the hotel staircase. So painful, the wordless red-faced embarrassment of adolescence. With or without erupting spots.

Then their time was up. They had to return to a grey and windy UK, their bags crammed with unwashed ski stuff and cuckoo clock or mini-tankard souvenirs. Perhaps one day another 'Jane' would enter their sad, 'schoolboy' lives, this time with a different outcome. In the meantime, they needed to get some experience. To meet a whole range of girls, whether they liked them or not. To feel easy around them, get to know a bit about what went on in their heads. To learn to tell a few jokes, even to learn how to dance. To become more attractive by trying harder at getting their spots to disappear…

Hanging around in the park, playing football and riding their bikes in male-only company, having suddenly lost its appeal.

Chapter 9
Moon Struck

James's boyhood wasn't always painful. Not in an everyday sense, anyway.

Running alongside his fear of heights and horror of cramped spaces; the feelings of alienation; the bizarre yet also gratifying need to spy on adults…the awkward mystery surrounding an absent and tragic brother…stretched a second path. Where life did appear to be normal for a boy of his age and place in history. Sometimes the two paths ran parallel, but then could also merge or cross. Certain days, the best days, hovering light-hearted and carefree, like feet skimming spongy grass, like hands pulling on the string of a red balloon, trying to escape. Like floating on your back in still waters.

James's psyche caught within a submerged labyrinth. On the outside, he like his peers, merely having to find 'ad hoc' coping mechanisms for surviving the minutiae of their daily lives. Within a structure designed for the good of all young people. The brutalising cycle of home, school, homework, weekends; home, school, homework, weekends…but then climaxing each year with that heady anticipation of the summer holidays counting down to those six weeks of sun-filled promise. The joy of the wait always outweighing the reality of the 40 days of wilderness freedom.

Somewhat less magnificent, the holidays of Christmas and Easter, colder, wetter, more uncomfortable times of year, a third in length. Always better than school though. Better than in years gone by when, as he had learnt in his history lessons, boys like him or even younger, were working up chimneys, their lungs caked with soot, or in noisy, unsafe factories. Long hours knee-deep in hazardous machinery. Much better now, therefore! A time to be truly grateful.

He remembered that in good weather, sometimes alone or sometimes with others, he used to go fishing for minnows in the River Crane or read comics, the Beano and the Dandy on a little wall in the garden. On chillier days, as well as reading, he would dedicate time and effort to the Brooke Bond card sets he collected, which featured the likes of famous people down the ages or native British birds or flags of the world…

It seemed such a long time ago now, before 'the trip that wasn't', that he played endless football with his friends in the park, rode around the nearby streets for seemingly hours on his bike, which used to belong to his father…and if for only a brief period, even joined the Boy Scouts.

On Fridays, how he looked forward to devouring an ample portion of plaice (or haddock) and chips. Wrapped in pages ripped from *The Daily Mirror* and covered in greaseproof paper. Generously doused in salt and malt vinegar. Spread across his lap…sheer bliss! Heralding the two days of (relative) freedom to follow.

This, in years to come, after having watched Ready Steady Go on the TV, presented by a quietly spoken, heavily fringed Cathy McGowan, marked the end of yet another five-day stretch of school torpor. 'The weekend starts here', she would remind him at the start of each new programme (at around 6 o'clock). Sacred words that caressed and tickled his spine…words that in truth very rarely led to anything much, though.

A heartening thought then that James, for a good part of his life, still managed to carry out all the expected things designed for a boy of his age, without much in the way of trauma.

During those highly anticipated long English summer holidays (in reality passing frustratingly fast after the first two weeks had slipped by), there was also the pull of the local outdoor baths. Housed in a building, as he was to find out later was Art Deco in design, complete with impressive twin staircases and cavernous hallway. James went perhaps only four or five times a year, usually at the weekend, but each one of those occasions remained indelibly stamped on his young mind. The water inevitably freezing. Yet on a good day, as close to a Mediterranean experience as you could get anywhere in England, with its welcoming area around the pool. Made up of pinkish paving stones from where (for those with any kind of imagination), you could laze, sleep or sunbathe in Ancient Roman-style splendour.

By now, James too had made the discovery of girls, in his own way and by himself. He loved it there. For the fact that his parents never went, for its blue-green water and for the atmosphere. For the multiple presence of girls, as he had never seen them before. A place where he could marvel at their diverse body shapes, their glistening wet hair and skin, and when close up, showing tiny goose-bumps on arms and legs…in and out of the water, out of their school uniforms, out of their jeans and jumpers…in skimpy bikinis, imagining they were younger versions of Honeychile Ryder.

He listened in on their bursts of carefree chatter and laughter, and as for the more attractive ones, noted the open pleasure they exuded when conscious of the attention they were drawing from an admiring male presence, which straddled every age group. Some men, openly, and some in a more furtive manner behind newspapers, in case their wives (or teenage daughters) happened to be looking on.

Harriet, of course, didn't count in any of this…

When not in the water, the poolside thus, providing a perfect place for James to witness the comings and goings of others from behind innocent dark glasses. Who could tell where he might next target his gaze? No need for lurking on staircases or hiding behind doors…and all the while listening in on other people's transistor radios, perched hither and thither, as they poured out the top twenty or thirty hits of the day. James sometimes pretending to read the next dampish page of 'The Catcher' (The Catcher in the Rye), from which he had become inseparable…

The afternoon's revolutionary blast of pop culture planted a firm and delicious wedge between his generation and that of his parents. Now certain the two really had come from different galaxies. Impossible to meet, let alone merge. Having reached a point of no return. Thinking little of future implications, because the music always kept him rooted in the present moment, rarely beyond the duration of each song. As Bob Dylan reminded him once again:

"The order is rapidly fadin`
And the first one now
Will later be last
For the times they are a-changin'"

The Beatles once again reading James's mind before setting words to music, as the girl in their song finally decides to leave her family:

Quietly turning the back door key
Stepping outside she is free…
She's leaving home after living alone for so many years…

Meanwhile, James, having never got around to deciding whether he should subscribe to a Mod or a Rocker lifestyle (still a bit too young) was by now experiencing a deep yearning for California and the hope of one day following the Hippy trail, something that appeared to quash every other desire that had come before…

In compensation, while he waited to grow older and find answers to such tough decisions, Harriet had sometimes under duress, agreed to take him to the nearby Gaumont or Odeon cinemas. After the spy movies, it was the never-ending wave of American Westerns, a rival yet much older genre of film, which soothed his overworked brain. Watching cowboys on television too. 'Bonanza', 'The Big Valley', 'Rawhide', 'The Monroes', 'Laredo', 'The High Chaparral'… A constant stream.

He didn't know why or where it had come from, but he always found himself taking the side of the native redskins or the poor downtrodden peasants with their huge sombreros and Spanish-sounding names…something at the time he never questioned. Deprecating the arrogance of the swaggering John Wayne stereotype, of the cowboy settlers, the sheriffs, the invaders, the 'stealers' of land. From his 'own' people, with their glorious imperial past and riches rooted in the exploitation of others, or even worse, the slave trade, with the excuse of exporting Christianity. How they always made it sound that their way of doing things was superior as if set in 'commandment stone', and speaking with God-given authority.

As for the pop music and the westerns, James's attitudes slipping even more effortlessly into the broad strokes of a prevailing Hippy philosophy.

Once or twice, he would take a glimpse into a possible next chapter of his life, when he too would be escaping the kindly meant yet total, spirit-breaking dullness of home…off to read English literature at university. Everyone telling him now how gifted he was, an intellectual and academic now, one of the privileged few. So proud they all would be of him, family, teachers, 'friends'. One of a mere handful in his year group and the only one in his immediate circle.

James knowing, however, that it wasn't down to a superior functioning brain, encasing a laser-sharp intellect. Yes, he was bright enough, but likewise aware he had also struggled with subjects like maths and science. Subjects, which interested him far less than the 'Arts'.

No, it was more to do with a talent arising from the pain of intensity, which had always stuck to him like slug slime. Something, which had opened the door into a world of art, music and literature…directly through the emotions. Allowing him an instinctive grasp of the themes and characterisation in novels, poetry and drama, long before the undertaking of detailed research, on intellectual acquisition.

A predisposition, therefore, which cut through syntax and semantics, historical and social context and the techniques and styles artists displayed. All that he would learn about and study later. Together with a boundless imagination, which permitted him a rich and alternative 'way in' to the joy of reading, watching and listening, and at the same time providing him with an escape route out of real life, his life.

Music, with its lyrics, from soulful melodies to primitive rhythms in which he could float his mind. Recognising all that was beautiful in its fullest sense. Forests, lakes, Cornwall. The female…in the shape of Emma Bovary, Elizabeth Bennett; Guinevere, the Lady of Shalott; the real-life Dorcas Glidewell alias Marazion; and the butterfly girls who emerged out of hibernation each summer as they flitted in and out of the open-air pool. Encountering that never-ending gaping ache, that beauty awakened and inflicted…

Then came the Moon landing. The Moon, yet another beautiful creation. Astronauts Neil and Buzz, the first 'dudes' ever to walk upon the surface of that cratered white ball we all squint up at, in its monthly transformations. Marvelling at its constantly changing shape slices and its mystical pull of the tides.

The Eagle touching down on the edge of the man-named Sea of Tranquillity. The Moon, a light bulb dangling in space, a quarter of a million miles away, that pretty, yet pockmarked satellite snatched and colonised in a single day by none other than…the star-spangled US of A. Patronage for all the wrong reasons: to show the Soviets that it was now the Americans ahead in the space race. Locked into Cold War madness back on planet Earth.

Two heroic spacemen proudly planting their national flag on the Moon's powdery surface…the stars and stripes…red, white and blue. On a plaque, bequeathing the words composed in earthling English: 'Here men from planet Earth first set foot on the moon—July 1969 AD—We came in peace for all mankind'. Why leave such a stupid message? For all the passing aliens?

For the Russians and the media, more like!

Yet another show of conquering vanity, reminding future (non-American) space folk…to bite the 'moon' dust! As if, they would ever get the chance…

In James's mind, it all linking in with his earlier obsession with spies from either side of The Iron Curtain, with 'Cowboys and Indians' in the movies. A simplistic world divided into goodies and baddies, right and wrong. Winners and losers, superiority, power and possession…the unwritten rules (and mentality) of the pathetic school playground.

On that historic, moon conquered day, new neighbours had just moved into the house two doors along, and James, frustratingly, would never be able to separate this major lunar event from the fact that he had had to watch those unquestionably breath-taking moments alongside these outsiders. As on a tiny patch of planet Earth, a TV set had suddenly 'exploded', resulting in a likewise loud knock at the front door and humble request to watch the live events at James's house.

This petty invasion stopping him from getting comfortable (he liked to stretch out, in a highly ungainly manner, his long limbs over the floor, while clasping his hands behind his head.) It had stopped him concentrating on the mind-blowing events unravelling across the, albeit grainy, television screen. It had stopped any sense of awe he might be feeling, in its tracks! Having to share settee space with strangers, smelling their alien smells, the boy emitting strange hiccuppy sounds from his throat, that weren't exactly hiccups (so had to be something else); the girl scarlet-faced with acne, over brimming with teenage embarrassment…

Fortunately, Harriet was also there to make conversation. Harriet. His underrated sister, once again to the rescue.

Chapter 10
Harriet

Harriet took an alternative approach to life. Borne out of a different mindset and a lively personality, which rarely caused her to dwell for too long on existential matters. She was confident and pragmatic which in turn, allowed her to look forward with courage.

There had been a good few years in fact when brother and sister had grown apart, for she was practically a young woman now, still thinking of James as a gangly and often annoying young boy. With a face that rarely smiled. From her perspective, he still seemed stupidly to cling to boyish ways, whereas she had warmly embraced every emerging sign of womanhood as soon as it arrived.

Up to then, all things considered, it had been good having someone younger, smaller, less worldly, around the place, with whom she could show off her latest accomplishment, tell a funny story or share a morsel of grown-up knowledge. To have a younger brother she could 'practise on' as regards a new experience or discovery. She realised from the start, that in terms of factual knowledge, he seemed to know a lot more than most, but forced herself to think of it more as a family trait rather than something he alone had inherited.

However, the unconscious need for him gradually evaporated altogether.

She knew other people considered James highly intelligent, but decided early on, that she, for one, was never going to demean herself by letting him know that she had ever noticed. For her and doubtless many others, being brainy wasn't exactly an attractive characteristic, as for most people, it conjured up a world of thick-lensed spectacles, old-fashioned pullovers, and a head poured over a pile of dusty books. Grateful, however, that he rarely embarrassed her in front of her friends, having heard many stories to that end. Only that, he sometimes looked detached and bizarrely serious when they called round and that frustrated her. And especially when their father was trying (very hard) to share a rare joke or two with the family! This did not come naturally. Why was her brother so devoid of a sense of humour or come to that, an ounce of human kindness? If only to pretend…

Harriet had also observed…well in truth, as a result of someone pointing it out to her…that if you looked a bit more closely, James was turning out to be quite good-looking, definitely an improvement on the earlier 'version'. Something else upon which to decline comment…

In any case, it was patently clear that he was 'weird'. Kind of belonging to another time or place, but nothing she could actually pinpoint. Like he wasn't actually in the room, even when he was! Like he was living out an alternative life in his own head. Nothing she could do about it though, if that's the way he wanted it to be! If it came to it though, in an emergency she was more or less certain that she would still go to his rescue…and make sure to give him a lengthy lecture afterwards about not getting into that situation again! If only to show the world, that she too could have her say and still have James under her thumb.

As far as she could remember, they had never hugged or exchanged kisses or said that they loved each other. Not even with their eyes. Never exchanged niceties. To her knowledge, that sort of thing probably didn't take place in other families either, so nothing too odd about that. Fortunately, no member of the Newhouse family had ever been seriously ill or away from home for more than a few hours for anything other than work, school or shopping, their situation therefore rarely warranting that kind of effusive behaviour. They lived to set rhythms. Life bulldozing ahead in a seemingly straight line.

Now, she had her own bright future to seize…once again, what they all did was up to them.

'Attractive and lively' would have been her friends' description of Harriet. Nearly always good company and full of fun ideas. At school, her friendship 'group' had included a tight inner circle of three and then a few part-time hangers-on, who, when convenient on both sides, like one of them falling out with another girl or having to cope with a friend's absence, would spend some (privileged) time with them. Not quite the cleverest girls in the class, but had, nevertheless, gained widespread admiration further down the school, for their worldly maturity, and sophisticated confidence. For having 'arrived' earlier than the rest.

Her fair hair she always wore loose. Except in the science labs, where when she was 13, the precious hair had encountered the cruel blue flame of a Bunsen burner. The beautiful ends frayed and singed in a split second, emitting there and then a horrid smell, which seemed to linger for months…

Never relinquishing the fringe or centre parting, she would hurriedly draw the rest back into a ponytail, until it looked nice enough to wear loose once again.

Her best feature probably being her mouth, especially when she smiled, which opened to reveal two rows of near-perfect teeth. She had deep-set grey eyes…and a slightly retroussé nose like that of her mother. And like her mother, Harriet was neither too fat nor too thin, not too tall nor too short. Displaying nothing that might single her out particularly, or cause people to mock or stare…consequently a nice-looking, fresh-faced girl.

Harriet never quite able to determine what her father had passed on to her in the way of looks or personality.

If her appearance was agreeable to her, she did nonetheless, vehemently disapprove of her name! Knowing no one with that name, not in books nor real life. To her, it seemed ridiculously old-fashioned, more like a boy's name which had to be changed at the last minute to fit the disappointment of the arrival of a baby girl, and yet she chastised her mother over it, guessing that it would have been her choice alone, and nothing to do with her father.

Never bothering to question her on the matter, though, as she was afraid it would inevitably turn out to be something to do with being named after an ancient 'Henriette', some boring dowager duchess, a hitherto unknown member of Margaret's absurd (and probably non-existent) pseudo-aristocratic relations!

How Harriet despised them…if they really did exist…and for the nonsensical grip, they somehow continued to wield over her mother. Blocking out any potential closeness to her and the here and now. Was there such a thing as a normal family? It definitely wasn't this one…

Perhaps that was the source of James's 'otherworldliness', she once thought fleetingly.

When Harriet was 18 years old, she fell in love. Or so she believed. It knocked her for six. Properly in love, like in the movies. With all the right ingredients: heart all of a flutter, head struck by a passing moon beam…Much, much more powerful now she realised, than the teenage love she had impossibly lavished on the likes of Cliff Richard, then the Small Faces and a bit later George Best…such posters long ripped off her bedroom walls.

She lost weight without trying, she couldn't concentrate, her life meaningless without seeing the young man in question at least five times a week. He remained in her head, heart and soul from dawn to dusk. She drew up mental plans for their future, which didn't appear to involve many practicalities, more in the way of a set of scenarios. These would capture the two of them spending shared time in places like riverbanks and near-empty cinemas, as they whispered fanciful words of love, he plaiting wildflowers in her hair, she feeding him nuts or popcorn. They would of course go on feeling like this forever, unlike anyone else who had gone before them, those older, grey and dull people who couldn't possibly comprehend what real love was. Life's losers.

Growing old together never part of the fantasy. Love, exclusive province of the young…and yet she was certain at the same time that he would never leave her, and that she would never leave him! She conjured up the names of meals she would cook for him…unlike her mother…getting to about four. For the first time in her life, she wrote lines of crappy poetry in one of her brother's discarded exercise books, and pondered upon her lover's reaction, on receiving his first perfumed letter from her…

She forced herself to read novels by Barbara Cartland. A bit old-fashioned but not so difficult, after all.

Harriet, by now working in the branch of a local bank, having become proficient as a shorthand typist. She caught a glimpse of Adam, the first man of all (for that was her chosen name for the silent beau) twice daily if she were lucky. In the mornings, as she waited for the bus, and then on her way home, as he was leaving his office, which was located close by. This sorry state of affairs staggering on for nearly a year, through sun, wind and hail (still no looks or words having passed between them) until that awful, unimaginable day when, with fate casting its cruellest blow to date, she happened to see him, hand in hand, with another woman, a beautiful woman at that. She hated her. Far more sophisticated than she was or could ever hope to become…as the carefree pair hurried down a flight of steps and got proudly into (what was probably) his new car.

The indisputable proof that he had abandoned her. That in time, she would have to accept that in all probability, he had never even noticed her. All that wasted love and devotion, which had consumed her for so long.

Her cheeks burned scarlet with life's latest slap. Her insides collapsed. The lace-veiled dream shocked into shreds! True love erased in a split second! A soul destroyed. The indescribable pain of abandonment, the likes of which no one before her had ever felt so profoundly! Mortification. The whole business later also left her feeling very stupid, but at least she had wisely never shared this ridiculous fantasy with anyone. Her saving grace.

Never again, no never again. Even for a real person one day entering her life, that is, someone who came to know her and say he loved her.

Within just a couple of years, however, we find Harriet married and living close to the home of her parents. In a three-bedroom end-of-terrace house, complete with garage and back garden. A couple of years after that, the mother of two vivacious little boys.

Chapter 11
Narnia

James eventually entered his happiest phase to date. As an undergraduate. University, a place, which as far as he was concerned, took care of practically everything. Combining intellectual, creative and cultural pursuits, in those days, a privileged lifestyle designed for young people of that persuasion. Greater social fluidity, well to an extent. Sweeping away, in an instant, much of the tedium that had punctuated life with his parents, especially after his sister had left home to get married. All the silly rules and practices gone, and now the promise of adventure. Something completely different.

A new life, according to the gospel of his favourite pop songs and poetry. On days off, you could now get up as late as you liked, even if it meant skipping meals. Staying up all night to work on a neglected essay. Staying up all night to cram for exams. Or to party. Unlocked doors. A lot of sharing. No one wagging 'that' finger at you! Merely a residue of rules to uphold now, those fashioned for the good of all. Allowing James to operate above (or beneath) the family radar, grabbing each new opportunity, as soon as he felt ready to let himself go there.

However, more freedom meant breathtakingly scary and James wasn't what you would call intrepid. The fear rarely withdrawing its claws, even in heady times such as these. It was more a wiping of one's slate. Starting again, at a time which also happened to mark a change in the law, which was about to confer adult status to those of James's still tender age, down from 21. History in the making.

Friends with everyone, friends with no one in particular…just as he liked it.

Scene: his first tutorial.

In a high vaulted room, a raised right hand. Very pale. Property of an auburn-haired girl in a beige jumper. Albeit, females, a minority species, in and around the place. A small, mellifluous voice began:

"Yes, well in my case, it was probably *The Lion, The Witch and The Wardrobe*…I really enjoyed reading that book. Soon after, it just becoming a much bigger experience, when I came to realise some of my friends were reading it too. All a bit stupid really. We became obsessed. We even made a pact. Oh God, I wish I hadn't started this now. You're all going to think that I'm some kind of weirdo. Oh well, here goes. Oh just before I go on to make a total fool of myself, I wanted to add, and I don't know if this happened at your schools, but our teacher had given us all…I think we must have been aged about 10 or 11 then…a really long list of books we had to read at home."

"Extra homework, but no one ever actually checked that we were doing it. You know, mostly nineteenth-century titles, such as *Treasure Island, Little Women, Oliver Twist, Jane Eyre*, that sort of thing. The so-called classics…We got no help with them and I know I never got to reading more than half on the list…books with all those rambling sentences packed full of clauses, taking up half a page each. *The Lion and The Witch*…definitely not part of it."

"There were about five of us…and we decided, well, it was the idea of my friend Jane…that every evening, before going to bed we should climb into our own wardrobes at home. Then somehow summon up all our willpower, as we pressed our hands against the back panel…it was actually the bedroom wall in my case…wishing beyond all hope, to find ourselves together in Narnia, like the book's four children. We really believed in the possibility of magic. Hanging on to the (fictional) Professor's every word. We wanted nothing more than to find ourselves treading the crunchy Narnian snow and talking to the likes of a Mr Tumnus. We tried again, night after night…each of us, reporting back the following day that, alas, nothing had happened…"

"But surely you had all missed the point. Lewis wrote the Narnia stories out of his own firm set of Christian beliefs, to highlight the power of good over evil, to promote a message of love thy neighbour and the power of forgiveness…" interrupted the clipped tones of a pompous young blockhead.

"Yes, well, I know that now, but Professor Lincoln asked us to name a book that had made a powerful impression on us as children. It was magical worlds we needed then, not Christian doctrine…" she retorted quietly but firmly.

Their youngish tutor (young as far as the then image of a university professor stretched) knew it was probably time to step in, to thank the sweetly spoken… Jennifer…for her colourful account, commending her bravery for 'getting the ball rolling'. It wasn`'t easy baring one's soul to anyone, let alone to a group of high-flying strangers, sitting in deadpan judgement and having nothing to do with being right or wrong. More to do with being authentic and generous. Now their discussion could really take flight, as they went on to analyse the power of the written word in literary terms. He thanked her again.

James would never forget that short, hovering on the awkward, scene (one of a growing pile that would leave its mark upon him over the three years) clearly unable to detach the girl Jennifer from it. It had gained her a sort of baptismal permanence in his consciousness. Noting, from the very start, that she hadn't needed a 'truth stone' or the mystical influence of a barefooted Marazion, to open up, regardless of where she happened to be and the potential menace of a hostile, predominantly male reaction.

She had accepted James's praise, and the two fast became friends, unusual in itself for him, sometimes lingering after lectures to discuss the day's themes, characters or writing techniques. Even suggesting, shortly after that inaugural act of courage, that James met her boyfriend, Denis. She thought they might 'get on'…

James surprised that after only a couple of weeks at university she was already referring to someone as her boyfriend. He couldn't work out whether he minded. Perhaps it did niggle him a little, or even more than that.

The three undergraduates, soon becoming seven or eight, often meeting by the riverbank in the centre of town. The atmosphere relaxed and inclusive, as they sat and stretched their legs, sharing crisps and peanuts, making wittily crass comments about their chosen courses and lecturers. Some revealing their plans for the next few days. Most of the group making progress in wanting to get to know one another, at least superficially. A few smoked, what James assumed to be, French cigarettes. Flared jeans and tobacco, two instances as to how his own life would also be changing. Not quite there yet.

Jennifer, or Jenny as she was now insisting, was the only girl present, as she sat nestled up to her boyfriend for the duration, hanging on to his arm as well as anything he had to say. A Jesus-looking Denis, with some of the male students already having considered growing their own hair (now removed from home discipline and parental deprecation), this trend including long sideburns.

The conversation often returning to the current music scene. James noticed early on that Denis always spoke frugally, almost monosyllabically, and yet it was he, who remained the central focus throughout. At the centre of a gravitational field. There are people like that, which he was discovering for himself. You cant always put your finger on the reason why but everyone feels the pull. Whether the honorary 'sun god' was aware, was difficult to ascertain. He didn't appear to be working at it…never overtly charming nor particularly warm. Charisma.

His girlfriend Jenny filling in all the missing bits for him. She then went on to invite everyone round to her rooms, later that evening. An offer well received, as the following day happened to be a Saturday! The big lie-in!

Like the fast-changing skies, by 9 o'clock that evening, Jenny appeared quite different from when James had first caught sight of her. Now a far more exotic creature. With smudged kohl around her eyes and newly released pre-Raphaelite hair tumbling past her shoulders. She wore sandals and a long floaty dress, of different shades of green. Only the voice remained the same.

Denis had also put on a show. Nothing to do with fancy dress, but still managed to look like a sort of twentieth-century pirate, sporting a pair of gold earrings (fully visible whenever he tried to push his hair back from his face.) A bandana round his forehead. James found it hard not to stare. The others, as they arrived, appeared to accept such unconventional behaviour without question or surprise. Once again, an atmosphere of inclusivity and acceptance.

Someone had smuggled in a crate of bottles containing 'fine claret', which Denis wasted no time in inspecting…but then surprised everyone by having himself produced a few bottles of French champagne, which he swiftly opened, making a toast to 'their brave new world', words they all reaffirmed. Jenny was in charge of the music…Led Zeppelin, Leonard Cohen, Bob Dylan, Donovan, The Kinks, Yardbirds, Animals, Rolling Stones, some Pink Floyd…take your pick.

Champagne, claret, music and conversation drifting haphazardly into a sea swell of well-being. Followed by some painfully awkward dancing, some might add, the kind that the English in particular do so well.

At one point, Jenny and Denis disappearing for half an hour or so…

There would be many such gatherings that first academic year, each one slightly different from the one before. New people staying for the weekend, guest passes for parents, brothers and sisters, invites to friends from other universities and so on. Followed by a trail of young women, whom James and his peers had encountered around town, as their knowledge of the local area grew.

It wasn't just partying, however. Sometimes the shared night-space evolved into powerful discussions, which swept them into the void of philosophical thought. Tackling those seductively big questions, which had no answers, leading on to more big questions. Fed by the vast pitch darkness on the outside and the dark red wine getting to work on their brains. Wittgenstein and Bertrand Russell. What was beauty? Did God create man, or did man create God? Friedrich Nietzsche and Schopenhauer. What was the point of living? A. J. Ayer and Martin Heidegger. Were we intrinsically good? Herbert Marcuse. Was life really about trying to survive and reproduce, and not much else? Did language itself hold any answers relating to the human condition? Darwin and Einstein; Chomsky and Sartre. Then, why…? Why…? Round and round spun an insane web. Arriving nowhere new. Mental gymnastics.

Eminent names tossed in pretentiously (and not necessarily at the most appropriate moment) for good measure as if belonging to close friends. No one knowing enough to be able to launch a serious counterattack upon any claim. To be able to say, 'You're wrong…that was…' All sounding highly impressive though, had someone been drifting through. A world away from bus stop moans about the weather or someone huffing over the price of bread. Oh, were they proud, just listening to themselves…drunk on too much wine and their own pseudo-intellectualism. Playing out the imagined and revered roles of those who had gone before them.

Such was their right. It was they, who would go on to analyse the works of Shakespeare, Austen and Dickens…the literary giants. A class of their own.

On other nights, it was just about the music. On one's own, or in no more than twos or threes…sometimes even stopping to ponder the words. Occasionally, one of the students…Tim…organised poetry readings (not so different from listening to the songs) in his room, which in time became a popular option, on top of all the university-led literary societies and outings on offer. With the group's 'blessing', Jenny joined an amateur dramatics society, which regularly took her away. They were soon planning to put on a production of Twelfth Night. She could hardly wait for her new 'family' to go and watch.

Denis continued to cast his own spell over them. By the end of Michaelmas, a tight knot of friends had thus formed around him. Except for a few more mainly sporty inclined stragglers, who came and went…and James. James wanted to be with them, of course, and for the most part, he was. They were good fun. They regularly surprised him, many coming from more affluent backgrounds than his own, which opened his eyes to different ways of seeing the world. He enjoyed their pursuits. When being silly or hedonistic, but also when they were serious.

Enjoyed the intellectual rigour needed to 'keep up'. Like them but not enough like them. He remained, with one foot dangling out of their vast and cramped bed of friendship. Never quite knowing the reason for his lack of commitment, only that he had to remain true to himself…

They didn't seem to mind. He liked them even more for that.

Before long, he too had started smoking Gauloises, with their distinct blue packaging and illustration of a winged helmet. He had also developed a genuine appreciation for red wine, grown his hair long…and had already slept with three or four women. Life was good…

Chapter 12
Harriet's Visit

During the summer term (Trinity), Harriet, now a Mrs Harriet Garner, invited herself to spend the weekend with James, wanting to catch a glimpse of student life, to go see for herself what all the fuss was about, but also declaring to her brother that she had some important news to impart. In any case, Brian was away on his annual fishing trip…five days at a mosquito-infested lake, he had said, somewhere in France. Definitely not for her.

She looked well, James thought. Wearing a matching top and skirt, and her hair styled in the shape of a bob. She really was a 'woman' now, and there was no going back. He had picked her up from the little Edwardian-style railway station, as promised, and they were now enjoying a pub lunch at the Rose and Crown. If Harriet was taken aback by her brother's radically altered appearance…hair, clothes, quasi-swagger…she never showed it.

Sitting opposite her, he found himself (possibly for the first time) studying her face, checking to see if she also smiled with her eyes, to see what happened to her mouth when she laughed, whether they shared the same shape nose. Never having bothered until now to focus upon the height of her cheekbones or length of her ear lobes, or note whether she had any visible moles or freckle patches. Why would he? She was his sister.

He supposed that's what he was trained to do now with the vast array of characters (both real and fictional) he was encountering vis-a-vis his studies. Teaching him to be conscious of device and allusion, to absorb albeit the tiniest detail and so on. Second nature to James, of course…all that spying when he was younger…now even more so. Reading between the faint lines of her forehead, mindful of any tiny gaps in her teeth and pauses in her chatter, not just in the choice of words. Mindful that she was playing nervously with her fingers under the table…

They had last been together at Christmas, back home with the Newhouse family, brother and sister dumbfounded (and somewhat humbled) by the effort, that particularly their mother had made that year…neither child living permanently at home now. The newly acquired, gaudily rich decorations, red, green and gold, had found their way into each of the downstairs rooms. Whereas in the past, it had always been just the one room transformed into fake Christmas cheer. Now multifarious cards draped like bunting in the hallway. Glittery fairy lights poked out of the branches on their most flamboyant choice of tree to date. Margaret had also allowed them to eat off her precious dinner service, something she said she had inherited from her French family. No one ever having seen it let out of its formal glass-doored cabinet home.

Their father having gone to the trouble of purchasing some new board games: Monopoly, Scrabble, and Backgammon…

It was where and when James had come to 'know' Brian a little better.

Unsurprisingly, he hadn't taken to him.

Having concluded about three months earlier, from the day of the wedding itself. It was an instant aversion, and very likely mutual, in spite of the day's necessary smiles and formalities. James believed he saw him for what he was: vain, shallow and attention-seeking. All boldly written across a podgy face with its permanent hint of dimpled smirk.

What did Harriet see in him? Would future children, especially if they were boys, turn out to be miniature versions of him? James shuddered at the thought!

There was something in the way of tangible evidence coming just a little later when the wedding photographs finally arrived. James unable to find a single one where Brian wasn't looking directly at the camera, in contrast to several of his sister where she turned devotedly towards her new husband, with the hope of the two staring into each other's eyes. The photographer having failed in his professional duty to deliver any gloss of romance passing between them.

Then there was his stupid speech, which he had carelessly left behind, shot through with semi-concealed, self-flattering anecdotes, but delivered in such a guarded way, you had to be a 'James' to uncover the reality…his 'very lovely bride' a kind of after-thought. Perhaps James was being less than generous, nasty even, instigated by the sudden shock of sibling loss. Perhaps his critical skills had become over-whetted…

As far as he was aware his parents hadn't objected to the match…and naturally Margaret would have approved of the fact that Brian was some kind of city accountant…and even more so, that his parents regularly holidayed in the South of France. The genteel smack of respectability warming her soul.

During the Christmas visit, Harriet found the courage to let James know (and no one was more surprised than her) that she was actually missing her only brother…not all the time, of course, her life now full of other things, more responsibility…but specifically when it came to his fast wit and deadpan sense of humour, his originality. Confessing how while growing up, she had obviously taken him for granted. There again, didn't all siblings do just that? With no one now to replace him. Not quite understanding the direction in which he was going, but proud of him, nonetheless, especially of his academic achievements. Had she never told him before? No, probably not.

What she didn't reveal, however, was the extent of her missing him, a fear, that after university, he would go and live somewhere far away, even leave the country for a while…she felt they were only now just getting to know one another a little. A delayed beginning to the new version of an old story that she didn't want to end.

James, touched by this unexpected revelation, experienced a pang or two himself of something that also bordered on guilt, only without the same depth of feeling. It's just that, for now, life was good with or without his sister.

He had been looking forward to seeing her, nevertheless. Curious of what she would tell him about what it was like, that alien condition of being married.

They later admitted, and in different ways, that it felt like they had never really belonged to the Newhouse family, James inevitably more so than Harriet, and yet both unable to point to something tangible they could refer to, to back up why this should be. All based on mere feelings remoteness. Their parents had provided them with a sense of security, as well as a roof over their heads. They had fed, clothed and cared for them. Steered them through the storms of adolescence.

Discipline had conformed to the accepted model of the day. Simple, straightforward. Look after the pennies…wish not, want not…a bird in the hand…silence is golden. Treat others the way you would like them to treat you…What child could possibly want for more? Perhaps their mother and father had not sufficiently shown an interest in the new culture of pop music, long hair, love-ins and mini-skirts, let alone try to understand it. However, to their children's knowledge, neither had any of the parents of their peers. Who in their right mind wanted parents, who still pretended to be young?

After the Rose and Crown, they went on to the cinema…to watch a spaghetti western, something like *The Good, The Bad and The Ugly*. They had fun trying to keep a tally of victims shot dead throughout the film…never agreeing with the other's figures. About halfway through, one audience member sitting in front of them, clearly someone with a limited sense of humour, threatened to call the manager, as a reaction to their intermittent giggling and whispering. Another tiny, shared experience, adolescent in tone, the makings of a future family anecdote…

That evening, James had planned to introduce his sister to Jenny, Denis and a few of the others. Not sure if it was going to be a risk worth taking. However, she had told him that she wanted to see something of his new lifestyle.

Needless to say, Harriet felt like an alien. From start to finish. Everyone was nice and welcoming, of course, if only because she was James's sister…but she couldn't get to grips with what made them tick, more so as a group than when chatting to them individually. Their witticisms and innuendos, bouncing off one another, their esoteric political references, their seemingly infantile (yet oddly counterbalanced by a somewhat sophisticated) sense of humour. Conversation punctured with classical references…one of the group even spouting something in what must have been Latin, she deduced, to which they all guffawed. A super brainy knot of close friends, each trying to outdo the other in depth and breadth of knowledge, slapstick and satire. Even though she usually thought herself bright enough. The music likewise offering no respite nor antidote. The world her brother now inhabited, the world that made him happier than she had ever seen him. Precisely what she had wanted to uncover, but now troubled, threatened almost, by the distance she was allowing it all to come between them.

Their carefree and intimate time in the pub and the cinema wiped out in a few minutes.

James was vaguely unaware of any of this. Stupidly proud that he had seen Denis place his hands briefly on his sister's shoulders, affectionately stroked her hair, and at one point, engaged her in a private little conversation all of their own in a corner of the room. As though he had singled Harriet out…

When it came to saying their goodbyes the following afternoon, Harriet reminded James that she had something important to tell him. Had he forgotten? Was he just being too polite to ask? Not wanting to reveal her own fears or insecurities, that he just wasn't really interested in anything she might have to say, she casually announced that she had something to hand over, that he might find of interest. First the news though. She was expecting a baby…and he was the first to know, well, first after Brian, and she hoped very much that her husband would agree to call him James, should it turn out to be a boy, if only as a middle name. Her brother congratulated her in an unpractised, rather stilted way, the only way he knew how, borrowed from scenes that he must have absorbed from watching a play or film. He was, of course, genuinely happy for her…merely poor in family relations and self-expression.

Harriet wouldn't have expected any more than this in any case.

She thanked him for 'everything', and just before reaching the platform, handed him a bulky folder, that she had been hiding in her bag. Telling him to read it later when he was on his own; that he absolutely had to send it back to her by the end of the week. She made him promise. All the necessary information he would find within the bundle of papers.

Repeating, in a more relaxed tone now, that she had really enjoyed the visit, and, in particular, just how much she had enjoyed meeting Denis, by far the best of the intellectual bunch. Had she not been a married woman, well who knows? Her statement surely intended as a joke, though as an attempt at humour, did sound a little bizarre coming from his own pregnant recently married sister…

Chapter 13
Home Truths

James was grateful that there were no meetings or parties that evening. Even a liberated student needed to be on his own from time to time, to rest his overworked resources, or just to gather stray thoughts. He hadn't forgotten, however, the bulky folder his sister had handed him, still wondering what it might contain, and why she had made it sound so important. He might as well open it straight away.

On untying the somewhat frayed ribbons that bound it all together, quite a few papers of different kinds fell out. He put these back together, as best he could except as he was to discover, pages were not numbered and there were few dates to go by…

What he discovered was uncanny. How unsettling to read his own name JAMES NEWHOUSE on one of the pages, meaning that he was also part of it.

Peter was born on the…at…Memorial Hospital. He was admitted into the care of Dr Barnardo's on the…of…aged 9 months. He was cared for in Australasian Hospital in the Barkingside Village. His father, Raymond Newhouse, visited him regularly most months, until the baby was transferred for long-term care to… Hospital in Hertfordshire on the…

Enclosed in this letter is a copy of Peter's 'Admission History', compiled at the time and gives reasons for his admission to Dr Barnardo's care, family circumstances that led to this and brief details of his family background.

"Peter suffered from a range of congenital health problems. These included a left-sided microphthalmia; a high arched palate; a systolic murmur at the apex (heart); he had 13 thoracic vertebrae, 13 pairs of ribs and 6 lumbar vertebrae. He was prone to feeding problems, infections and cardiac difficulties."

"Applicant: Miss... Lady Almoner from The... Hospital for Children...Street, Chelsea."

Father: Raymond George Newhouse
Mother: Margaret Newhouse nee Claremont

The Applicant does not hold a very high opinion of either parent, for it seems that they have tried to evade their responsibilities to Peter, who is a handicapped child. The father, however, is sincerely distressed about Peter, who is the second child of the marriage. The mother is said to be of rather shallow character. The older sibling, Harriet, is an intelligent and attractive little girl. The mother knew the father when she was 16 and was married to him at 20. The marriage has been a happy one and the home, which is being bought on mortgage, is clean and well-kept; part of the house is sub-let. The parents looked forward to the birth of their second child, but Peter was born with multiple congenital malformations of the jaw and ribs; he also had a congenital heart condition. He presented a severe feeding problem and after a short time, the mother took a great dislike to the baby; she became overwrought and hysterical.

At the age of two months, Peter was discharged from hospital but was readmitted the following day because the mother could not feed him. He remained in hospital, as the mother could not be persuaded to resume his care. On one occasion, she said that she hoped every day to get a telegram saying that the child was dead. At length, she agreed to visit him once a week but when she did so she wept copiously. We were then asked to take him. By now, he was six months old. At this time, a doctor at the hospital stated that the child did not seem to be mentally retarded 'though too young at present for accurate assessment'. Later that month, Peter developed chicken pox and was transferred to a local fever hospital. It was feared that his life might be in danger if he were returned to his mother and we agreed to accept him.

Meanwhile, the parents had him examined by the local mental health officer, who did not deem the child to be mentally defective. The parents then made strenuous efforts to have the child cared for under the National Health Scheme but without success and they accepted our offer'.

Australasian Hospital:
'Report on Peter, aged 12 months, weight 16lbs 6oz.

Multiple congenital abnormalities; feeding difficulties at times, now improving.

Illnesses since admission: tonsillitis, bronchitis.

Interests or achievements: none.

Behaviour and sociability: cannot yet sit up. Lies in bed quietly playing with toys. Contented baby.

Family contact: Father has visited 3–4 times in the 3 months since admission.

When Peter was aged 20 months, it came to our attention that a third child had been born to Mr and Mrs Newhouse: a healthy son, named James.

Report on Peter, aged 2 years 2 months, height 35 inches, weight 17lbs 7oz.

Details on health and habits: General health poor. Extremely retarded and often will not take feeds. Nasal feeding necessary. Chronic constipation. Multiple congenital malformations.

Illnesses since last report: otorrhea; bilateral otitis media; balanitis; boils on scalp. Medical treatment necessary.

Hobbies and interests: nil.

Behaviour and sociability: does not respond or play with toys. Noisy at night otherwise lies quietly in cot.

Family contact: Father visits regularly, approximately once a fortnight and telephones regularly. Stays for about 2 hours each visit.

From the last report:

'Peter, now 2 years, 11 months.

To be discharged.

A letter written by Peter's father Graham Newhouse to Dr Barnardo's Homes.

"*Dear Sir,*

Thank you for your recent letter.

I would like to take this opportunity of thanking you and all concerned, particularly the Matron (Miss…) and her staff, for caring for Peter during his long stay at Barkingside.

Yours sincerely…"

An enclosed certificate showed that within 2 months of the writing of this letter and Peter's transfer to the Hertfordshire hospital, the 'horizontal only' life of the poor little boy had ended…

Peter was dead.

James sat motionless for what seemed like a couple of hours in frozen time. Trying foolishly to make sense of what his eyes had just scanned, but apparently incapable of transmitting to his brain. There were also other papers with columns, showing the monetary contributions that his father had made, all set out like an invoice, a record of hire purchase of little interest for now. He couldn't read any more in any case. He half hoped to find a photograph, but no image spilled out of the folder…remaining both disappointed and relieved that there appeared to be nothing more contained within.

How could it be, how could it be? In spite of the juvenile spying and Harriet's revelations about a missing brother, which he had practically cast aside the following day, James was now in full white shock. This was the awful and tangible proof, nothing real until now. Nothing beyond the exchanged whispers.

Now a little boy's name, names of key people and places, dates, medical notes, signatures and witness statements. Testament to the fact that he really had had an older brother no one spoke of, in what should have been his shared home. A tragic little boy, who had given up playing with toys, when still a baby. Now dead, but whose unnecessary existence had ruined the neatness of the Newhouse way of doing things, their way of perceiving the world. The keeping up of appearances. Little Peter…James wanting to go on shouting out his name now…physically deformed, mentally retarded, a human 'thing' they felt they had to hide away. Therefore, nothing to do with them…it hadn't really happened at all…nothing more than a cruelly extended, dystopic dream…and somehow, James and his sister Harriet had been their parents' silent accomplices. They should have stood up to the silence!

Little Peter left to a system, left to strangers, but at least strangers with a higher vocation, enabling them to do what his own family wouldn't. Then his father's dark and shameful visits to 'no man's land', kept separate from the rest of their daily lives. Unreal. Whispered reports lasting no more than a few seconds. Each awful mission accomplished ticked off the calendar.

James, brought up on a diet of middle-class decency and courtesy, rather than strict religious dogma, now felt something far deeper raging silently inside him. Untaught and unlearned, but there nevertheless. There perhaps from the beginning of time. A pure instinctive surge…one of those few times in life, when the spotlight of truth shines unwaveringly on Right and Wrong. Each a chasm apart, obvious and perspicacious. What his parents had done…and not done…was wrong. Wrong, beyond the concept of crime…but that like the basest of crimes, had to stay hidden from the world.

He accepted that his older brother was probably destined to die young.

He accepted that his illnesses and handicaps would have meant a huge shock for the most saintly of parents. He accepted that his own family would always have had to rely on medical support…and finally that Peter would not always have been able to live at home with them.

What he couldn't bring himself to contemplate, in the case of his mother, was her total rejection of the baby she had given birth to. How it was considered that the baby's life would have been at risk, should he return to her. How his father, with ongoing martyr-like weakness, had consistently backed up her position. Displaying a bare minimum of responsibility towards their faceless boy; his own flesh; the embarrassing list of monetary contributions; the trail of paltry visits, during which he played out the farcical role of part-time father…all the while saving his conscience from ruin. Doing the bare minimum for the sake of his brittle, unfeeling wife, to placate the authorities, to go on living with himself.

All of a sudden, James decided he had to get out of his room. Surrendering, like Denis, to an unusual and irrational urge to be with strangers.

Not long after entering a run-down-looking pub, not the cosy Rose and Crown this time, he found himself, like in a scene from a film, in the company of a colourfully dressed older woman. She had waddled (and wobbled) over to his little table and introduced herself. Chrissie, he thought she'd said, and telling him there was no point the two of them just sitting alone. Why waste time being sad? James let the encounter wash over him. The two ordered more drinks and started up a kind of conversation, which drawled on and on, each rarely listening to the other, each proffering their own homespun take on life.

In the woman's case, the world was a cruel place…her boyfriend, albeit eight years younger had recently walked out on her…How everyone had warned her against him. How from now on she was just going to live in the present moment. No more men in her life. She would learn to go without.

With little persuasion, he agreed to go back to her place, having partially forgotten who he was and what had caused him to flee his room. Outside of himself now, a puny lamb to the slaughter. She told him that she rented a bedsit ten minutes from the pub, so not much walking was involved. After tottering up a flight of stairs, they drank the remains of some wine from a bottle left on the worktop, smoked a couple more cigarettes and made unmemorable love on her unmade bed.

Then James followed an unasked-for dream: he was both its protagonist and the replacement child looking on…All was beginning to make sense now. The replacement child, who went on to disown his father for marital loyalty and cowardice, but always judging that his mother was worse, far worse, safe, removed and rescued from their awful secret, his father through a hazy mix of guilt and duty still having to show up. Face the reality. Men having to deal with everything then, anything not nice. The drains and the vermin. The bins and the bills. The now middle-class French princess was safe in her ivy-clad tower. Once a month or once every two weeks, regular as clockwork, he returned to their misshapen son, to save her from bad memories. Until Peter was no more. Doctors having correctly predicted from the outset that his life, in all likelihood, would be a short one…

Chapter 14
Getting Active

As promised, James sent Harriet back the folder with its unhappy revelations.

Then returned to his goliardic lifestyle, speaking to no one about it. From the outside, everything looked just the same as before, but for James, it felt that something big, very big, had died. An inner light he didn't know was there, switched off. His life changed irrevocably. He too now carrying the silent weight of family guilt.

It was there on falling asleep as it was on waking. Just like the 'Fear', that had always accompanied him, he would now carry this everywhere too. James not able to talk about their secret brother not even with Harriet. It hadn't seemed real all those years ago. Perhaps even a touch exciting. Out of the ordinary. A tragic baby prince locked away in a tower. A distant family member incarcerated for his own good…but that was only for novels, legends and fairy tales. Thoughts of a discussion with his parents totally out of the question. The once anticipated summer vacation now loomed darkly as that meant having to be at 'home' with them.

As much as possible, he strove to look out and listen. To recover his balance. He honed into the current wave of political activism, with students leading the way. News fast gaining current folklore status. Friends, acquaintances or the older brothers (and sisters) of fellow students, who had taken part in marches, sit-ins and other forms of protest, across England and elsewhere in the world.

He liked the sound of that. Living on the outside of himself for once. He had meditated for far too long. He now wanted involvement in big or even not-so-big causes. To raise awareness and be a champion of radical politics. To be part of a movement. Expanding the hippie message of peace and love. Joining the fight for civil rights. He read about some students at Cambridge, who opposed the tactics of the Greek 'junta', and had recently made a stand resulting in charges of 'riotous assembly, the assaulting of a police officer and the possession of offensive weapons'. Jenny knew one of those students personally…her cousin's cousin.

If only in his head, James raising the revolutionary flag of Karl Marx, whose grave, incidentally, had just been vandalised.

To let out a heartfelt cry for change.

There were many antidotes, in effect, for the pain of fear and guilt. Quick fixes. Readily available! Music, which could blow your mind, alcohol, psychedelic drugs, even the intellectual challenges of evenings spent in stimulating company, in addition to the miscellany of books he was reading outside of the course's literature syllabus. *The Bell Jar, A Clockwork Orange, A Man for All Seasons*. Novels by Herman Hesse and Thomas Mann. Robert Tressell's *The Ragged-Trousered Philanthropists*. James couldn't believe how simple it was, yielding to the warm seduction of those parallel parts of university life, always on tap. Dons (and fellow students) just letting him get on with it. No one pressuring him or chasing him up. Easy come, easy go. Provided of course, he handed work in on time and passed each of his exams. That never being a problem for him…

Even more than all that, just how effortless and edifying, finding women to sleep with, regardless of the fact he never came close to anything in the way of love: women from the town, girls he encountered on other courses, and just the once, his 40-year-old char lady. Most of the time, them searching him out. Mostly casual 'one night only' couplings…pain's fleeting reward. Any emotional pleasure gained was rarely felt beyond the following day. Always in need of a repeat performance.

Friends Jenny and Denis, still at the centre of their expanding solar system. They liked him and he liked them, all without words. Perhaps more than he was aware.

In fact, one evening shortly after the 'reading of the folder' episode, Jenny burst into James's room, tears teeming down stained cheeks wanting only to not be alone, to sit on his bare floor as she cradled a bowed head in white hands. He gave her the floor space and the silence she craved. A sorry pile of dark green, enveloped in swathes of auburn hair, explaining nothing, at least not immediately, but with James, instinctively guessing what was troubling her. He tried to get on with his latest essay without success…

It had to be about Denis.

She had presented Denis as 'hers' to the world, like a proud trophy she had all her young life worked hard for and deserved, albeit quietly. As much deserved as her place at university. In thanksgiving, going on to please him in every way imaginable. Yet everyone sensed that he belonged to no one but himself. A maudlin James still reflecting on what might have been, had his friend never showed up there in the first place. Seeing himself once more as a replacement, as second best, a consolation prize, or mere after-thought. As regards Denis, however, he decided that there really were people like that. People, through no fault of their own (not seeing then that he might be one too), who became troubled souls in spite of their universal appeal. He had, of course, read about them as characters in plays and novels. It was going to be a hard lesson for her to learn. Some might be of the opinion, that it was paradoxically, an extension of his charisma. For her, and others like her, an opportunity to achieve the impossible. In the irrational hope that love might change him.

Denis was just that bit taller, a bit better looking, a bit more erudite than all his clever peers, in the main God-given attributes, just as his life was a beautiful gift he didn't quite know what to do with. In his search for answers, he therefore set out to test, taste, dabble (and then seemingly drown) into everything. Jennifer's singular devotion by now a painfully slow act of suffocation, as Denis required maximum freedom of movement, in order to function. Couldn't she see that by loving him her way, she was cruelly pinning him down, glueing his wings together, a once vibrant and exotic butterfly, now straining to escape the display case?

Couldn't she see what everyone knew, whether they had heard of him or not, that he was Dionysus?

Jenny's sob-filled convulsions and soft, low grizzling finally petered out with the rawness of her cheeks returning to ivory pale. James suddenly noticing that since first seeing her, back in that uneasy tutorial, she had become painfully thin. Yet still Renaissance beautiful. Her apparent fragility now causing a rare burst of sympathy on his part. He poured her some dark red wine, wrapped his long, military-style coat around her, and let her rest her head on his shoulder, and then joined her on the floorboards.

With some difficulty, he tried to imagine what she might be going through. He still didn't know much about women. He wondered how it must have been at the beginning. Denis would have singled her out for her unusual looks, the flowing auburn hair, her wide-eyed sweetness and her originality. She was also exceptionally bright and could be outlandishly funny. Both therefore caught up in that initial grip of shared passion. Sadly followed not so long after by the carelessly discarded remnants of his time spent with other women.

James wondered how she must have reacted to each discovery. All the usual evidence: left behind bits of jewellery, traces of lipstick that she herself never wore, wafts of stale perfume (real or imagined), the stray hairs not auburn. In denial at first, indubitably inventing improbable excuses for him. Self-defence and self-preservation. Then clarity gradually setting in. The long silences, his disappearing for hours at a time. His adventures becoming more provocative, as when James had inadvertently seen a partially dressed young man, leaving Denis's room one morning when Jenny was away. The drug taking by now firmly anchored, way beyond recreational, harder, more solitary…Perhaps his university days were numbered.

There were other tiny revelations, which became more of a big deal when all put together. The night when Jenny was away and James had stumbled into his room and found him alone in cold winter darkness, listening to a symphony by Mahler, tears pouring down his face. The afternoon, when some of the friends had spotted him in deep conversation with one of the local tramps, the one everyone referred to as 'the poet', seemingly unaffected by the body stench and slurred speech his new companion emitted. The long and desperate poem he had written that Jenny had found on his desk, unpunctuated lines that none of them could comprehend.

Hearing from Denis's younger brother, down for the weekend, how a few years beforehand, he had wanted to take up Ancient Greek at school (after categorically dismissing it as an option), but that he had already missed over a year of study. How, despite the headmaster's protestations that catching up would have been an impossible task, he had shut himself in his bedroom for the whole of the Christmas holidays. How he had taught himself with the help of an unreturned old grammar book that he found at home, absorbing everything (and more) that he needed to join the class…

James discovering that Denis could play the piano with ease, able to recreate practically any piece of music he had just heard.

James asked Jenny what she was going to do. Pointing out quite simply that this was the price she had to pay for wanting to be with someone like him. The joys and the pain. The 'agony and the ecstasy' he said, using the title of a book about Michelangelo, which he had recently read. There was no point complaining about it. Was she able to go on paying that price? If so, for how long? Only she could decide. Only she knew the weight of her inner strength, the depth of her continued love and need of him. There were no signs that things would ever get easier. "We cannot change other people," he heard himself tell her. Surprised that he owned (and was passing on) such grown-up wisdom. Sensing too that she was already aware of this, but they were the cruel words that she needed to hear from the lips of a true friend…

"Now I know why girls like you," she commented as if in a state of trance. "You always speak meaningfully, never 'tarting up' the truth. You use harsh-sounding words, but there is no malice in you or even competitiveness. I think you are unaware as to how you come across…that is also very attractive. You are the distant, all-knowing iceberg on the horizon, the greater part of you hidden. That is why girls like you as well…" and then looking up to face him for a few long seconds, continued, "You don't know what I am talking about, do you?"

A noble James let her sleep in his bed, while spending the rest of that long, strange night slumped on an armchair under a couple of blankets, with his feet resting on a pile of cushions he had placed on top of an old crate. Despite this state of affairs, they each managed to sleep well into the following morning and breakfasted together in the tiny kitchen on coffee and half a packet of lemon puffs.

The only 'food' he could find.

Jenny then left saying she would give herself three days…always something magical about that number…by then she would know exactly what to do. In return for his kindness, she invited him to spend the weekend with her at her parents' house.

She left a note for Denis, stating where she and James would be, and that she needed time to think. She would see him again on Monday.

Chapter 15
The Holidays

His first academic year at university came and went. James unsurprisingly passing all his exams, which gained him easy entry into a second year of study, a second year out of the family home. In addition to all the partying, he had worked hard and reaped the rewards. A year that had flown faster than all the rest. By far the most significant year of his young life, but one already fixed in past time.

By the time he got home, his parents had already left for Cornwall. To be fair, they had generously invited him to join them, but he found himself saying something like it was much better they enjoyed themselves without having to worry about him; that it would be like a second honeymoon, at which he inwardly 'died', unable to believe he had just spouted such unfelt nonsense…

He knew by now that he could survive on a diet of bread, cereals, baked beans, cheese on toast and canned soup (if it came to it) and sometimes remembering that it was good to eat some yoghurt, fresh fruit and vegetables.

Having protested at least a couple of times that they really wanted him to go with them, but guessing that he might have plans of his own, his parents told him that Aunt Hilda was also happy for him to go and stay with her. (She was his father's sister, the one who had always invited them over for Sunday lunch). That she was fine about cooking for him and about storing all the stuff that he had accumulated while at university. This was provided that, he would take their old dog, Ringo…such a stupid name thought James for a cavalier King Charles spaniel but they had let the grandchildren choose it…out for a walk every day. Hilda had recently suffered a fall, which meant she had to take things easy and James, being fond of his Aunt, decided that, under the circumstances, it sounded like a truly welcome offer. He had little money left and by living with her, as well as being wise financially, would buy him some space, in which to sort out what direction his life seemed to be going in, still uncertain about the future.

Hilda was a big-hearted person, who didn't take a great deal of interest in her physical appearance, but someone who, and much more importantly, had the knack of making everyone in her company feel a bit happier about life than they had felt beforehand. A true 'propper upper'. She smiled big smiles, rarely complained (unless in jest) and had a kind word for everyone. James used to wish she had been his mother instead of the cold and aloof Margaret, long before knowing about Peter, feeling more than a little envious of his older cousins' good fortune.

Yet it struck him now that she too had been complicit in keeping his brother Peter's life a secret from him…she too must have known everything from the start.

Taking the dog out for regular walks gave him not only fresh air but also the opportunity to revisit many of the sights and sounds that made up the backdrop of his childhood and adolescence. All of that he had never really considered before (except for the near-sacred open-air pool). Only vaguely aware they existed at all, a bit like the family furniture at home. In less than a year, his old life now trailed far behind him, in a kind of mottled and lumpy grey fog, a life which could easily have belonged to someone else. Revisiting or merely passing by old haunts, James found himself starting to piece the separate bits together. Maybe, due to all those books he had been devouring, always searching for connections, references, allusions and motifs. Not able now to let it all go.

That walk to and from school, which he had undertaken twice a day, Monday to Friday, month after month, year upon year. The only respite, being those long, dreary yet yearned-for holidays. Taking him past an ancient house, which continued to serve as a youth club, a place where, unlike his then 14-year-old friends, he was always too fearful of joining. They told him that, as well as the wide range of activities on offer, a lot of 'snogging' went on there, he not knowing back then quite what that entailed and never much cared for the sound of the word in any case…

How his life was to change!

It now happened to be the first time he had stopped to take a proper look at it, examine its façade. The building, although imposing, of course no longer frightened him, he having enjoyed a variety of sexual experiences. He suddenly pictured it in its original, much vaster seventeenth-century setting…when there would have been little else around. Gone then the surrounding nineteenth and twentieth-century housing, gone the railway station built partly on land, which had belonged to the generations of its past owners. All those years ago, it would have stood alone, dark and forbidding, and yet almost vulnerable, the little river still babbling modestly past, with just a couple of dirt tracks close by, having diverged from a wider, more accessible thoroughfare. Recalling that his history teacher had jokingly told him that for generations the house had belonged to the same fortunate family, who had started up a brewery there.

The events of the seventeenth century, when the house first appeared on what would have been a very bleak landscape, now fast unravelling in his mind. The death of William Shakespeare, the execution of Charles I, the Great Plague followed by the Great Fire of London, building already underway for what would become St Paul's Cathedral, colourful pictures of London life flowing from the pen of Samuel Pepys…

The dog walks also taking him across the park. From the age of 12, his mother had given him permission to take the shortcut through it to school, rather than have to go all the way around, the streets busy at such times with cars and people. Past scenes of this place came back to him quite easily. This time thinking of it more as an afternoon or early evening venue. He remembered his friends: Alan, Roy, Tim and so on. Their grumpy and frustrating after-school attempts at playing five-a-side football against some boys from another school, so-called matches sporadically interrupted by complaints of rule-breaking or play-acting from the opposing team.

Recalling that in the late autumn and winter months, he had to be home before it started to grow dark. Boys pulling out of planned matches (or other escapades) at the last minute or making weak excuses the day after to explain their absence. The highly anticipated conker fights held in mid-September, rarely fulfilling their promise. The small, vertical scar still positioned above the bridge of his nose, was a permanent souvenir of that period, when he had cut himself on the wire fencing. The park's wide paths providing the stage for some of his pals to show off newly learned stunts on their bikes, and then relive their embarrassment, as they tried hard not to cry if they had fallen off and hurt themselves. Public humiliation always far more painful and lasting than any resulting bump, graze or bruise.

He saw his younger self as audience rather than participant, even during the times when he was taking part…

James always present, but seldom properly enjoying any of it, still turning up for more social 'punishment', as if he had no say in the matter. There seemed to be no alternative. It now all appeared senseless. Why had he been so willing to put himself through it? To avoid even more hours spent at home. The life of a would-be loner…

Such scenes then gradually evaporated from his mind's eye; he was no longer conscious as to what had caused their demise, the eventual breaking up of the group. The result of a slow fizzling out perhaps or a specific incident. Just where were those friends now? As far as he was aware, none had gone to university, so all were in jobs or looking for work, taking up apprenticeships, or now doing what their own fathers had been doing for the last thirty or forty years, and in some cases their fathers before them. Girls still not part of his consciousness at that time, a breed apart.

Except for Marazion. There again, she went beyond mere gender.

Did life really have a purpose, and if so, did that mean for everyone…or just for a selected few? Those who were aware, those who yearned.

He walked on and reflected, walked and reflected…with very little chance of ever reaching a satisfactory conclusion. With Ringo at his heels. No such worries for the spaniel. Neutered at a young age, he had all he needed: food, water, walks in the park…warm and generous female laps at home.

"It's so nice having you here, James. You're a good boy, well no, sorry, a young man, now. You don't say much, but it's been a real comfort for me, all the same, you staying here with us, now that your cousins are all married. Having someone to prepare meals for and so on…it's silly, isn't it? I know that's what you are thinking. That I am just a silly old fool. It's just that some people are simply meant to be carers and companions, in order to feel realised. I must be one of them. In any case, your Uncle Douglas will be back in a couple of days…but I've been thinking…why don't you stay on here for the rest of the holidays? I know there's stuff he wants to get on with…and could probably do with a little help…"

"Best check with your parents though. They will think I have kidnapped you, otherwise. There again, if you prefer, why don't you come here two or three days a week…I don't see what they could have to say against that…only if you want to, of course."

Her cheerful voice trailing off as she hobbled out of the room.

Chapter 16
Alexander Pope

"Well, it's about time you gave some thought about your future. Of course, your mother and I are proud of you. Always have been. Academic success is, well, a bonus. However, it's also got to lead to something else…you've never really discussed with us what it is you want or are planning to do after. We've been patient with you, given you ample time, hoping you would come to us with some ideas, not the other way around. To be honest, no I mean it, I'm going to talk frankly on the matter, although we stayed silent on it, we were both more than a little concerned about your choice of degree…English literature. We said literature! Reading fiction! What kind of subject is that? Something more befitting adolescent girls or sad old maids? It's only women, who buy or read novels, everyone knows that. You may be having regrets…but too proud to voice them. Have you thought of asking the 'powers that be' if it is too late to change to another course of study?"

Raymond's words reverberated against a wall of concrete silence.

A brief pause…and then continuing, "Showing you are well-read might be impressive at dinner parties but it certainly won't go on to pay the bills now, will it? As I said, perhaps we, as parents, are at fault and should have persuaded you from the very start to take up something more worthy instead; I don't know, the law, for example, architecture even…you were quite good at drawing as a child. You are clearly very bright. Crime will always be with us…as will the need for new buildings and public spaces. I suppose otherwise, the only thing open to you, is staying within academe…what else is there…you know how much we've had to tighten our belts to send you there…?"

This was part of the last somewhat restrained and yet very much verging on the desperate 'conversation' that took place with his father…his mother had more than likely instigated it…before the restless young man boarded the train that would return him to a second wave of much-anticipated freedom. The exchange had been, predictably, one-sided. James had dealt with it by maintaining a deadpan face and staying quiet throughout. Leaving Raymond either disappointed…or perhaps still hopeful that the silence signalled that his son was coming around to their point of view but still needed time to consider his options, or that he was just trying to save face…

This year, James, Denis and two others had opted to rent a house a short bus ride away from their university buildings. It soon became apparent that this wasn't going to be the only change. It emerged that Jenny wouldn't be returning, with Denis remaining tight-lipped as to the precise reason. Their group of friends sensing from the outset, that something must have happened between them during the summer and that he didn't want to talk about it.

As for Denis himself, he looked very well indeed, completely recovered from the previous term's emergency nose dive into self-destruction. He told them that he had spent the holidays partly at home with his parents, but that they had also managed a few weeks away in the south of France and then onto Tuscany. His skin still tanned, serving as evidence, and his once tangled or mindlessly plaited hair now clean and glossy.

All this left James feeling off balance. Queasy almost. He had really liked Jenny, and could barely imagine (university) life without her. He became aware as to how deeply he would miss her, and all her ways. How she would pop into his room, rarely thinking to knock. How she would pack wacky ideas into everyday conversation. Always full of surprises! Having even embroidered a couple of cushion covers for him with powerful words randomly borrowed from different languages. The continuous love and patience she had shown Denis.

That lasting image of titian or auburn…was there a difference…hair spread over pale shoulders, when she'd sat on the bare floorboards of his room…It almost seemed as though her absence had tarnished forever the memory of that momentous first year when James learned for himself that life could also…sometimes…reach beautiful.

No longer feeling like a life-changing episode now, more like one he had exaggerated or made up in his head or merely experienced in a long and shimmering daydream. Only partially aware that he was being histrionic. He realised now, that it was Jenny, even more than Denis, who had symbolised for him that year and that change of lifestyle. He felt hollow again, freshly conscious of the once all too familiar emptiness, crouching deep within his stomach (as well as in his head) biding its time together with the ancient fear. Fear, and its grisly partner, Emptiness.

Denis's physical transformation, therefore, rather than fully pleasing him, left James more than a little perturbed. He was discovering something akin to 'Schadenfreude', but not from a book definition this time, as was the case for so many of his important finds. Subconsciously blaming Denis for Jenny's absence, for all her recent pain. Discovering firsthand that his negative feelings did not apply exclusively to adversaries. Now with one friend gone, probably forever, and his other friend back at the centre, a reborn Adonis, whose mind would shine even more brightly than before. Had Denis, in his present socially acceptable form, merely sold out? Having prematurely given up on the human animal that lurked within, and in what he once believed?

James shocked yet again at his own reactions. He was both judging by appearance and jumping to conclusions, wanting to cast blame. Trying to make others fit his own desired scheme. Ignorant thoughts, he knew that more suited to the set in their ways middle classes. Why had he needed so badly, for Denis to descend into hell, to live alternatively, in the first place? Never consciously wanting harm to come to any of his friends, and Denis, the one whom he (and everyone) most admired, the one who had charmed them from the start. He'd not reflected on that before. Why we sometimes relish the hardship of others, stretching even to those we know we like? At the same time feeling empathy or pity for them. Madness.

Perhaps, it was because together he and Denis had spent hours ploughing through books about the lives of anguished poets and suchlike. Analysed and then discussed their lifestyles, which led to their creative works. One seemingly impossible without the other. Often while drinking Sambuca, all the while pretending it was Absinthe. How they had talked of living out the fates of their literary heroes.

For some reason, Denis's new guise pointing to the fact that he was not up to carrying it through, after all…

Just why was it, that James had needed someone to make that journey to hell for him? Someone outside of books. Because he was too afraid of going himself, of what he might find there, of an impossible return? Reverting once again to the role of cowardly sidekick cum spectator…a mere dabbler in things forbidden. Fear and Emptiness brandishing their superior swords yet again.

On that occasion, he got no further than that in his thoughts about Denis or Jenny. In fact, he decided to stop thinking altogether…to wait and see where a newly rejigged friendship with Denis (and the others) might take him.

It took him, bizarrely, back to the early eighteenth century…and the writings of Alexander Pope.

In spite of much holiday idling and relaxation, Denis had apparently kept his brain busy in a practical way. He'd spoken (advanced) 'schoolboy' French on the Côte d'Azur and had even started learning Italian from a pretty girl in Viareggio. (Incidentally, Denis was never boastful; he merely dropped bits of news and information into the conversation as he went.) His friends could hardly believe it, however, when he announced at the start of the new term that he'd already looked ahead to the books and writers they would be studying that year and had happened to find a few dusty copies of a once celebrated poet's work in the family library. Not only come across them but also that he had begun to sift through the works of a certain Alexander Pope.

He spoke about subsequent pencil sketches he had drawn of the poet. About how he had been inspired by a portrait of Pope by a celebrated artist of the day, who had captured his likeness when about 30. A pensive Alexander staring into the distance, full-lipped, eyes large and moist, his cheekbones well defined. Some of Denis's more credible attempts he had taken with him to university, with which he intended to 'decorate' the walls of his new room. Sketches complete with that turban-type thing artists and intellectuals used to wear back in the eighteenth century. Replacing last year's tatty posters with the caption 'I drink, therefore I am', which some witty member of the group had scrawled out 'drink' and replaced with 'stink'.

There was, however, mused James, no Jenny around to make such a turban for her beloved! Something to which she would have no doubt turned her hand…

Denis spoke of how, late one night, he had come up with the idea of forming an Alexander Pope Society as soon as the new academic year was underway. How he wanted to share his discoveries. Apparently unconcerned as to whether or not it would prove popular. No, he already knew it wouldn't, clearly for a restricted elite, only for those of an 'Oscar Wilde type' sensitivity. People like them. He was, of course, doing it for himself…

While his friends looked on somewhat taken aback by this sudden release of unnecessary energy. What did a tiny, as they had just discovered…Alexander Pope suffered from severely stunted growth…and physically deformed poet (due to a hunchback) living well over two centuries ago…have to do with them or even more pertinently to the now refashioned Denis?

It therefore wasn't long before Denis had covered his walls in quotes, written out in fussy and curly lettering:

"Blessed is he who expects nothing, for he shall never be disappointed."
"What Reason weaves, by Passion is undone."
"You purchase pain with all that joy can give and die of nothing but a rage to live."

Together with and adorning the mantelpiece, a beautifully bound copy of *The Rape of the Lock*, full of its owner's comments and musings, readily available for anyone to pick up and peruse. There was little uptake.

Opened at the page, where you could find highlighted lines depicting a boat ride on the River Thames in all their mock-heroic glory. An even more satirical nod to the day when Denis and his friends had shared a similar experience on another stretch of the same river while taking it in turns to read aloud Rimbaud's Le Bateau Ivre.

The transformation now complete.

"But now secure the painted Vessel glides,
The Sunbeams trembling on the floating Tides,
While melting Music steals upon the Sky,
And soften`d Sounds along the Waters die.
Smooth flow the Waves, the Zephyrs gently play,
Belinda smil`d, and all the World was gay."

'And all the world was gay!' Bathos as smooth and elegant to Denis's ears and soul, as the craft on gently glittering waters.

Belinda, or should that be Jenny…?

James learned a lot about Alexander Pope that year, obviously through the Age of Satire lectures and even more intimately through membership of the society that he was (albeit unconvincingly) helping to form.

That the poet named Alexander like his father before him, was born in 1688…paradoxically the same year of the Glorious Revolution, which restored full-blown Protestantism to England in the shape of William and Mary.

The Popes, however, true to their surname, happened to be Catholics.

Up until then, enjoying relative religious and social freedom and living in London, with the future poet's father running a successful linen business.

By 1700 (Alexander would have been 12), they moved out of London to Binfield in Berkshire. Laws were by now harsher, applied more tightly and this meant that no Catholic could live within ten miles of the City of London.

As far as James was aware, Denis was neither Catholic himself nor had Catholic nor any religious leanings or affiliations but remained fascinated by his friend's passionate condemnation of the historic lack of religious freedom, the utter unfairness of the system. All leading to the subjugation of a fledgling genius.

James was also amused that, surprisingly, Pope (like Denis?) went on to become a great favourite of the female sex. In the main, high-class literary-minded women, who populated or regularly visited Twickenham, where he then chose to reside, just ten miles outside the City. They admired him for his superior intelligence, sparkling wit, knowledge of the classics, and his mastery of modern languages. Perhaps even more so for a wicked, almost spiteful streak, which could pour from his pen, when he took to lambasting the writings of certain highly regarded writers of his day. Attacks often personal in nature. With some friendships remaining and others permanently with daggers drawn.

All this left James still loitering on the margins of 'fanhood'.

Part 2
Eight Years Later...

Chapter 17
Patched; Fixed

A lot had happened during those intervening years. Much 'slaughter under the bridge', as James, on better days, worded it in his head! Much of it unremarkable, so naturally of little consequence…and yet alongside that, some stuff bordering on the sheer implausible.

James now occupied a very different 'place' from where we left him. Not always caring to remember, in what order that heavy chain of events had taken place. Some bad things worse than others to carry around, but all unbearably significant. Geographically, he had not gone far afield. No postgraduate ventures into dark continents, no tempting invitations from ancient penpals to discover what life was like living by the Pacific Ocean, or in the Australian outback. He had simply taken the train back to where he had come from. Except for when 'they' came, every now and then, to take him away for a spell…but these were not long journeys either. The English countryside.

He had been ill, very ill in fact. For a very long time, and then every so often regressing for a few weeks or months, before he was able to say yes again to life. The treatment had been arduous, as was his progress.

However, he did eventually manage to emerge from the tight, hellish shell that he saw around him, a shell he and life had galvanised in tandem.

On a happier note, he had more recently acquired a house, which looked out onto a centuries-old patch of green. Manifesting a continued need perhaps, for therapeutic surroundings. A beautiful Georgian property, with a pretty courtyard garden at the back. He sometimes wondered if Alexander Pope himself had ever walked by or even visited it. How would Denis have reacted to that, he mused, smiling faintly. A quiet sense of humour returned. This was to be his home, not only a fixed address but also a sanctuary from which to face the world and to which if venturing out, he would return, triumphant or not, each day. The heart-pumping excitement of some warmth and cosiness after such a long, debilitating illness, much of it lived out in clinical settings.

A new home no one could snatch back from him. He hoped that one day his sister Harriet and the two nephews that he barely knew, might agree to pay him a visit. Not very likely for the time being.

Once again, like when he was an undergraduate, it was time to start thinking about what he wanted to do, where his life was heading, each day seeming to race by now, when before time had seemed to drag, undefined except for light and dark. He acknowledged his unique and privileged position…everyone told him so…in a vague, abstract kind of way, but couldn't genuinely feel it. Anyone else would have jumped for joy at the news of such an inheritance. However, he remained detached from his circumstances, still mostly looking at his life from behind a murky screen.

Then came the time that he felt ready…to take up from where he had left off…he had hollered the word YES, three days in a row. (Jenny's magical number 3.) Not so much 'carpe diem' as 'seize BACK one's life'! 'Rise, take up thy bed and walk!'

For the reader's information:

In those eight gruelling years, Harriet's philandering husband had abandoned her and their two young sons.

Denis had virtually disappeared and Jenny had taken her own life.

James's parents had died in a car crash on the way back from Cornwall, one on impact…the other a few weeks later from sustained head injuries.

His mother Margaret had left a huge inheritance, which no one had known anything about…to share between both children. Fortune's wayward wheel. Double-spoked. Double-spiked.

It was a Thursday and James was making his way to St Raphael's Roman Catholic Church. Well, to the adjacent presbytery actually. It was a nondescript day, a bit grey, not particularly cold. He smiled to himself, shaking his head as he went, accepting that arranging such a meeting was also madness, still wanting to go through with it because he had learnt that, sometimes, it was good to follow up on an irrational whim, to do something a little crazy and out of character. Something small, yet radical. A dynamic act, especially for someone like him, who over-thought everything. Thinking too hard trapped you, held you to the spot, made you inert. He knew that now. He was travelling blind to see where such an encounter might lead. Purposeful.

He had been quietly grateful to the medical teams, who, with stoical diligence, had delivered him back to a place of hope for an acceptable life to come. Aware that the rest was down to him. They had listened to him ad infinitum, administered a whole range of potions and pills, furnished him with the tools of their trade, and shared advice on how to crush underfoot any looming or unresolved anxiety as if it were a low-lying, deadly creature…

He had much to carry forward. He imagined that what he needed now was the company of a wise individual. Someone totally detached from the world of white coats and slick advice, those specialist achievers and highflyers, socially buoyed up by their prestigious medical degrees. If only someone like that really existed…and locally. A Merlin, a Dalai Lama, an Elizabeth I, a Solomon, a Marie Curie, a Bertrand Russell…someone who could lend a wise ear, an independent voice, someone who spoke from a different wellspring. Someone to take him a few squares forward at a time on the mysterious board game of life.

A person like that, he could just pop round to speak to of an evening.

His unlikely wish did paradoxically 'come to pass', in a considerably less than grand manner. The result of his own unconscious listening into part of a conversation, which had recently taken place in an adjoining garden. He made a mental note of a certain name, which happened to be 'dropped'. That of a holy man, of a humble Father John O'Flaherty, parish priest of the local St Raphael's Catholic Church…

There was a small park across the road, and not wanting to arrive at the presbytery any earlier than the established time, James decided to make that his first port of call. Not quite understanding why he had left so early in the first place. It was his second visit of the day. He'd also visited the park before, remembering…because he always forgot…that it was endlessly uplifting, to be in the company of trees. He seated himself on a vacant bench, unrolled the newspaper he had just bought, and scanned the day's headlines: 'Maggie's Defeat on the Buses', 'Battered Tories Hold Out' and so on. Then, putting it down again, preferring to watch a couple of young women and their children in the nearby play area, all of which he found unusually charming…

His watch told him that he had just five minutes, and he made his way up the private road, which led to the priest's door. Then before ringing the bell, a last-minute sinking of the soul. What was he thinking of? Just what was he doing there? Why had he returned? A place that had nothing to do with him. How he would also be wasting the time of a presumably busy man. He suddenly remembered how he and Denis had often discussed the ongoing human need for religion. How he himself had always been antagonistic towards it. Bracing himself therefore against being sucked into any kind of devious plan to get him to join the church, thus giving him a final boost of last-minute courage.

A very short, curly-haired, florally dressed Mrs O'Sullivan opened the door, seemingly unaware that Father John had made the 2 o'clock appointment. She wasted no time in stating with and harsh tones what was probably a Belfast accent, who she was, what her role in the house was. The young man didn't possess the look of a normal parishioner (whatever that meant) and with tilted back head, eyeing him somewhat suspiciously…she then stated, "You'd better come in then. You'll find Father in his study, just along there on the left!"

Fortunately, a much warmer welcome awaited him once inside.

"Oh hello, James. Sorry I wasn't able to see you this morning. Always so much to do. I'd almost forgotten the time. Getting a bit too carried away with Sunday's homily as usual. Homily? It's like a sermon…this week on the subject of hypocrisy, and how we shouldn't judge others. Can I try a bit out on you? Don't be alarmed. Just want your opinion. Yes, do sit down, over here; the blue chair's a little less lumpy. You see to tie in with the scripture readings this week, I want to get the 'faithful' to see that stealing isn't just something that involves a so-called criminal…well, I happened to remember a little story I heard when I was much younger, in fact. It's somehow stayed with me and goes something like this:"

"Little Kevin's mother and father, a couple who took great pride in their parenting skills, were alarmed when they received a call from their son's head-teacher, saying that they strongly suspected he had taken some felt tip pens and sheets of card from the stationery cupboard without permission, with a view to smuggling them home. Such behaviour, stealing, was, of course, a very serious matter and so the head, Mr Murphy had no option but to call a meeting with the child's parents."

"The parents duly turned up at the school, very concerned and yet stating that it couldn't possibly have been their precious son, because…his father regularly supplied him with paper, pens, pencils, glue etc. that he himself brought home from the office…"

It was this simple gesture, a kind of fleeting invitation into Father John's world, the taking of a stranger into his confidence, that first impressed James and bound him to John. The priest also admitting that there would be a good few of the parishioners in his church, who still wouldn't 'get it' if he left it at that. Everyone helped themselves, if only occasionally, to bits and pieces from the workplace, didn't they? James suddenly remembering his own forays into the school stationery cupboard. Opening those precious pots of white, almond-smelling paste, used for glueing. Breathing in its heavenly scent. Hardly the same as stealing from a person, a shop or even a bank. Or was it?

However, he surmised that that's where John, in a kinder, more sensitive world, would have liked to leave it, to get people thinking in a different way. By themselves. To take responsibility and radically question their own behaviour, motivation and actions, especially in the small things.

The tale also caused James, just for a moment or two, to think about people he had once known. How they might have reacted to the story's message. Different again. Arguing how the State, all the big institutions and companies, from the most powerful down, used underhand means to retain privilege and wealth and continue to exploit the masses. Therefore, supporting a dog-eat-dog environment, designed exclusively for the strong and the rich and so what difference would it have made if a few pens and sheets of paper went missing every so often? If it kept the workers docile.

Friends from the past with anarchic leanings. People who clearly would not have been quite so impressed, so won over by the priest's story and its simple message of personal honesty in all things, great and small.

Chapter 18
James's New Chapter

I turned up at Star House on a Monday and quickly learnt that the family also called it Casa Stella. It was a nice place, unexpectedly cosy, in spite of its size. Quite unlike the other houses I had just passed, much grander in every way. John had said there were various people living there, so I had no idea who I was going to meet on this, my first day.

It happened to be Lorenzo that I first encountered, Giulia's nephew. Strutting, almost, in the spacious hallway…dressed in an airline-type uniform, navy blue jacket, that he was putting on, white shirt with those epaulette-type things, striped tie with pin. He didn't say much, seeming a little vague about who exactly I was and what I might be doing there.

Well, of course, he was…I wasn't even sure of that myself. He didn't seem to mind though, at that moment being more concerned about producing a perfect parting for his hair and having another go at the knot of his tie. After an initial glance in my direction, when he did speak to me, it was all the while looking in the mirror…then all of a sudden realising that he'd better get going; he was 'on duty' from 2 pm. Calling out that Zia Giulia was away at least until the weekend and telling me to go and meet his parents, who were in the kitchen on their lunch break.

By which time a dishevelled Father John had also turned up, somewhat out of breath, but still managing to apologise profusely for his lateness. He had taken it upon himself to show me around and make all the necessary introductions, uncertain as to whom he was going to find there. It was always like that at Casa Stella, he said.

As Lorenzo had stated, Domenico and Carmela…how will I ever remember all these names, I wondered, let alone get to adequately pronounce them…were at the kitchen table, halfway through what looked like a type of vegetable soup.

I urged them to remain seated, thanking them for their hospitality and assuring them that we would catch up later. They both spoke at the same time in a mixture of English and Italian, so I had to guess my way through what they were saying back at me.

Once John had given me the guided tour of the house and garden, he said he had to get back to the presbytery…the bishop was due to pay him a visit, something about checking the parish records…and so leaving me to my own devices. Everyone just so busy, it appeared. Unlike me. Endlessly free from appointments, duties, timetables and deadlines, never having to worry about work or personal finances. Leaving me to make up and fill in each blank day as it arrived. Always trying to colour it in, and yet giving up too soon. So much the better, I reflected, but again, sometimes not without its own difficulties, something not quite right about it, isolating. Something I knew rather than felt.

In truth, having reclaimed my health and free from worldly concerns…simply made me feel useless, an alien species. From a different galaxy.

I unpacked the few clothes I had chosen to bring…clothes perhaps meaning more to me now than they once did, probably due to the influence of my former university friends, especially Denis, who always appeared to know what to wear for any occasion. How to dress up, when to dress down. In my case, not much to do with fashion or even other people, but more to do with an attempt to cultivate a personal look which on rare occasions, even bordered on the eccentric. Only a few other possessions had made their way into the suitcase: toiletries, books, watches, cassette tapes, and tape recorder. My own place only fifteen or twenty minutes away.

I soon spotted that Giulia had left out a bunch of keys on the kitchen worktop, all clearly labelled: front door, back door, store room, garage etc.

I no longer drove a car. Hadn't for years. Yet another thing to get going again.

There was also a note left on the bed, addressed to a certain 'Giacomo', that I guessed had to mean me, even though there was one here now to confirm that it was the Italian version of my name. The note exuding an unexpected warmth of tone and instructing me where everything was. Information about who to call upon, if in need. Letting me know that her nieces would be back later. That the family usually met for supper around 7 pm and I was free to join everyone downstairs in the kitchen, whenever I wanted. I probably wouldn't be meeting her until the end of the week or beginning of the next, but she was looking forward to it. And so forth.

It turned out that my rooms, a big square bedroom, olive green in the main, equally big sitting room, much smaller kitchen and bathroom, came with a large quite ornate balcony, which looked out onto a vast expanse of garden. Definitely, the prize feature. There were even a couple of garden chairs, folded and propped up against the outside wall, no doubt in anticipation of warmer weather to follow. I had no head for heights, but at the same time, this particular balcony didn't appear threatening, wasn't too high up, and in fact, it felt somehow liberating, to be able to push open the double doors and fill my lungs with fresh air. I looked forward to watching the sun rise and set each day, not sure yet if that was even going to be possible.

That first week, I found myself going out for walks, or simply biding my time at a nearby pub. Generally getting to know a bit better my immediate surroundings, even though I was already fairly familiar with the wider area. Catching up with neglected reading. Following domestic and world events on the TV, tuning in to Newsnight or Question Time and when all that became too much to bear, I lay down on the bed, listening to music. Downstairs, I forced myself to chat to members of the family, especially Lorenzo's sisters. All light-hearted stuff. Father John was going to be proud of me. I was making every effort to engage and blend in. For my own good of course. A wise investment for a 'richer'…in every alternative sense of the word…future. Apparently.

All the while, picking up clues about Giulia. Her prolonged absence adding to the mystery of who she really was. Just second nature, on my part, to attach an exaggerated importance to the few people, I judged to be fascinating. Perhaps because she was away, I was 'overthinking' her and getting her wrong. She would probably turn out to be just a slightly odd and kindly soul. No more than that. There were such people in the world. Like my Aunt Hilda. Providing yet another occasion for me to look back on my own past foibles, and writhe in guilt and embarrassment. What kindness had I ever shown?

There were, however, clear signs imprinted of Giulia everywhere. Building on my first perception that she had to be an unusual woman. Simply for having opened up her home, to someone like me. Without knowing anything much about me. Father John, of course, having promised to reveal as little as possible. I reflected upon such generosity and naivety in a world like ours.

Whether I meant to or not, I was now back playing detective, already in possession of a sample of her handwriting, due to that note, and privy to her turn of phrase. Clearly highly organised, possessing a bold yet caring nature…

There also happened to be a large portrait of a woman with very dark shoulder-length hair, hanging just outside my suite of rooms on the top floor. I had noticed it the day after moving in. It had invited me into its shadows, and I instinctively knew that it had to be her. Regardless of the fact that no one had shown me a photograph or described her. I wanted to stare into that face, its expression as enigmatic as that of La Gioconda, but something stopped me from lingering for too long. Of course, having no idea why this was…

Over the next few days, I would go on to learn about Giulia's eclectic tastes in art, books and music. With the copious photos, dotted here and there in almost every room, confirming the identity of the woman in the portrait as her. (Not that she appeared in many of them, however). The family insisting from the start, that I was free to enter any of the rooms on the ground floor and borrow her books if I wanted to. Giulia was always keen to share them with others, they urged. Especially to go on and discuss them with her after. Not that there had ever been much uptake within the family.

Then there were the scraps of information, casually divulged by their housekeeper, a Mrs Mogden, a funny and likeable character, who spoke in broad 'Londonese', even when she was trying not to. With me, concluding (for the time being at least) that this Giulia was coming across as a bit too good to be true. A bit precious. The others, for some reason, never allowed themselves to say anything negative about her, not even in jest…

However, I knew that I was 'ready' for her. Giulia, I mean. Having in the last couple of days, already sensed a powerful attraction. Unsure as to what I meant by that, or why it mattered, or where getting to know her might take me. Furthermore, I felt happy that she hadn't entered my life until now. Any earlier, I might have messed things up, or missed out completely, on the 'fruits' of such an encounter.

Aware, of course (and not for the first time), that I was letting my thoughts escape unbridled, so stupid. Potentially hazardous. Come to that, I might not even like her! There were things I already thought I didn't like about her! Even for considering her worthy of all this attention. That is, they were not straightforward feelings…going deeper and beyond the 'Oh, she seems quite attractive for an older woman. I might try my luck…it's worked before'.

I sixth-sensed (and hoped) that my meeting her might deliver something of existential significance, perhaps along the lines of a friendship, something powerfully platonic. A noble kind of love. With a woman. I'd never really experienced that, outside of a book. Just recognised a new and prickly taste…or need…in my mouth, under my skin.

I had a couple of sessions with Father John during that first week…quietly amused that I was now permitting myself to put that creepy (for those, who haven't been raised as Catholics) title 'Father' in front of his name when thinking or talking to or about him. It got me thinking a lot about his lifestyle. What it must really involve. Not all his jokes did I find amusing, and many of his little stories could definitely stray beyond rambling, but somehow I knew from the start that I was in the presence of a worthy man, someone genuinely trying to do what he thought was best for me, and everyone else. Someone who lived out his beliefs. Who lived exclusively for others. Which begged another question, what made such a person tick? Where did it all come from?

I didn't understand the concept of a spiritual vocation. Not able to extricate it from the idea that it just had to be the result of some kind of prior brainwashing. For a Catholic priest, it seemed all-encompassing. They had to agree to give up practically everything the rest of us see as normal. All that made life worthwhile, bearable, painful even: personal freedom, pleasures like close friendships, family, sex. Not just for a while but forever. It was like the opposite of living at all…

Like death, then?

Chapter 19
In the Abercorn Arms

"Jimmy lad, Jimmy, over here, I want you to meet someone. Look, this is Dolly. Doll, this is my young friend Jimmy Boy. Dolly's just come back to these parts, haven't you, darlin', the place where she grew up. Look, I'm gonna buy the two of you a drink, and then I'm afraid I must skedaddle. What's it to be, Jimmy, the usual? Another gin and tonic for you, Doll girl?"

He went to order their drinks at the bar, which was rarely busy at that time of day.

"Good. There we are then. Will catch up with you later. Watch what you say, mind. Don't want to feel my ears burning…ha-ha. Bye for now. Au revoir. Toodle pip."

Within a couple of minutes or so, the generous and affable Sean was making his way out of the pub, waving back at his friends through the steamy window, as he wandered off along the wet pavement.

Oh God, thought James. He hadn't seen this one coming. The return of the feeling of sinking. Trapped. Something he knew he couldn't get out of. Wasn't that how it was in pubs? Their main appeal. Meeting new people from all 'walks' of life, as you shared a joke or drowned sorrows together. No one had forced him to enter. Now, any excuse to disappear would be overtly fake, downright rude in fact. He'd only just got there. Now, having to spend at least fifteen minutes…until finding a way out of it…with this elderly woman…a total stranger. That was what his culture had taught him about good manners. He still wasn't very good at small talk.

Could she, in fairness, be feeling pretty much the same? She too coerced. That thought not yet able to pierce his consciousness…

However, as is often the case when we anticipate the worst, James needn't have worried. It was she, who started up the conversation. Without him realising, that he could be on the verge of making a new friend, notwithstanding the obvious differences. Friendship…and even love…never confined to people of the same age.

"My name's actually Dorothy. Gosh, he takes a few liberties, doesn't he? I suppose it could have been worse; he could have called me Dotty!" she said laughing. "I've met him two or three times in here now. He's harmless enough. Very kind in fact. His ears must be burning already, ha-ha. I'm guessing you aren't a Jimmy either?"

James looked across the little table at her. She wore no make-up except for the two stripes of red drawn across her mouth. Her face and mole-spattered neck showing the unasked-for signs of ageing. Yet it was a nice face. She had probably once been quite pretty, he thought. Noting that having a kind, smiley character can often help to make a person appear better looking than they actually were…Dolly's blue eyes still managing to produce a twinkle, whenever something amused her. He thought she must dye her wavy hair, however…perhaps the only artificial thing about her…because there were no traces of grey amongst the brown. It was chin-length and she wore it loose, to frame her face. Her cheeks were nice and soft, almost downy.

"No, you're right. No one's ever called me that, not even at school. He just took over…and I went along with it. So, I'm James, very pleased to meet you, Dorothy."

"Well, since we are here in the pub, let's say that I'm happy with Dolly, after all. Sean has, I suppose, re-baptised me. My first proper acquaintance since returning to this place after so many years. I'm here to stay now, to the very end. It's been a dream of mine for at least 30 years. What's kept me going? Don't even properly know why. Then suddenly just sensing I had to be here, like my life going full circle. I belong here and the town belongs to me. It's just the way it is. Oh and just for the record, as a respectable woman of a certain age, I would never have walked into a pub on my own anywhere else. Even though I don't seem to know anyone here now. A false sense of security I suppose."

James half realised now that he was already feeling relaxed and aware just how easy it was to be in her company.

"Ah, but that means you need to find a new dream now…Dolly…not always an easy thing to do. Because we never believe, that those dreams are going to materialise. You're happy then if I call you Dolly, ok? We all need at least one dream to keep us going, surely?"

"You've got a very wise head on your young shoulders, I must say, James...I hadn't really seen it like that. Just happy for the first time in ages. Carefree and enjoying the moment. Don't feel the need for another one yet. I take it you have a dream then?"

At this, James hesitated for the first time since meeting her. Ultimately deciding to laugh it off and change the subject. Asking her now about her life here the first time round.

"Well, what do you want to know? It spans nearly two decades. Let me see. What might interest a nice young man, like you? I lived here up to the age of about 19, I think, to around the end of the war. I had been very fortunate, to get a place at the County School...the chance of a grammar school education seems to have disappeared around here now...and after that, I got a job as a shorthand typist...Perhaps the most dramatic thing I can tell you about my experience of the war years is that one morning, I must have been about 13 when we went upstairs from spending yet another night in the cellar, looked across the road and incredulously, the three houses immediately opposite were no longer standing. Gone. Swallowed up. Disappeared into the night leaving behind the smoking piles of rubble. The only proof that they had ever existed. That was the war for you."

Dorothy remained silent for a few moments, staring out and away from him from blue-glazed eyes. Then once more, she took up the story, as though it were from a life belonging to someone else.

"Mere rubble left behind. That's all. Leaving a gaping hole opposite, like missing teeth in the vast cavernous mouth of the morning. Three houses razed to the ground in one air attack. Our neighbours opposite all killed in the blasts, but with me thinking for a long while after, that it could so easily have been us. Only a few yards across the road. So hard to make sense of it. Why them and not us? I still think about it, well, it comes back more in the form of dreams these days. It was towards the end of 1940, and there had been the usual bombing raids during the night. For us children, the novelty of war having long worn off. That was how life had become, with us adapting to a new kind of normal. Most nights back then we just slept on mattresses on the cellar floor. That is whenever we heard the sirens."

Dorothy's expression became wistful and the pace of her words now much slower...

"I can still remember the dark and dank smell of it down there. Before the war, the cellar had always been more of an Aladdin's cave. The place where Dad sent me to fetch up those brown bottles of ginger beer, like at Christmas or family birthdays. With him always calling out to me to mind the steps on the way down…! He had a building firm and employed about ten men."

"So, why did you leave and are you living anywhere near that house now?" James asked, genuinely engaged by now in her personal story.

"I got married, James, as simple as that. My husband was a widower and already had a place of his own about thirty miles away, and that's where his work was located, so of course, that's where we lived. All taken as read. I never did learn to drive. No need, I suppose. No one has ever asked how I felt about having to move away, and I suppose in a funny sort of way, that helped me not think about it. Any feelings of regret obviously lying dormant for years. I am so fortunate though, on balance. I realise that now. What do they say, that ancient proverb…where there's life, there's hope…and here I am. My parents had always taught me to count my blessings and that patience was a virtue…"

"In fact, I am now living just a couple of roads away from that childhood home. Isn't that wonderful! I bought the house a couple of months ago and I'm deliberately taking time to relive all the memories, even better, rediscovering little things I had totally forgotten about. Learning as I go…on my walks, talking to people at bus stops or in shops; or in here of course, to anyone who looks as though they might remember something of those times…always hoping that not everyone has moved away…or worse. Like putting pieces of a life together as if from an old jigsaw puzzle. I like young people too though…we all have so much to learn from one another."

"The other day I turned up at my old primary school, St Mary Magdalene's. You must know it, that one near the bridge. The headmistress took it upon herself to show me around, saying that the fourth years were actually working on a Second World War project called 'Bread and Dripping'. Isn't that lovely! That's what we used to eat; a family favourite during the war and post-war rationing!"

"She's asked me to be guest of honour later this year, to do a talk about my childhood and wartime experiences. I've been jotting down memories as they come to mind. It's strange but back then, no one wanted to think, let alone talk about the war once it had ended. We all looked forward to happier days. Even my son, years later, would perform a funny kind of fake yawn if ever we did refer to it. (Dolly doing just that.) No one wanted to hear about it. As though it were our guilty secret to hang on to. I'm getting the feeling though, that it's changing, and that younger generations are beginning to regret not having learnt more about it from their own parents and grandparents…"

The two continued their conversation, with even James telling Dorothy a little about his own life to date, albeit in a highly selective manner. She turned out to be just as good a listener as storyteller…interested in everything he had to say, and in all probability, in what he was trying to keep from her. That she would leave for the future.

"Oh, if only Edward…" her voice melting away.

In fact, when James next looked down at his watch, he realised that he'd been in the pub for well over an hour. He had found in Dolly a kind of treasure trove of local (and human) information, events and scenes from a not-so-distant past, but one that to him in 1980 felt centuries-old. She couldn't have been much older than his own parents and like her son, the one she seldom referred to in her musings, neither James nor his sister had ever shown any real interest in World War II either…

Their lives seeming to hold something unanticipated in common.

Chapter 20
Light on Water

It wasn't long before James and Giulia were spending shared time together, snatched time. Theirs a mutual attraction, equal, pre-ordained. Mental and physical, playfully and profoundly sensed by James during the lead-up to their first encounter. Something in the air. A semi-conscious understanding of the playing out of fate. Possibly the same for Giulia, when learning his name from Father John.

Both opting for a clandestine love, despite the permissive society. It therefore prompted a need for signs and symbols to assemble and decode. Certain footwear left outside a bedroom door. A white flower in a vase in the hallway. An upside-down photo in Giulia's study, which now always remained unlocked. And so on. Compelling each to read into the language of the day, which signalled if they were free to meet, talk or love that night. Theirs, a passionate encounter, delicate rather than romantic, but which they each sensed could be dangerous too, transcending much-buried pain on both sides.

As for James these days, it wasn't so much the ancient fears of lofty heights or cramped places…more to do with inner space. He could now avoid those 'unnecessary' experiences, such as having to enter those sealed, windowless lifts that he hated, always choosing to take the stairs.

Instead, it was that murky stuff, which cloyed, lingered or regularly resurfaced. Uneasy thoughts, memories and emotions. The carrying on of family guilt.

Theirs, a shared chapter in a story, which masked and encompassed the fears, which gnawed away at them. Creating a sweet release from all that bound or weighed them down. Each recognising the other's personal song, each seeing him or herself in the other. Warm comfort more ancient than the capacity of human language, which can never totally hit the target.

The simple joy of glimpsing the other by chance on the stairs…sharing a secret smile…the anticipation of their next encounter, no matter how fleeting…and all the childish, coded fun they shared.

Not a relationship, which had prompted thoughts about past or future time.

Then one afternoon and 'out of the blue', Giulia invited James to Venice. She had already visited the once prestigious marine republic and felt that it was the right place in which to disappear for a while. The city of 'masks and light and water', she said. A time for them both to drown in its mysteries. A floating city, which everyone sensed, would not be there in years to come. Its days numbered from the start of its humble awakening. She said that she had taken an old school friend there, after giving her the choice of Venice or Lourdes. Laura was in the final stages of cancer. Laura had chosen Venice…

On a lighter note, Giulia making much of the fact that James's name and surname translated back into that of the legendary Venetian adventurer and lover Giacomo Casanova himself…and they could now retrace his steps and test out his 'notoriety', she joked.

They would set themselves little tasks, such as counting and crossing as many of the 400 bridges as possible, tiny bridges in the main, which connected each of the City's numerous little islands. Then go on to explore the vast and secret waters of the lagoon. Aiming to be, in effect, both tourists and true Venetians. Separately, they would write little poems set against the backdrop of places they visited, to share once back in England.

She would take him to church. There were well over 100 to choose from…

All this oddly reminded James of that precious first year at university, where essays apart, you had to work hard to keep up with the pace, originality, and wit of those around you…a mix of cultured dons and fellow students…something stimulating he welcomed from the start, even though it all tended to unfold in unstuffy ways. Against a backdrop of larking around, drinking and exaggerated posturing.

Likewise with Giulia. So much to learn from her, but he also wanted her to learn from him. His own brand of 'originality'…it had to count for something. A sign of generosity on his part, as well as a touch of pride and vanity. He admired her intelligence, which as well as all her cultural knowledge, also included knowing when it was wiser to stay quiet…a rare phenomenon.

At Casa Stella, first the planning. Each wanting to keep their 'storia d'amore' to themselves for as long as possible. Hence, Giulia would leave for Venice a couple of days before her lover's departure. Telling everyone that she was meeting up with an old friend in Verona, which wasn't too far away from her true destination. The family, as always, never allowing themselves to ask follow-up questions, as regards her little 'trips away' but each separately concluding that it must have something to do with that 'mystery man' she visited from time to time…a story conceived in their own heads, built on repeated bits of flimsy evidence. Hastily construed and then safeguarded where the mind easily alighted.

James bought an 'open' airline ticket, leaving him free to decide when to return, either before or after Giulia. She making no demands on him. No stepping on toes. No manipulation. That would have ruined everything and in any case, it was unnecessary. James wholly taken up with the idea of visiting Venice, La Serenissima, especially with her…having never been before, strange in itself…and there again there was his already bizarre connection with the place. When he looked down at a map of the watery city, he spotted the symbol of 'yin and yang' (or perhaps it was their own hands), in the arrangement of its islands.

Recalling the time (a good few years beforehand), with some degree of embarrassment, when his sister had told him about the results of a 'personality survey' she had carried out on his behalf in one of those magazines she was always reading. (After first doing one on herself.) It had turned out that the place in the world that most related to him was indeed the City of Venice! Life again playing out one of its neat little tricks.

Sometimes out of the chaos and pain, as if by magic, he already knew that things appear to come together…like the spinning and weaving of a poem.

What nonsense…and yet…delicious nonsense, as he was now heading towards his 'rightful' place, to spend a string of carefree days and nights with the most extraordinary woman he had ever encountered. A mature and, in his opinion, beautiful woman, whose mouth smiled while her eyes narrated sadness. An adult Marazion? Had that been love all those years ago? More likely a kind of rehearsal for what was to come. Was this even love now, or something flimsy and ephemeral, a perfect bubble, set up to burst? Was love misting up his own vision of her, making mischief with his fragile mind?

He then turned his thoughts again to that huge, bewildering and primitive phenomenon…maternal love. A mystery no one fully understood. Least of all him. That instant love. The instant bonding. How each new mother believed her baby to be the most beautiful in the world, while others nodded in fake agreement, seeing all the while how disappointingly prune-like it was. Unattractively puce and crumpled, with its dull floating eyes. Then the flash of pain stabbing his stomach, the return of an image of his mother Margaret first (and subsequently) looking down at the poor imperfect creature in her arms, not part of the deal. This, he duly extinguished, choosing his former reverie about his lover…By now knowing exactly how to crush underfoot such an unwelcome chimera.

The love instinct therefore playing out for the survival of the human race. Designed by nature for nature. We humans seeing beauty that probably isn't there, for each new life to thrive…prompting us to feel this 'deep love thing' above everything else.

Did Giulia's uncomfortable beauty affect others too? Or was he the only one capable of acknowledging it?

This was how it worked, when we 'fall' for someone…in order to 'kick start' the above process, until the moment, when our dreamy eyes suddenly open wide and pierce the truth, see things as they change, as they really are. This, James could not and would not accept. Not when it came to Giulia. Impossible to envisage her not looking, sounding and being as she did now.

Neither could he properly answer those other questions, which never completely went away.

What he was certain of, however, was that if love meant wanting to marry her, then no. Not now nor ever. About that, he could be wholly rational, uncharacteristically decisive. Far too limiting…for them both. Domesticity. It would let in the ordinary, downgrade their lives to mere roles, killing off any remaining love, which once bound them. A poisonous drip, drip, drip. An image of his parents' faces now floating back into view. Versions dead or alive? He wasn't sure. The sight of which, in either case, causing him to shudder.

Meanwhile, Giulia had travelled on ahead, turning up to meet him two days later at the Santa Lucia railway station. Telling him (during a lengthy embrace), that she had a surprise for him, that they were not going to stay in a hotel after all. Quite by chance, just before going to find one, she had started up a lively conversation with an elderly woman in a nearby café, who on hearing that Giulia was going to be spending a few days in Venice (and soon to be joined by a male friend from England), invited them both to stay with her. "Far too big an apartment now for just one person. Once it breathed full of people of all ages…It's behind the piazza, on the second floor of the big palazzo. I will take you now…" she had said exuberantly.

It appeared that such things only happened in a place like Venice, thought James, or when one was so drunk on love, the magic continued to spread…outwards and beyond. He tried to imagine the same set of circumstances back home. That is of inviting someone, you had only met a few minutes beforehand, to share your home…and found it impossible. Not part of the national character. People too insular, untrusting and phlegmatic. People who only looked down or straight ahead, never to the sides and beyond, or more importantly to the skies. Being Italian, Giulia had accepted at once, charmed by such an unexpectedly warm offer.

Had she not done the same for him in England a few months beforehand?

Both Giulia and James delighted to discover, that their two designated rooms could be accessed internally by a semi-disguised adjoining door…and that the building, which was centuries-old, offered up high ceilings in every room, full of decorative paintings to stare up at; at swirls of cavorting cherubs in a shell pink and pale blue paradise; at all the stylised animals and related symbolism, which underpinned ancient myths and legends. At Mother Mary, set amongst the low-lying 'puff ball' clouds, as she held her precious baby son…

A real home, once bursting down the generations, with the noise and clutter of family life. Its stories and conversations trapped in the walls, now tightly stored in musty pockets of air. So much better than staying at an impersonal hotel no matter how prestigious. They had their own key and so could eat, or not, when and where they chose. The same with sleeping, or going out. James was impressed and felt ripe for adventure. This was all part of it. He assumed the role of honorary Venetian, as he took up his place by the waters of the Rio della Misericordia. Like diving head-first into a painting by Canaletto.

Nothing however could have prepared him for the view of the city when on the following day, the 'vaporetto' swept and swung them around the lower part of the city's reverse S shape. From where they began to make out Santa Maria della Salute to the left…and further up the Canal Grande, on the other side, the magnificent Palazzo Ducale, already bathed and gilded in the morning light. Giulia looked up at him and read his heart, "Sublime, isn't it?" James's spirit lifted even higher by the warm stream of her words. Recalling writer Truman Capote's comment that 'Venice is like eating an entire box of chocolate liqueurs in one go'. So bloody what! Maybe it is what we all need! The sickly image kicked quickly away.

(Even more so, what did that say about a Venice with Giulia?)

Later that night, he found himself going over a recent incident. An antidote to overdosing on all this love and beauty and wonder. Just a couple of months beforehand, despite meeting Giulia, already conscious of the effect she was having on him, he had felt the sudden urge to abandon Star House. Not knowing then if he would ever feel ready to return. Another minor relapse? Something to do with Denis or Jenny, or perhaps with them both. And or his 'stranger-like' parents. It had all come about after Giulia's suggestion that he might want to help her transform her wild garden.

Man created in any case for life on earth, not a celestial paradise…

He had, of course, made the return journey…simply unable to stay away.

Chapter 21
The Choir

James and Giulia walked everywhere, except when travelling by water. Their clothes seemingly getting looser as the days came and went. Old Father Time now having to fit in with human needs for once. Getting up late, or with the sunrise, planning only the next few minutes or hours, loafing around in cafés or visiting little artisan workshops. Going on safari-type escapades. On a quest to spot owls and kestrels, herons and cormorants, all the gliding and swooping waterfowl on offer. The turquoise and orange flash of a solitary kingfisher. The sight of lavender, in the form of a pale mauve carpet, spread across the heavily doomed wetlands.

The magic continuing to enfold them.

As on the day, when they were crossing Piazza San Marco, and became aware of a group of adolescent girls, who suddenly stopped what they were doing and broke out into song. In fact, a medley of songs delivered 'a cappella' across diverse languages. Impossible, then, to guess where this impromptu choir came from. The singing went on for ten minutes or so until two of the girls broke free and began to hand out flyers, to the (by now) gathering crowd of onlookers. Showing them when and where they would be performing later that evening, apparently in a little church not far from the piazza, after which they dissolved into the morning mist.

James and Giulia each separately sensing that they too would be there among them.

Although a good few days had already passed, they still hadn't taken the customary gondola ride. Both fearing an inevitable awkwardness about finding themselves on show to the rest of the world. Inevitably steered by a tanned gondolier with film star looks, who would deliver up the usual menu of truncated arias and an embarrassingly long stemmed rose for Giulia, on behalf of her presumed love interest, as he rhythmically struck the waters. Neither appreciated that kind of approach or the need to go public. Never wanting to become tourist packaged, or caught for eternity, albeit anonymously, on someone else's camera film. However, they also knew by now that to explore the tiny, back street canals from a water perspective, the gondola was the best option. It was only going to be the once in any case.

Therefore, when the time came, an amused James looked on as Giulia was exchanging words with their assigned gondolier, as he (Carlo) nodded repeatedly to her requests…

"What exactly did you tell him?" James asked as they stepped into the wobbly craft.

"That in order to save him any later embarrassment, we were brother and sister, and so there was absolutely no need for him to churn out the usual pseudo-romantic claptrap, O Sole Mio…and the rest!"

"And what will you say to him when he realises that I don't speak any Italian, surely a little strange, me being your brother?"

"Oh, just that we were separated for many years. That we've only recently come to know one another…not too far from the truth, don't you think?"

"So now I will have to restrain myself from kissing your neck…for fear of arrest," commented James, pretending to be crestfallen.

"Just as well," she replied, laughing, "or else you might miss something priceless. If I can wait a couple of hours for your kisses, then so can you!"

Leaving the busy Canal Grande and its 'vaporetti', they spent the next few hours, undisturbed, as they glided through the maze of watery backstreets, feeling pleasantly relieved, removed at last from the tourist-infested city. Pointing, commenting on and giggling about any little domestic detail, which happened to catch their attention…

Starting with the basket of shopping making its precarious way up to a third-floor balcony and then the manic dance of each line of washing hanging out to dry, high above their heads. The mottled reflections of buildings, flickering on the evergreen water. The tiny wrought iron balconies, which were crammed with plants in terracotta pots, with their gaudy red, pink and orange flowers. Every so often, the appearance of brightly painted little boats lining one side of the narrow and nameless canals. The distant sight of what looked like a floating vegetable market.

The perpetual rows of indelible tidemarks on the walls, a warning of past and future flooding. Ordinary people, real Venetians this time, going about their business, as they made their way up and over the seemingly infinite number of tiny bridges, with their bags and baskets. People, who had learnt since birth to live alongside the rising sea levels, to the surrounding presence of saltwater, which regularly soaked city pavements, filled shop floors and basement cellars and silently ate away at their foundations.

The intoxicating smell of the water, which surrounded them. Its music, now coming in the form of regular and reassuring guitar slaps against the sides of the gondola.

It was now evening and James and Giulia decided to stop for a bite to eat and a glass or two of champagne, at a café on Piazza San Marco, before setting out on foot for the little church where the choir would be appearing. The sky was already pitch black, and both sat mesmerised by the elegance of their young waiter, in his manner, movements and appearance…straight back, perfect teeth and hair, how he deftly held the tray (other arm tucked behind his back) and placed two dainty dishes of 'mousse au chocolat' on their little round table. An impressive choreography from start to finish. How he kept words to a minimum. The role of the humble waiter elevated to an art form. The evening transformed once again. A tiny scene presumably lost on everyone else.

They thought they knew how to find the venue. They had the name of the church and the name of the 'calle'. However, Venetian addresses are notoriously complicated to outsiders, not based on any comprehensible logic. Locals' directions were likewise unreliable, and Giulia had to confess to James that she didn't always understand what bystanders were telling her, as their dialect was very different from where she was from. It seemed by now that they had been walking for ages, and round in circles, even though they sensed they were close. The effects of the champagne also playing a part, perhaps. Just so frustrating. They had both felt the urge to be in that church. There would hardly be any point now in continuing, as the little concert would soon be underway. A missed opportunity, so disappointing…

They were on the point of conceding defeat, having lost all sense of direction when James suddenly turned round and declared. "Look, that must be it. That poster on the wall. Ha-ha, can you believe it? We've found the church after all! It's tiny."

"Or it's found us," replied a happy, yet somewhat restrained Giulia. Each saved by the magic, unconcerned about how they would find their way back.

There was to be yet another surprise for them that evening.

It very soon becoming clear that the choir in question was none other than that of a highly regarded girls' school, Giffins, situated very close to where they lived back in England…

The next morning, a sombre Giulia told James, who was already soaking up the early sunshine on the balcony…that she had to leave Venice. Only for a couple of days, though. That the manager from the hotel next door had just sent someone round with a message.

"I have to go straightaway, I'm afraid. I have already packed a few things…but I'm sure you will be fine. There is always the Signora Zanin you can ask, should you need anything. See you on… Wednesday, then!" at which she planted a cold little kiss on his cheek.

How strange. The last thing James would have expected. As though a tiny bomb had exploded. He felt numb and bewildered, knowing that he had no right to feel either. They shared a silent understanding that they were always free to come and go as they pleased. However, he was only human, and couldn't prevent a shabby barrage of questions from invading his head. *Where was she going? Had she known about this from the outset? Who was it who had made contact and how exactly? Why did she not give him a more detailed explanation? Why such a frosty goodbye…and why the rush? Could he not have gone too, to see her off at least? Would she really only be away for two days*? So, it continued…Human frailty.

He dealt with each question, one by one, though each returned to haunt him. She had looked genuinely unsettled by the departure, but at least had not tried to fill his head with a made-up story. It must have had something to do with her past life, something that he was no part of, so why get upset? Giulia was a strong person, and yet he was becoming aware of a more vulnerable side, as their liaison developed. He hoped she was not in any kind of trouble, and yet again, if that were the case, why hadn't she trusted him to help her?

Chapter 22
The Tourist

Having little desire to return to England, James decided to make the most of this unexpected situation and play the role of quintessential tourist. He had, so it appeared, two full days to follow famed trails, to experience parts of the city he still hadn't visited. Places he may not even have got to see at all if Giulia were there. Used to being on his own, and replete with life's coping mechanisms. By now, second nature. The therapy had taught him that much. Body and mind restored and reconnected in an instant.

He hired himself an English-speaking guide for the second of the two days, as he wanted to see and learn more about the 'ghetto' in Cannaregio. However, today preferring to be by himself, dissolve into the crowds behind anonymous black glasses, and discover where the flow would take him. La Signora Zanin had already mentioned some evening concerts that might interest him.

He could also devote more time to reading up on the extraordinary lives of famous Venetians of the past, the likes of Marco Polo, Antonio Vivaldi, Carlo Goldoni…not forgetting his own infamous namesake.

Thoughts about Giulia didn't go away, however. How could they, their having just spent a crazy week of love? He picked up a book she had left on the bed, something to do with an ancient walnut tree in Benevento, and wondered again who she was, who she really was, and why when still a child, she had ended up living in England, cast out of her own country. Unlike most other people he had encountered, she never spoke, not even fleetingly about her past life, about who her parents were… A wordless no-go area, made clear from the start, even with him.

He knew her character though, her being, her essence: that she was lovely, kind, unusually passionate (judging from the cool exterior), clever, witty and well-read. Very religious also, if her weekly (and sometimes more often than that) attendance at Mass was anything to go by…She had to be in her late thirties, and easy guesswork told him that she didn't have a husband (past or present) or any children. No one at Casa Stella had seemed willing to open up any more about her past, but perhaps they didn't know a lot either in spite of their close ties. He had given up enquiring, and yet still grateful for any carelessly dropped bits of information. Were they really blood relatives? With so little in common. No one actually looked like her either. Very strange.

On the day of Giulia's departure therefore, James, went 'out and about', threading his way through the reams of tourists, who were in the main conspicuously American, with their loud, drawly accents and equally loud choice of clothing (especially the men's.) They got into everywhere: swarming across the Rialto Bridge, inside the Palazzo Ducale, and outnumbering the pigeons in the Piazza San Marco. To get away, James eventually took a boat out to the island of Murano, where he watched as the glass-blowers exhibited their mesmerising art in humble and stifling workshops. He had already bought Giulia something that morning, a book containing five plays by Goldoni and soon fell under the spell of a glass-beaded necklace that he visualised placing around her neck and for which he inevitably paid well over the odds, the number of Italian lire making the cost appear even more phenomenal.

He then headed off by waterbus to Venice's famous Lido, which about 70 years beforehand, had generously gifted its name to the outdoor pools springing up all over England. Just like the local 'lido' he and his sister had enjoyed while still living at home…another life ago.

It turned out to be a long flat sliver of land, full of sandy beaches, which acted as a barrier for the lagoon. James was fully aware that he was following in the sacred steps of poets Goethe, Byron and Shelley. A little more recently, in the footsteps of Thomas Mann, whose novels he had started reading while at university; remembering just how funny he had found *The Confessions of Felix Krull*.

The sun continued to pour down its rays, while the contents of the bottle of Bardolino he had ordered gently misted his brain, as well as oil his soul and imagination.

Allowing him to visualise, in the style of an Impressionist painting, all those who arrived each year in their hordes to be part of the acclaimed Film Festival. To catch a flickering glimpse of the starry screen gods and goddesses of the moment with their busy entourages…and tons of devoted fans straining to venerate them. All hungry for a sighting, a whisper, a touch, an autograph. A chance to declare to the world, 'You'll never guess who I saw…in Venice' and therefore if only for a few moments, shine in their own misplaced and according to James, pathetic glory.

Quietly grateful on that particular day…a day he now owned…that the narrow strip of island wasn't packed at all and that he could linger or wander exactly as he chose, leaving him free to gorge on ideas as to how von Aschenbach must have felt in those same surroundings. While frustratingly at a loss to invent a new face for him…it was continuously that of Dirk Bogarde in the Visconti film, which rose up to meet his gaze, a film he had watched on at least a couple of occasions, each time leaving him heavy with sadness.

The thriller Don't Look Now was next in the queue of his cinematic memories. Although of a different genre, it too was set in a melancholy Venice. With its painful themes of love, death and loss. Reminding him of the crazy things that so many of us do to escape the inevitable, to escape the unbearable nature of reality.

A new image then appeared. This time from his own life. Crouched in his mind's eye, lasting only a few seconds. That of two of his university friends, as they walked almost floating, hand in hand, across the sand. In his direction. Followed soon after by two more blurred figures, those of his parents skimming into view, they too advancing towards him, and then all of a sudden dissolving into the sunny haze. All there to pay him a surprise visit.

It didn't stop there at the Lido. That surreal and unasked-for return of ghosts from the past. When back in St Mark's Square (just like Laura in the film), he was sure he caught sight of the same little blonde girl dressed in red, as she dodged in and out of the city's ancient architecture…the workings or manifestation of Jenny's rule of three.

Probably because of the ubiquitous sand, his thoughts then turned further back in time to Cornwall and Marazion. Was she also about to make a return? No visitation yet, and James suddenly knew why…it becoming perfectly clear…that all along, it was Marazion, who had heralded the coming of Giulia into his life, corresponding to an earlier version, a child straining to grow up, and yet still unready to emerge from her itchy chrysalis. A girl without a family of her own. No sightings indicating that she was still alive somewhere, and thinking of Arthek…

He had drunk a lot that day, far more than usual. His skin had soaked up too much sun.

In the evening, still affected by hazy visions and far too much red wine, James made his way to a church, to listen to some Vivaldi. Easy, uplifting music, which wafted cosily familiar around his head, lifting his spirits. He had always loved the sound of Baroque violins and despite the fact it was a season of concerts laid on more for tourists than for the buffs, it didn't appear to bother him. That is after all what he was. A mere tourist. Music was music in any case…beautiful live music so much the better. The concert morphing into theatre, as the musicians entered the church, dressed in full eighteenth-century costume. Everything coming together. The evening's programme offering up the expected Quattro Stagioni but also featured some of Vivaldi's lesser-known lute pieces. Quelle surprise! On top of everything else today…

The improvised stage at the top of the central nave, a dazzle of the men's pony-tailed wigs and waistcoats, which highlighted the elegant cut of silky pastel-coloured jackets and matching knee breeches, the lacy frills and flounces, the slightly high-heeled shoes. Pale apricot, lilac, sky blue, oyster pink, ivory. How wearing such clothes…no doubt agonisingly uncomfortable…caused the musicians to stand, sit, bow, maintain perfect posture and play their instruments. Albeit stiff and stifled. Then the women with their damask elbow-length sleeves, their trains, hooped petticoats, and too-tight bodices, which both squashed and then lifted, with each new breath, their breasts above low necklines. The masks, their bowed heads, their powdered faces and patches. The seductive language of the fan. Did anyone know that a Giacomo Casanova was in the audience?

The ever-present workings of magic…if you knew how to watch and listen, to think, to fantasise.

The day's reading causing him to ponder how life must have been two and three centuries beforehand at the Pio Ospedale orphanage. How Vivaldi, composer and musician, known as the Red Priest (partly due to the unusual colour of his hair) had stepped in to transform the lives of the illegitimate daughters of the ubiquitous courtesans, turning the most talented into choristers or musicians in highly acclaimed orchestras. An ongoing act of altruism or carried out for interests of his own? More likely than not, a bit of both. James fixed them in his mind, as they played out their spared lives on musical instruments hidden behind screens, out of modesty and respect for a morally superior audience…hypocrisy that ran wild.

These were the fortunate ones, left as babies at the Ospedale and placed in the ominous 'scafetta', a kind of box-like compartment…which when shut allowed the nuns to retrieve them on the other side of the wall…all abandoned by mothers who were unable to look after them. A box perpetuating the big respectability lie. Baby girls brought up by the nuns, supported by benefactors. With the likes of Antonio Vivaldi composing hundreds of concertos and oratorios for them, once they had grown. Anna Maria, Chiara, Nicoletta, Lucrezia and so on. All devoid of surname.

Less fortunate, however, the new-borns tossed into the Canal Grande. Venice, elegant playground of the 'bel mondo'.

Giulia returned as promised after a two-day absence. In a turquoise dress, one that he had never seen before, and what appeared to be a new leather bag draping her left shoulder. She and James picking up seamlessly from where they had left off, with no further explanation on her part. The same as before, only that James thought he had detected a little more strain in her voice, her face slightly more pale and drawn…

Chapter 23
The Replacement Child

Back in England, the weeks grew quietly into months, and James's life slotted itself into a neat pattern of (what was for him) hard labour in the garden, broken up by bouts of pleasurable relaxation and everything in between. If anyone was thinking that it must be time for him to go home, no one alluded to it…Almost one of the family now, he had even managed to pick up a little more Italian.

He read widely and profusely and kept a Casa Stella journal. In which, for his own amusement and amongst other jottings, he had penned lengthy descriptions of everyone, most verging on caricature, some full of bathos. Inspired no doubt by his earlier brush with Alexander Pope. All the while causing bittersweet memories of Denis to return…

The piece that he was just finishing focussed on Serafina, Lorenzo's young Sicilian wife, who had recently come to live in England.

In his description, James had turned her into a timeless Greek-style goddess that he had begun to 'worship' soon after her arrival, making her the focus of daily prayer rituals. He had to be careful, however, that no one in the family came across it, or any of the other pieces, as they could be open to misinterpretation. Anyone who took what they read literally. Lorenzo in particular.

Somewhat surprisingly, he had not written a word about Giulia. He was 'living' her instead. It was she, who had stolen his soul, and while this feeling continued, no written record was possible or even necessary. She filled his gaps, and he believed that, in spite of her own deep spaces, he occasionally filled hers.

In the end, he decided to leave the journal with its 'incriminatory' descriptions at his other home fifteen minutes away, which with or without him, continued to look out onto the triangular green.

He went out for regular walks, which included (usually on the way back) visits to what by now really had become his local, The Abercorn Arms. It suited him totally. An old-fashioned, friendly kind of place, with little in the way of drunken fights…although alcohol-fuelled arguments occasionally erupted, as customers spilled out at night onto the cobbles. There were the usual drug pushers and 'it fell off a lorry' merchants doing their rounds, but business was low-key in nature, practically invisible to those who knew little of the local subculture. To those who thought such things, if they really did happen, only went on elsewhere. Or to those who preferred to turn a blind eye. Including James. He had no taste for any kind of drug now, illegal, family doctor prescribed or otherwise. Nor for fights, nor involvement in matters that he considered were nothing to do with him. The police having rarely turned up in his own life.

In spite of all the earlier dreams of alternative lifestyles or of blazing a trail in the name of social revolution, he had remained indubitably middle class. He was lazy. He was cowardly. Stuck in the concrete of his own situation, which ultimately suited him. Which consequently left him feeling ashamed and yet it seemed he was unable to do anything about it. Surviving each passing day was energy-sapping enough. A constant and repeated drain.

He continued his liaison with Giulia and dug up vast areas of the Casa Stella garden. She had a crazy notion about transforming it into some kind of earthly paradise, including the creation of a large pond and decorative fountain, and much more. He, the unlikely gardener, was bizarrely helping her with it. It turned out to be unexpectedly satisfying, however, in spite of any resulting fatigue, back pain or aching muscles. Physical signs that he was at last engaging in something practical, useful. The early morning start, convincing himself he was now taking a dip into the ancient rituals of the once ubiquitous agricultural labourer, the following of peasant rhythms. He got used to the wind and rain and the ferocious bite of winter. His days, guided by sunrise and sunset and at last appearing to hover on meaningful.

Meetings with Father John came to be ever more relaxed in nature. Each man uncertain as to whether they were for James's continued therapy or purely friendship-based.

It didn't appear to matter in either case, their conversations having touched upon many subjects. From a current news item to comments on popular culture, and then to poetry. From plans to redecorate the presbytery at last, to discussions about the sacrament of Holy Orders. Sometimes John needed extra help when Father Paul was away for example…a priest's work is never done…so would ask James to sit in and answer calls in his office when having to visit the home of a needy parishioner. Sometimes to sort through papers in the bottomless drawers of the priest's desk, finding everything from sweet wrappers to unsharpened pencils, to yellowing order of service booklets with their faded photographs.

The part-time secretary often absent due to the chronic health condition of one of her children. Neither John nor James, however, wanting to define (or bring an end to) this unlikely, ad hoc arrangement. What the dean or bishop might have had to say about it was a different matter…an agnostic rifling through church drawers and Catholic practices.

James vaguely anticipated that he would stay for at least another six months and then reassess his situation unless Giulia or one of the others had different ideas. He knew in any case that he would continue to visit them. Father John, this house and the De Martino family had entered his life at such a crucial stage of his odyssey back to good health. How could he not feel a special attachment to them all? Even to the pond that he was helping to create. He too would be leaving his mark there.

A new sensation…gratitude…yet another sign of recovery.

New friendships, lighter in nature, were also blossoming elsewhere. Especially at the pub. James, who had always veered towards the intellectually minded, was now broadening his range of companion type. It felt good. It felt liberating. He had only recently detected about himself (followed up by a customary bout of self-loathing) an ugly snobbish streak, not so much a class-based prejudice like that of his mother, but more to do with a desire to be with people he considered erudite, cerebral like himself. It had sprung from an early and yet healthy need to learn from others. Then had turned in on itself. Prejudicial and ignorant on his part. Why had he not seen this long ago? Perhaps there had never been anyone close enough to point it out…or that he had chosen not to look or listen.

It explained to some extent what had kept him from getting close to his sister Harriet. In spite of shared childhood experiences. She had always been bright, lively and positive but without feeling the need for books or 'higher things'…so he had callously dismissed her. It also partly explained why he had not stayed in touch with former school friends.

Now he was living life in a much freer and open manner. Open to diverse possibilities. Enjoying the pub's guest bands on a Friday night (a return to some of the music he had grown up with), sharing chats with visiting musicians, listening in on the current batch of silly jokes circulating at the bar, the more stupid, the more he allowed himself to laugh…What do we call Postman Pat when he retires? Knock, knock, who's there? What did the barman say to the horse, as it entered the pub? Even the unacceptable ones, by society's frosty standards today… Why does a woman need legs? And so on.

Listening in on (rather than contributing to) the never-ending barrage of banter, the range of often dodgy or suspect political opinions, engaging more easily with people of different ages, types and places. Each in any case with his or her own story to tell, his or her unique set of circumstances. Not so difficult after all. They too merely trying to steer a way forward…

Dolly, by now a regular, had become a firm favourite as she offered him yet another layer of support, personal support, which bordered on the maternal.

All those years trying to tackle Hamlet's dilemma of 'to be or not to be', his cliff-top life seeming to dangle from a flimsy thread. Living on near empty, accompanied by the fear, forever gorging off itself, and the overwhelming sense of guilt he carried everywhere. The fact that he hadn't shown love or gratitude towards his parents, for not becoming closer to Harriet, his same flesh and blood; harbouring an absurd guilt for being the replacement child. Not really wanted after all. The one who felt unworthy of this role and title…completely hidden to those looking in.

Was he really such an improvement on Peter, his older brother? He the son that they had decided to keep and show, over the one who had to remain hidden from view. As they tried to make themselves feel better about the tragedy. No embarrassment to follow them around, no one to stare or make fun of the family connection, or worse still, show pity. No one to ask awkward questions.

James, having sensed the existence of this tragic little boy before laying eyes upon the evidence. Visceral. Like a missing twin.

Despite all their plans, little Peter had, however, continued to affect every nook and cranny of their lives. To seep through all the cracks of acceptance and respectability, especially at home. The uneasy whispering, the tenseness of parental behaviour, the left behind scraps of knowledge, that Harriet had dared pass on to James, she too overwhelmed by the responsibility placed on her own young and narrow shoulders. James's immature pestering to know more, as he carried out juvenile spying activities. Followed up by an amalgam of growing self-centredness, denial and indifference. His doing nothing about it. What could he have done? A 'rescue' out of the question. Even much later, still too afraid to approach his mother, for what more he might discover, too afraid to understand her version of events and accept what his parents might have to say in defence of their actions. Not wanting to hear it. Years later, still waiting for the right moment…and then, suddenly, that moment was gone for good. The awful news of the car accident.

The horror of that crash, an event beyond the bounds of his imagination, of his way of seeing his world. Things that happened only in the world of other people. How he would have wanted to forgive his mother and father for their shortcomings…how he had felt the need.

Many years had passed. There just hadn't been time.

He reread *Sons and Lovers*, and it struck him for the first time that like its author DH Lawrence, he too would have made his peace…one day. The writer, who had likewise needed time to fully grasp his father's complex situation, having always recoiled from him, who had grown up loathing him for as long as he could remember.

Then the more recent guilt he had had to deal with, this time of a different nature. Margaret, his mother, hadn't been making it up…those aristocratic connections…that he and Harriet had never cared to pursue, to share in the pride and fascination of her family history. An ugly, but also immature lack of concern for her on their part. The cruel insensitivity of adolescence.

Everything becoming clearer, in the days following the reading of the will, the discovery of a fortune, which had now passed down to him and his sister, through that same family. All real. A fortune he at least had not deserved. Separating him even further from the rest of humanity. A fortune, which rewarded them both with an easy future; guaranteeing them lives, which would have nothing to do with hire purchase agreements, rising interest rates or the misery of unemployment. Allowing them both a permanent and sturdy 'roof over their heads'. His father's words springing manically to mind again. The inheritance had blown his already battered brain.

Who was he to judge his mother, his parents? What right did he possess to condemn? Not everyone is born strong and able to face, with stoicism, nature's horrible tricks. Look at his own inertia. He remembered an off-the-cuff remark, someone saying that God sends people only as much as they can cope with. So what about his parents and Peter? It had not been fair on Peter, of course…who never asked to be born…but would the little boy have fared better living at home with them? To this question, something that continued to gnaw away at him,

James stubbornly still of the opinion that yes, his ailing brother would have somehow, in the deep, dark recesses, sensed the difference. That vulnerable baby boy encased in maternal arms, to die a little over three years later, enfolded in those same loving arms at his family home. The only home he would have known. Love and warmth, and the scent of familiar skin would have made a world of difference…

The image causing him once again to sob without tears, releasing another brick of pain that had been building. The anger still impossibly there.

He also knew he still had to deal with the death of his friend Jenny. That he would keep for another day. He had in these few months already journeyed a great distance.

Chapter 24
James and Dolly; James and Harriet

"I hope you don't mind me speaking out, but from what you've told me, I think you've got more than a bit mixed up over the years, tied yourself into unnecessary knots. All this replacement child nonsense. I'm surprised the so-called experts haven't made you see this…even your pal Fr John, or have you never discussed it with him?"

Not giving her friend time to reply. "It's been on my mind a lot recently. In the first place, people never used to be able to plan their families, well not properly. For so many women, babies would have arrived every year or two, one after the other, neither planned nor unplanned…that's just the way it was…and as we know many died along the way. Of course, things are very different now. But I really don't understand why you…so intelligent and well-informed about everything…beat yourself up, seeing yourself as this tragedy on legs…weighed down by a silly title that you can't shake off…for something that had nothing to do with you…"

"The sins of the father, or should that be the mother?" James quipped coldly, but Dolly continued regardless.

"Condemned to a tragic existence for something that you are not responsible for. You might just as easily have come into the world if Peter had been ok and lived at home with the rest of you. Child number three. What is so strange about that? What if you'd been born a girl…would you have still felt the same? Or is it only a boy then, who can replace another male child? I know that your parents, your mother in particular, could possibly have gone about things differently, but who knows what was going on in her head and in her heart? Something she felt she was just not strong enough to handle…"

Dolly continued, "Of course, different people see things differently…Is it kinder to kill a fox that's been seriously injured, or try to save its life? What kind of life would it have afterwards? Surely that counts for something…"

Then on seeing James's baffled expression.

"Ok, perhaps I shouldn't have brought animals into it. And she certainly didn't abandon him somewhere in a cardboard box. She didn't kill him. She just let him go, let the professionals take over. They knew from the start that his life was going to be a short one. And I think you said that your father always went to visit him. But there's no one right answer. In these shocking situations…Oh, James, if only I could persuade you to stop heaping guilt onto your parents, then…don't you see…there is no guilt for you either to carry forward. What about your sister? Does she also crucify herself like you? I hate to see you like this."

Dolly, remaining in full flow…

"Also I've noticed that you get a bit too caught up in your reading and research into writers' lives, and in them see tragic connections. Fiction means made-up plots and characters, and as interesting as we may find them, they don't really have anything to do with us, do they? Those writers seem to be a troubled bunch too! What's that thing you told me? By that clever Frenchman. Carve out your own destiny…and he is right. You've spent far too much time thinking about things that happened in the past, things that are impossible to put right. It's all futile. You have to stop going around in circles…it's unhealthy. Serving no purpose other than to cause you even more pain…it's as though you are afraid to move on, afraid of the future…that you cling onto the pain because you don't know what to replace it with, or even worse, that you get some kind of warped pleasure out of it."

A seemingly unmoved James finally replied to Dolly's long rant of home truths, her no-nonsense approach. By now in an alcoholic haze and letting out in a low, slow drawl, "Oh, don't waste time worrying about me, Dolly. Most of what you say is true, I get it. I know you are really trying to make me snap out of it. (He tried clicking his fingers with his right hand, without success). There's other stuff though I haven't told you about…One day perhaps. You make it sound so easy. But it's not like dealing with one thing at a time, crossing it off a list and then going on to tackle the next. They all merge and interlink. Re-form. Just as you think you've gouged one out, like someone's eye in battle, it somehow grows back."

With his slurred speech suddenly gathering fresh momentum, he added, "The version of me you are seeing tonight across, may I add, this rather sticky table (over which for some reason he continued to run his fingers) is a huge improvement on the one of just a couple of years ago, maybe a couple of months even. I'm still working on it, and although to you it must all seem pretty gruesome, I've actually come a long way!"

"Back then, I wasn't even able to get up in the morning. Wasn't able to face the world. Month in month out. I never had any plans for the day ahead; never went anywhere. I never saw anyone, well, no one who meant anything. It was my cleaner, bless her, who would go shopping for me and make sure I had something to eat. Day…after day…after day. On top of everything else, I soon discovered that not having to work for a living, especially when you are so young, is a curse… OK, so you don't have to wait hours for the bus or have a crowded train to catch, or clients to satisfy, or reports to write. Deadlines to meet. So hard to say that to people; they just don't get it. Just thinking you are rubbing your…he wanted to use the term 'unjustifiable' (but simply unable to elucidate the word's six syllables)…good fortune all over their stupid faces. That's because they think that if they had lots of money, then all their problems would be gone forever."

"Neither though did I have the courage or the will to give it away. To charity, to a good cause, to the poor or whatever. I still cling to it, in spite of the heartache it causes me. Ha-ha. It's not just about Peter. In the end, you realise that life doesn't let you get away with it, the good fucking luck. We are all doomed to suffer whatever our circumstances. The causes might be different, but the results are the same…we can either live in denial and bury the pain…or allow it to disable us, destroy us even."

"But I don't want you worrying about me" …and then changing his voice to sound like Sean… "Another gin and tonic, Doll girl?"

Both James and Dolly, it being quite early on in their friendship, and before James's trip to Venice, had downed much more alcohol than usual, neither being habitually heavy drinkers. Which might have explained why their conversation grew uncharacteristically maudlin, devoid of its usual jokiness and span of discussion topics. It did reveal, however, that Dolly had become very fond of James, and that still unbeknown to him, he was becoming her replacement child.

She too was holding on to a clutch of memories involving her own precious son. A son she had not been able to help or protect either.

About three months later:

"Well, lads, here's your room. Do you like it?"

"Yes, thank you," replied the older boy, dutifully.

"Have you really been very ill, Uncle James? Is that why we don't know you?" The braver, slightly younger one asked.

A somewhat disgruntled Harriet then appeared, "That's enough now, we can talk about those things another time. Right, so you've got an hour…go down to the games room, yes, it's in the basement, and let your uncle and me go over our plans for tomorrow. Off with you both!"

At which the two brothers vanished in an instant.

"Thanks for that. I do want to talk to them, explain, but it is probably best I find out what they already know…and what you think they can cope with. Harri, I must say though, they are wonderful boys. You've done…are doing…a great job with them."

"Yes, I think I have under the circumstances. An absent father, no grandparents to call their own…and as for their uncle…well!"

He hit her playfully with a convenient pillow, which she threw straight back into his face, and a mock fight broke out. James took that as a sign that she really had forgiven him.

"Come; let's go downstairs, we can talk better in the library."

"You mean where you've put up that unwelcome 'silence' notice…?"

He threw a cushion at her this time…

"Ha-ha, yes, that's really droll!"

It was all beginning to feel a bit like the old days now. Older sister running affectionate rings around younger brother. Her tone of voice then suddenly changing.

"The school has been so supportive. I don't know what I'd have done without them, especially the deputy. As you know, the boys, they're 13 and nearly 12 now, are weekly boarders, the best of both worlds, some might say, back every Friday evening, and so not too much time to miss them…or for them to miss me. It's only about four miles from the house; I can always turn up if I need to. They wouldn't admit it, not in a million years, but I think they really like it there, and the whole setup as it is. Like finding the right balance."

"Monique has been great too. I have told you about her, haven't I? Hope she won't be wanting to return to Toulouse in a hurry. She's there at the moment, to see her family, but back in a week's time. I had to tell her off a few times at the beginning…it seems a long time ago now…you know for little things, like eating biscuits on the bed, letting the boys off cleaning their teeth and so on because they made such a fuss about it. But now she's a real asset. I don't know what we would do without her…we've sort of become…like friends, even though she's younger of course."

"And guess what, she's taught them so many French songs…they're feeling much less inhibited now about the pronunciation. You know what it's like, an English person trying to speak French…excruciating to listen to! Just why are we so inhibited? But she knows she's not allowed to do their homework for them…only test them or explain something. She plays things on her guitar for them too, which makes the singing…and the learning…easier."

"I'm still finding it difficult with the local women though, that brigade of upstanding wives and mothers. They are nice enough, I suppose, to my face, should I see them at the school, or in one of the shops. It's just so obvious what they are thinking behind those fake smiles and awkwardly polite chatter. Inviting a relatively young divorcee to one of their precious dinner parties, was simply out of the question. Obviously, their husbands would be at risk from my evil clutches. Or vain creature that I am, maybe it's not me, but Monique, ha-ha, I'd never thought of that! Little do they know that the last thing I'm looking for is a replacement man in my life!"

"I've tried inviting them and their husbands to my place but each time they begin to make pathetic excuses about having to decline the offer, so I just gave up. At least they don't take it out on the boys. To be fair, they do invite them to their own children's parties and so on. They probably feel sorry for them. I can live with it!"

"But what about you, James? How are you really? You look much better than I was expecting…"

"You know, Harri, I think I can truthfully say, that life has rarely felt this good, well at least on par with that first year at university. In a completely different way of course. That all seems quite unreal now. For one thing, I think that you and I are back together, for good I hope. I'm right, aren't I? (Harriet grimacing and shaking her head in mock disagreement) Yes, we are. Admit it! Life at Star House is good. I like the family, though they can be a bit strange. Yet

I quite like that. I like the fact that I'm almost part of it but then not really…what's so bizarre is that they help me without knowing it. I have made some decent friends at the pub…"

"It shows…"

James making no particular mention of Giulia, Father John or even Dolly.

Chapter 25
November Pain

James had never liked November. "Does anyone?" He wondered flatly. It felt almost as bad as January. With the nature gods hard at work: reducing trees to mere silhouettes…eerie and skeletal freaks. Releasing untimely frosts, ripping up precious minutes of daylight. Taking us prisoner, making us orphans, zipping a steel grey sky across us. The faraway taste of spring was now impossible to ponder. For the likes of literary heroes Chaucer and TS Eliot, April may have been 'the cruellest month' but on this matter, James would never concur.

He named the day Slug Sunday. It seemed by now that it had been raining all month…and that meant that multifarious slugs were out in force, baring their dark horns.

Whereas an upbeat Father John reminded him that, it was the month to remember those who had gone before us. James replied, "You mean the dead?"

"Yes and no," came the bold response. "A month dedicated to the Holy Souls in Purgatory, who we believe, with the prayers of the faithful, will finally secure a place in heaven, and therefore everlasting life."

Amen.

Back to the real world, it was that time of year, when immaculately turned out members of the 'great and the good', laid wreaths at The Cenotaph. Commemorating those who had laid down their lives in bloody battle. For all of us here now.

It also fixed the month on the calendar when James's parents had died, with this year's November already turning out to be characteristically bleak. For a different set of reasons…

Despite all his recovery know-how, there were limits as to how much James could blot out or handle at any one time. Ever conscious that progress regarding his own mental health had always emerged during the months of spring and summer. He now felt spent. With the memory of past long winters beginning to resurface, it seemed that the old fear monster was close by and flexing his claws…

That year proved different, however. Worse if anything. On the evening of the 23rd November, a terrifying earthquake took place in Italy, more precisely in Irpinia, which happened to be near Giulia's first 'home'. An earthquake, paradoxically lasting no more than 60 seconds, and yet so violent as to leave years and years of widespread human and geological devastation in its wake. Also ripping Giulia away from him, so he took it personally. She just took off, abandoning everyone and everything at Star House, including her precious students. No more than a few hastily written notes 'to whom it may concern', left behind on the hall table. Without having even informed her friend and 'padre spirituale' Father John, he like the others, reduced to hearing the news only after her sudden departure.

James feeling the first twinges of a fall back into the sinkhole of depression. That wretched creature, who had been biding its time, returning to pull him down and wring out those last precious drops of life force. The victim now obliged to launch a counterattack, with no stomach for a return to that horrible place. The battle was underway.

"She won't be away for long, surely," pronounced her deflated and resentful lover to himself…

He was, at the same time, angry with himself, for having grown too dependent on her. On her just being there. As though in some outlandish way, she was there…just for him. So that whenever he felt the need, he could place his hands on her proud shoulders, and kiss the top of her head. Like when he had first touched her. How she had looked up at him with her beautiful eyes…something bordering on the maternal.

He decided to keep himself busy. He would follow the example of his unsuspecting 'teachers', the others at Star House, who were always doing something useful, and who never appeared to question anything concerning Giulia's behaviour.

James however remaining doggedly puzzled. Why exactly had she gone? What was it that she intended to do there? Had someone made contact with her? If so, who? Why had she not spoken to him about it?

As some will already know, depression can travel fast even when you are throwing everything at it. In lots of different ways. Trickling insidiously into the darkest reaches, causing thoughts to run riot and emotions to explode. Draining. Compelling us just as much to look outside of ourselves, as well as inside, to grasp the universe and scrutinise our shamefully tiny place in it. James found himself yet again raking over scenes from the past, and looking towards the next century, and then to the next millennium, with the sudden realisation that, perhaps it wasn't only him, but that all humankind was reeling and losing its way. A shared universal cry. A short-lived comfort.

James, once again Atlas, bearing the early weight of planet Earth on his shoulders.

Followed by a flash of manic consciousness, questioning the ancient Greek gift of democracy. Despite his own century's great strides towards freedom, a so-called better life for all. The birth of the National Health Service and Welfare State. Ground-breaking success following the battle cry of free education for all. The mammoth achievements in science and technology. The discovery of antibiotics, a miraculous Moon landing. Better and better, higher and higher, for everyone. The phenomenon that was Bob Dylan…

However, what had James done or what was he ever likely to achieve against such a backdrop? Nothing. Nothing. Nothing. His life limply dangling, marked by inaction. Stagnation. Being ill. Getting over it. Getting ill again. Incapable of properly moving forward. A social parasite. Had never even fathered a child. Would leave nothing behind other than anonymous bones.

A slow countdown to the third millennium had already begun, and people occupying future time would know or come to know that this had been the century of two World Wars and the Holocaust. Once again, nothing to do with him. Let off the hook…

The century of Western-style capitalism, marked by the Arms Race and rampant materialism. The futile search for more and more of us to obtain more and more of what we do not need. Weighed down with the stuff that poisons and consumes us. Disconnecting us from our roots. Feeding our baser instincts, our herd mentality. Drawers and cupboards, garages and sheds…filled to bursting with flashy gadgets and novelty devices, many unused or unrepaired, things we never hold more than once in our greedy hands, our planet and our heads spinning ever faster. Wardrobes stuffed with piles of rarely worn clothes, shelves stacked with shoes that we might never wear. Boxes and boxes of shiny, discarded toys bought to keep our children quiet because we have forgotten how to talk to them. Totally out of touch with who we really are.

The decadence of Ancient Rome revisited, as the British Empire continues to crumble. James not excluded, trying to fill up the empty hours of a life without purpose.

The consuming of drugs and drink of all kinds, smoked, swallowed, sniffed up dilated nostrils, jabbed into veins, a process to make life seem palatable or more exciting. So that we can, for a short while at least, blot out the boredom, life's unfairness and ugliness, persuade ourselves that we 'belong' and are like our friends, that we have friends…that we really do like ourselves, that we are alive. Money needed for things, buying us the illusion that we are 'part of the action'. Even more pathetic the absolute need to show all this to others. Putting into practice only the 'to have' and not the 'to be' side of the human equation. Self-esteem at its lowest.

More and more competition, individual and universal. Mountains of food but millions going hungry. Never-ending conflicts in the Middle East and Africa. The knowledge and power to destroy our planet a hundred times over…

What was James doing about it? Nothing. Flailing, failing, at the centre of nothingness. Useless, spoilt, wealthy, overeducated, gravitating around himself. Stuck. Sick. Feeding his own misery.

Missing Giulia.

Christmas was coming. 'We are now in Advent', as an annoyingly happy Fr John referred to it. Four weeks of intense watching and waiting, of preparation. 'Necessary time for getting our lives back in order, back on track'.

Did anyone actually do this?

There was a lot to do however at St Raphael's. James made himself useful, slightly buoyed and feeding off, to some extent at least, the priest's childlike enthusiasm for this Christian-minded season. John discussed with him how and why people pray, stating the importance of ancient ritual and proudly backing up his argument this time with some scientific evidence (not merely the usual reference to the passing down of faith and the fruits of the spirit), as he informed his friend of a recent experiment:

A cohort of cancer patients, all at about the same stage of their illness. Divided equally and at random into two groups. Other people began to pray for those in the first group, with all the patients unaware that this was happening. After a given amount of time, it became clear, that in nearly every case, those in group 1 went on to live longer, live better…

John went on to assure James that God really does answer our prayers in unimaginable ways. The power of prayer at work in the example of the cancer patients had not surprised him at all. God our Father, with the help of the Holy Spirit, coming up with better solutions than the ones we are seeking. In ways that we are not privy to at the time and made apparent only when we look back. The gift of hindsight.

With great effort, and even though winter was fast approaching, James continued to check on the state of the garden at Casa Stella and attempted to get to know Giulia's nephew and nieces a little better. None of which was easy, except when chatting to the youngest, Tina; he really liked her. Through her, he learned more about Italian customs and traditions, which he found genuinely interesting. It took him out of himself, for a while at least. Then there were the nights of little or interrupted sleep. The mornings when he had to make a super-human effort to roll out of bed, to drag himself downstairs. To eat, to take a shower, to go for a walk. To the outside world, apart from Father John, who by now had become his 'confidante' (rather than confessor), all was fine. He was pleasant and helpful. Showing no outward signs of loathing November, of wanting to hibernate, or even of missing his own beautiful muse…

At The Abercorn Arms, he took the time to find out more about Dolly. Began to listen more attentively, attempting to look outside of himself. He discovered that her only son, her beloved Edward, had died at the age of 27. It turned out to be a painful account. Her heartache was profound, and yet she had a way about her when talking of personal tragedy, that made it sound interesting rather than embarrassing for the listener. James almost enjoyed listening to her talk about him. Despite the obvious pain and parental guilt that she still carried, she spoke lucidly…and managed to be philosophical, even humorous. Sometimes straying from the pain, by including the odd little joke or anecdote. Without blaming others, without bitterness.

Her husband had died the year before his son's demise, had died in the full knowledge of the problems surrounding his son but of course Ed was still alive. Such timing indicating that there was still hope. The two older children from his previous marriage having never taken much interest in her precious son…

Chapter 26
Ed

Du Cane Road
Alone as a spectre
I was cannoned down Du Cane Road.
No buswheel embrace for macadam,
Infamous stretch of urban limbo.
A train gnashed past left flank, and
I knew the hospital came first.
Here, new baby bleated; there Alsatian howled.
Their cries mingling somewhere above Du Cane Road.
Matches, tobacco…100 grammes net, unopened,
A copy of Heavy Metal stared up from the bag.
"It's on the right, luv, in between stops."
"Hope they let you out," somewhere a voice pierced.
Fully equipped, but for conversation,
My feet conveyed me the rest of the way.
The forecourt magicking me to the movies…
The Italian Job, a triumphant Noel Coward perhaps,
(Rather than Alcatraz and Steve McQueen.)

I was told to wait, and I then came to.
So I was kept waiting by a sardonic screw
In spite of the drizzle. Mistaken for a probation officer
I went through the wrong door…
To face him, who dwells in shared cell 8 by 12.

"He said he wanted to be a racing driver. He loved speed. Nothing odd about that I suppose."

"Everyone liked him back then. With those angelic features, he looked a bit like a choirboy. He did well at school, and yet without ever putting in much effort, and got himself a place at the local grammar. We were so proud of him then, even Reg, for once. Probably because his older children had gone to the Secondary Modern. Ed liked playing football, going out on his bike, he loved swimming…just like any other boy of that age, really."

"Then for some reason…I will never understand it…things started going downhill and so fast we just couldn't keep up, didn't know what was going on or what to do. Something we had no experience of. Beyond our imagination. It all began when he stopped going to church with us. Ed only lasted a year at that school. First behind our backs playing truant, faking our signatures etc. and then refusing point-blank to go in. Hadn't done any proper homework in weeks. The head-teacher called us in and said that he was a silly boy, wasting a precious opportunity…but that he had by now run out of second chances."

"They found him another school, but that didn't work either. Once again, he just refused to go. Never really explaining why. Just that he didn't want to. After only two weeks, it was the same story. Looking back, I think that he had a big problem with authority. Someone telling him that he had to do something. Even quite a small thing. Perhaps I had spoilt him a bit…as my only child. He never wanted to explain or talk about it though. With anyone. I was at my wit's end, of course, and from then on… Reg left me to it. It got worse."

"Ed was still so young, but I soon discovered that he had started sneaking money out of my purse to buy cigarettes. Players, I think was the make, well it had the face of a sea captain on the packet. I can still see the face staring up at me…Reg and I didn't smoke, so I don't know where that came from. I never knew whether or not to tell his father…or give him just one more chance, which of course turned into hundreds."

"The education people sent round a tutor for him at the house. A couple of hours three or four times a week. Doctors never got involved. We never really thought of going down that route. That still left him loads of time to lie in bed of a morning, to wander the streets with his friends (after they had finished school) and a few of the mothers around where we lived started pointing a finger at me when they found their own sons smoking pot. From what I hear, these old friends have now become respectable, 'pillars of the community' so to speak…for them, it was merely a passing adventure, an adolescent phase…"

"But not for Ed. I only found this out much later on, oh, how could I have been so naïve, but I knew nothing about those things then."

"He somehow came across some hippie types, you know with lots of hair, much older than him, living in a squat on a road just behind the Police Station, haha, would you believe it? They'd taken over an old Victorian house, lots of arty people drifting in and out, or even staying, lots of music, smoking a lot of weed and taking psychedelic drugs apparently, with rock music pouring out of the windows at all hours. Deep purply walls inside covered in their own artwork. Well, that's how the police described it."

"From then on, very little conversation took place between us, except once or twice when he commented on how stupid most people…'straight' people…as he referred to them, he meant us I suppose…were. Weighing themselves down with mortgages, endlessly dull jobs and long-term responsibilities…total mugs."

"Time passed, and so many promises were made that he didn't or couldn't keep, but at the time at least made me feel that deep under all this bravado or foolish anarchy that he really did love me and his father. He wasn't doing it to punish us; it was just something bigger than him to contend with. I'm probably still making allowances, though."

"I can't remember the exact order of things, but life continued to be really tough. There were times when we didn't see Ed for weeks on end. When he was with us, he would sleep all day and be up prowling around the house at night. He kept his drug paraphernalia hidden in a bag. I never looked inside, just not strong enough. At least he never injected in front of me…I felt useless, staying silent. At mealtimes, when he was around, he would fall asleep at the table after a couple of mouthfuls, his head slowly nodding. He loved ice cream and ate a lot of it I recall. By now, he rolled his own cigarettes, using those Rizla papers. Taking his time…stopping and starting…during the procedure, as if it was some kind of important ritual."

"We used to find different types of pills, prescribed and illegal I suppose, carelessly strewn over the floor. He swallowed or smoked anything available, even though he only really wanted heroin. Intravenously. When the veins in his arms packed in, he would inject into his groin. Even Reg's huge pile of luncheon vouchers, which he used to save up, disappeared from the drawer. Reg said that he had had enough…that his son would have to go. Strange people used to ring the house or turn up on our doorstep. It wasn't long before Ed started to break into chemists' shops and take whatever he could grab, and eventually ended up in Wormwood Scrubs. Have you ever heard of a place with such an ugly-sounding name? Makes my spine tingle, whenever I hear it. I suppose it fits though."

"He'd been living on borrowed time. Let off repeatedly in magistrates courts. Each time looking and sounding like a public school boy. Slicked back hair, side parting. Saying all the right things. That due to having a highly addictive personality, he became addicted to 'smack', from his very first hit. He came across as so clever. Taking the opportunity to express how sorry he was for his actions, to the court, to us…his family, the police and society in general. How he would definitely seek treatment, accept any support coming his way. Start his life again. The sheer humiliation of it. Now it was incarceration. Our son's life had come to this. Reg refused to go to court on that occasion or to visit him later at the prison saying, '…best place for him, he might stop using those filthy drugs now…it will give him time to think about his actions, all the hurt he has caused us.'"

"I confronted Ed in response to his father's message…I can see his face now…but he answered me with a wry smile saying that the place was awash with drugs of all kinds and that it was in the main the screws who smuggled them in. So, you see, even if that was only true in part, it still felt like the whole world was against us. Ed told me that he had tried to read the Bible they had given him in his cell and that even though he had really tried, it didn't help, it wasn't for him. We sat across a small table, like you see on TV. Not able to hug or even touch. A surly looking guard searched my bag as soon as I entered that horrible building before they could let me see him. I do remember feeling shaky and shedding a few quiet tears. People looked on but no one came to comfort me. Why should they though? They must see scenes like this all the time. They're hardened to it."

"What I don't remember is what else we spoke about. That's a shame. I do know that it was all over soon enough, well that's how it seemed. They called his name and took him back to where he had come from. Did he turn to look back? (Dolly shrugged her shoulders.) He wrote me a few letters during his time inside. Out of boredom, I imagine."

"When he came out, he was put on probation. For the first time in years, I didn't feel entirely alone. There was at last a bit of help, in the shape of Kate.

Such a lovely, caring young lady, his probation officer. We agreed Ed could live with us. At least for a while. Reg wasn't keen but at least consented and said we would give it a chance. I now had a name, a person to ring…at any time, she said. I could discuss the events of each day with her. She would do everything possible to support him. Perhaps, looking back, he had won her over too."

"This worked OK for a while. He would go each day to pick up his 'script' from the chemist…but then one day, he just took off…and I didn't see him again for about six months. The methadone he was on clearly wasn't working. He just didn't want it. Needles were his big thing. Apparently, he would just sell it outside the chemist's shop, and with the money, feed his craving for heroin, smack he called it. I think, nowadays, they have to drink the methadone in front of the pharmacist. It got to the stage that he needed to 'score' just to stop feeling ill. Worse than flu. Gone was the rush. Every time the telephone rang, my heart sank as I wondered if it was going to be news of his death. I once, anonymously, rang a radio programme, out of sheer desperation…the guest expert telling me, in no uncertain terms from what I had told him, that unless Ed changed his ways, he would not see his thirtieth birthday or even his 25th."

"Oh, I forgot to mention Carrie, a sweet little thing, with doe eyes and an elfin face aged 17, who at some point Ed introduced to us. She hung on his every word…and probably took the same drugs as him. They did stupid things like flinging open the doors of taxis and jumping out, because they couldn't pay for the fare. She got pregnant with his child, but then suffered an early miscarriage. Within only several weeks of us knowing her, the police discovered her lifeless body on a bed in a squat they were sharing. She had choked on her own vomit. Her family hated us, and hated Ed even more. Who could blame them? I thought in a hard and selfish way, because I was out of my mind, that perhaps this was the shock Ed needed, though. Like divine intervention."

"I learned Kate's letter off by heart and most of the article in the local press. I can still reel them off…"

November 1978. Probation Service.
Dear Dorothy,
Jo Hammond rang me this morning to give me the sad news of Ed's death. I very much appreciate you taking the trouble to let me know. I don't quite know what to say in this letter.

My memories of Ed go back a long time, and to say that we had anticipated his early death does not make the fact any easier to accept, or the shock any less. I can only imagine the painful mixture of feelings you must be experiencing.

For myself, it is a return of the sense of helplessness in the face of an overwhelming problem. The feeling that surely somewhere, somehow there was something that could have helped. Recollection of a person who was often sick and tortured (and is now at peace) coupled with fine memories of Ed when fit, rational and humorous. Glimpses of what might have been I suppose.

Assuming you have no objection, I would like to come to the funeral if I can. I send all of you, but particularly you Dorothy, my deep sympathy,
Kate.

The Local News January 1979

Drug Addict Death after Overdose.

A drug addict who gave a false name and address to get drugs from more than one doctor died after an overdose, the Coroner's court heard this week.

Mr Edward Wickham, aged 27, was found dead in a squat on November 22nd, the day after being prescribed one month's worth of drugs by the doctor with whom he was registered under his real name.

In court on Wednesday W's room-mate at the squat in A Road, Mr K, himself a registered addict on methadone treatment, told how Mr Wickham had made himself a fix of Palfium, a potent analgesic, normally prescribed for the relief of inoperable cancer.

Mr K explained that Edward Wickham had crushed some tablets and melted them in a spoon before injecting them. In a five-hour period, he took three such fixes.

At one point Mr K went next door to visit a friend and when he returned he found Wickham kneeling on the floor. He did not look well. So, Mr K called a friend and then ran to the ambulance station down the road.

Mr Wickham was later found dead. Mrs Dorothy Wickham, the deceased's mother, said that she had suffered 14 and a half years of misery because of her son's addiction.

She explained that she had tried to help him by getting him into hospital on several occasions, but after a while, he always discharged himself.

When Edward ended up in prison, she thought that might help him, but was dismayed when he told her that he could get as many drugs in prison as he could at Piccadilly Circus.

Mr Wickham's GP, doctor DF, after prescribing the fatal drug, had told his patient not to attempt to inject it, as the tablets were plastic coated. He said he was angry that a young man, who knew so much about drugs, had done something like this.

He added that he usually only prescribed an amount of the drug to cover two weeks, but that Mr Wickham had told him that he was going to visit friends in Wales, and that he himself had seen such a startling improvement in his patient's physical condition. For this reason, he prescribed a month's supply.

"I really thought he was keeping to his regime," he told the court. What Dr DF did not know, however, was that Wickham had registered the name of Edward Falk with another doctor, giving his girlfriend's address.

It was not discovered what he did with the drugs prescribed by the second doctor, but no evidence was found of them by the pathologist.

Mr Wickham's mother expressed concern at the inquest that he had been able to get drugs from two doctors by using a false name and address.

The coroner, Dr JB recorded a verdict of death by misadventure.

"Come on, Dolly, let's get going. You look exhausted. I'll treat you to some fish and chips!"

Chapter 27
The Return of Dionysus

One afternoon, a rather elegant and bespectacled young man knocked on the door of Casa Stella. With a full-length camel coat draped around his shoulders. Already flashing a broad white smile, as he waited for the door to open.

It was James, who came to answer, the figure of Giulia disappearing back into the darkness of the hallway.

"My old friend, so good to see you! You look great. Much better than I was expecting!" Then lowering his voice, as he pointed into the house, "Who was that by the way? Oh I see, so that…is Giulia…"

Then in reply, adopting exaggerated public schoolboy type articulation, "Well, I'm only letting you in if you give me the password, old boy! Come on now…I'm a busy man these days!"

"Are you serious? I will remember it till my dying day!" insisted the visitor, letting out a jaunty laugh.

"Has to be word perfect, I'm afraid," replied a doubtful James in mock sombre tones. "Only the one attempt! Rules are rules!"

James's guest took up a theatrical pose, before releasing, with the help of a flurry of gesticulations and dramatic pauses, the necessary words to gain entry.

"For spirits, freed from mortal laws, with ease assume what sexes and what shapes they please."

"Good, you may now enter," conceded James, only now releasing a warm smile in the way of his old friend, as he began to lead the way into the house.

Once over the threshold, Denis suddenly pressed James against the door and kissed him full on the lips. With James successfully maintaining a cool demeanour, unresponsive. A simple act of bravado for old times' sake? A Denis still needing to make a memorable entrance?

"It was so good to hear from you, out of the blue, like that. How long has it been? About eight, nine years? So why the visit…the real reason?" James asked exuding an air of composure, as they sat down on opposite armchairs in the drawing room. Neither wanting to comment on the kiss. Of course, he knew that Denis had occasionally spent the night with young men he had picked up in the town, but nothing like this had ever happened between the two of them. Neither had he ever thought of his friend as homosexual.

"Well, first and foremost, it's for the pleasure of seeing my very best friend in the world, after far too long an absence…"

"You knew that I've been ill though, completely out of action. Harri did contact you, didn't she?" James interrupted. "And the awful business of the crash…"

"Yes, of course. It must have been hellish…for you both. My first impulse was to drop everything and go and find you…Harriet, Harri, as you call her now, felt it was better however that I let you recover at your own pace, doesn't mince her words, does she, that sister of yours? No hard feelings though. I am aware that in spite of my good nature, it's by now common knowledge that wherever I go, I leave, unwittingly of course, a murky trail of destruction behind me, like some sort of demonic snail! No, but seriously, I was truly concerned for your welfare, as Harri, bless her, kept in touch, telling me what stage you were at, how long everything was taking. I was always certain however that we, at some point, would be meeting up again. I don't really know why it's taken us…both…so long. But that doesn't matter now. Here I am."

"And secondly?" James inquired wanting the conversation to move on.

"Oh yes, I need a favour from you. No it's nothing to do with money," laughed Denis believing to have read his friend's mind, seen his jaw drop. "The publishing company is doing pretty well at present. I've just bought a house in fact. About an hour from here. I hear you beat me to it, but there has never been any need for competition between us, has there? Each beyond the need for infantile rivalry." He mused for a while… "No, it's to ask you…if you would be my best man? I'm getting married in the spring…"

Somewhat taken aback by his friend's news, James found himself unable to continue hiding his true feelings.

"You, Denis, Dionysus, god of wine and pleasure, you are getting married? That is outrageous. The last thing I would have predicted. Who would have thought it possible? Who is the…fortunate or more like…unfortunate…creature?"

"Her name is Penelope."

"Penelope…" James repeated as if in a trance. Realising sometime later, that his friend always used all four syllables, whenever speaking of her. To call her Penny would perhaps have reminded him of Jenny…but deciding it was best not to raise such a matter. "Come on, you owe me an explanation!"

"Which I shall endeavour to give you. I'm sorry, but this necessitates maximum seriousness. Though it's quite simple, you see. Up to now, as you well know, I've always followed my instincts, especially those baser desires. I've lived it all, seen, heard and tasted it all. Feels like I've led at least three lives, and I'm only in my early 30s. What I want to do now will seem commonplace, I admit. In an age that allows us greater choice than ever before, I want, I feel the urge, to create a family, a big family, if possible. I need to pass on my name, my blood, my best genes to the next generation…leave something of substance behind. Dionysus, my mythical namesake is, after all, also the god of fertility."

"You've come to the right place here," thought James with a wry smile…half surprised that his friend hadn't gone to add how the world too would be truly grateful for such a generous act on his part!

"Surely, when it comes to it, until science comes up with a better explanation as to why we are here, reproduction is that reason. So simple that I somehow missed it. But now I recognise that need, that human longing, the ultimate in creativity don't you think…beyond even books and art, beyond poetry and music?"

"And is the lovely Penelope aware of all this? Have you discussed it with her? What is there in it for her, other than years of self-sacrifice and endless drudgery? Sorry to sound banal, but you haven't mentioned the 'love' word. Does that come into it anywhere? Frankly, I don't think you, or me come to that, are capable of attaching ourselves exclusively to one woman…one person…"

Denis thought for a while, crestfallen.

"I see as regards my wanting you to be my best man, you are biding your time, stalling, unable to give me an answer. I will therefore allow myself to ask the question once more, and then alas, the search will be on for a replacement, albeit a far less worthy candidate."

James realising in an instant that he had sounded middle class and a tad too judgemental…is that what became of growing 'older and wiser', getting his own health back on track? Not something he would have allowed to seep into his thinking during those carefree student days. What right did he have to question Denis, adopting such a parental, almost superior demeanour? In an instant, he felt ashamed at what he had become. Just as well he hadn't mentioned Jenny, at least that! Did he even properly know Denis now? He clearly still didn't know himself…

Denis had been magnificent throughout, hadn't upbraided him…had merely allowed him his suburban say. Hadn't sunk to his friend's level. James thus decided to change tack immediately. To make it up to him. He stood up in the middle of the room.

"If that is the case, it is with immense pleasure that I accept the role of 'best man', YOUR best man, Denis Montague Beaumont, at your forthcoming nuptials. That I am both honoured and humbled by your choice, the perfect choice of course…you being a man of high intellect and exquisite taste. In the meantime, I wish you and the lovely Penelope, whom I hope to meet very soon, every happiness…"

"God, is this what the speech is going to be like…heaven help us!" interrupted a seemingly gobsmacked Denis. "Now, James, just calm down, be a good boy and go find a decent bottle of champagne, like the old days…"

At which point Giulia quietly entered the room. "Did I hear the word champagne? No, please stay seated. I'm Giulia and I'm so happy to meet you, Denis. Welcome to Casa Stella. So, you are James's dear friend from his university days. He said you would be coming to the house today. May I join you for a glass, and then I will leave you both to your memories?"

"Why, yes, of course," the two friends uttered, each in his own way. James then leaving the room to search out a bottle, with Giulia calling out to him that there was a fig 'crostata' in the kitchen. That it would go beautifully with the champagne…

"Actually I'm getting married, Giulia, and I've asked James to be the best man."

"Oh, that's wonderful news. He will take his role very seriously, I'm sure of that. When and where will the wedding take place…?"

"Here we are," James arrived back after only a few minutes with the bottle and an ornate tray bearing three nineteenth-century champagne coupes. "Let's drink a toast to Denis and Penelope, and to friendships, old and new."

"Hear; hear, to married love and lifelong friendship!" added Giulia, their glasses ringing out in musical trills.

"I like her," commented Denis once Giulia had left the room.

"She's a…wonderful person," agreed James.

Chapter 28
The Wedding Web

Giulia attended Denis's wedding too. James had first considered asking Dolly, having become quite close to her. He knew that she would have appreciated such a day out, meeting James's friends…all about the same age as her son Edward. In the end, he looked to his own needs, deciding he would rather spend what would probably turn out to be a long, tiring day, with his beguiling 'landlady'. James was curious to see how Giulia might function in an environment, where she knew no one and no one knew her. Having to fend for herself, for a great part of it, as he would be busy, carrying out the onerous duties of best man. He realised that he had only seen her in situations where she was in control, he never wanting (or needing) to make additional demands upon her.

Genuinely touched if not slightly surprised, that Denis had also invited Harriet and her sons…a silent burst of affection, signalling how much the 'groom' really did care about his friend. He was looking forward to reuniting with all those friends who, to a greater or lesser extent, had become pivotal during their first shared year of university. Remembering with fondness and strangely free of resentment how as a group, they had all mysteriously revolved around Denis (and Jenny of course) with some closer to the centre than others. A solar system of fellow travellers he, sadly, had made no effort to contact since, as he himself had fallen out of time and space…

The friends agreeing, in one of those surreal, 'deep into the night' conversations, that no matter how many special people you might meet afterwards, they remain on the outside, excluded from what has already happened. That there is something about a closely shared experience, which makes relationships uniquely powerful. You do not have to like everyone caught up in it with you or even find you have much in common any more. James had discussed this on an earlier occasion with Giulia and her friend Fiona, who had recently served on a jury at her local crown court, the expected two weeks gradually turning into five. She spoke eloquently about how she and the eleven other members would always remain uniquely connected. Something they all sensed if never dared express. Each would remember the same scenes, the same men and women, who entered and exited the courtroom every day (like characters in a play) each with their little foibles. Impossible to forget the pale faced defence lawyer, with his tattered gown. Jokes passing round the jury members about organising a whip round, so that he could invest in a new one. How the lawyer had later explained to them, as if reading the jury's minds, that it had once belonged to his grandfather, and that it was now his turn to wear it with pride…just as it was, with no patches or repair work. It marked three generations of barristers in his once racially persecuted family. It symbolised victory over attrition. It served as a constant reminder…

The twelve jurors in Fiona's account spending what turned out to be their last night (as they were unable to reach a unanimous verdict during courtroom hours) in a chic hotel in London, all the usual places offering accommodation being full on that occasion. The condescending judge telling them how unusual this was and how fortunate they were. A reward perhaps for their hitherto lengthy deliberations. A difficult case. That they needed to produce a majority (now down to a disappointingly acceptable 10/2) verdict. The following day resulting in a declaration of 'not guilty', even though each of the jury members sensed the defendant was as guilty as hell. Just not enough watertight or conclusive evidence. The dismay of the judge, as she had been counting on hearing a guilty verdict and delivering up a tough custodial sentence.

Fiona and eleven others, local people from diverse backgrounds, whose paths would otherwise have never crossed. Twelve good men (and women) and true. Twelve jurors united for life. Like the twelve apostles, called to act in an extraordinary way, sealing the fate of one individual.

Like Denis's year group of sunstruck undergraduates…

It was only recently that James and Giulia had resumed their affair, having been separated due to her reaction to news of the Italian earthquake. Huge reasons indeed. Not so easy to manage now, due to additional complications, Giulia having the two brothers from Italy, Matteo and Stefano to look after…which was also proving to be a drain on her energies. On everyone's energies at Casa Stella. Always too stubborn to give up. She would see it through, no matter what, help those unfortunate boys and emerge victorious. Something to do perhaps with the out-dated and yet ingrained virtues of patience and perseverance she had soaked up during her time at Fielding House and the orphanage in Italy before it. Having recently begun to speak to James a little about her time there…

It was not going to be the first English style wedding Giulia had attended, having been a guest at a few of her school friends' ceremonies and receptions. She therefore had some idea as to what to expect, in terms of the order of events and was no longer surprised by the appearance of a car complete with trailing tin cans and balloons, to whisk away the newlyweds to their honeymoon location…and other such crazy rituals. This wedding indubitably having little in common with Lorenzo and Serafina's stretched out celebrations, which had taken place in the summer heat somewhere along the Amalfi coast…

James well aware that Giulia knew how to be charming with strangers, not down to Fielding this time, but a characteristic she must have inherited in her genes. Speaking with the slightest hint of a foreign accent and sometimes employing unusual diction only adding to her appeal. She looked wonderful, understated in a coffee-coloured dress, with a navy jacket and shoes. Preferring to forego the English tradition of wearing a hat. She thought to herself that they looked ridiculous. They got in the way, ruined your hair, and then if you did take it off, you had to carry it around with you.

He and Giulia had already met the bride to be, Penelope, on a couple of occasions: once very briefly, when Denis was showing them around his new house in the country, and once again in a pub during a somewhat lively meeting, called to iron out the finer details of the special day. After which followed an even livelier lunch.

From the invitation, James had seen that her full name was Penelope Jane Hall which in James's head, had blurred into Penelope Jane Tall because that is what she was. Tall, with very long arms, legs, hands and feet. With just a trace of hunched shoulders, probably, due to having always towered over the vast majority of her peers. Regular features, fair-skinned, with bright blue eyes and chin-length brown hair. James had tried to imagine her a few years hence, with a winding trail of children following on behind, each little boy or girl, like a line of ducklings, a tiny bit smaller than the one in front. A latest already slightly visible inside her…she having bought into Denis's mad dream.

Back to the real world, James tried hard not to compare her with Jennifer. That would have been both futile and unfair to her replacement, who whether she realised it or not, was about to embark upon the onerous task of becoming wife to his brilliant, once tormented, and surely still complicated and mercurial friend. However, as is often the case, the more he tried, the more he found himself doing precisely that! It was clear to see, from the start, that she didn't exude any of Jenny's spontaneous warmth, and yet when she did allow a smile, he was surprised to see that it lit up her whole face.

Penelope 'Tall' was apparently the only child of two elderly parents, who obviously doted on her. Her father still recovering from a recent stroke. The pair were obviously happy that their daughter was finally about to marry and reward their own efforts with a grandchild or two. (In all likelihood knowing little yet of Denis's domestic ambitions.) She had always lived at home, going on to work for her father, in some kind of personal assistant capacity. In fact, that is how she had first encountered Denis, at a book fair. James could quite easily imagine how his friend might have plucked her from the rest. Pleasant, wholesome, well brought up, well-read and not in the least unattractive. Quintessentially English. The girl upon whom to hang his latest need, his latest quest. James (harshly perhaps in his head) still not having allowed Denis the benefit of having grown up a little over the years.

Oh, Penelope, but where was the long and flowing pre-Raphaelite hair?

The special day turned out to be quite windy and so on the subject of hair, while Giulia's hair danced flirtily around her shoulders, Penelope's elegant chignon stayed firmly in place at the nape of her neck. The bride was as tall and slender as an Italian cypress. If not also a little stiff and awkward. Having to remember to keep the smile going even when cameras were not pointing in her direction. A long tiring day for her, painfully aware that her new sun king- stroke-husband was playing his part seemingly effortlessly…impeccably turned out, with perfect hair, and a broad white smile. Even more polished and relaxed now than when he lorded over them all (in a range of guises) at university.

Everything went well. The rain stayed away, and the sun occasionally managed to sneak out from behind a thin layer of wispy clouds. Of course, there were a few tiny mishaps…there always are at such events. However, with a little wit and human guile, it is possible to turn mental lapses and Freudian slips, to the best advantage, creating a burst of unrehearsed humour (always the best kind). Fortunately, it had only come to the bride's attention, much later in the day, that as regards the ornate, multi-tiered cake, one side had partially collapsed. However, a quick-witted caterer had managed to hide any damage with some greenery she had found in the cottage garden, resulting in highly original and exotic photographs, which in years to come would also tell a story of their own.

A super attentive James was almost certain that during the speeches, he had discerned a spark ignite between Denis and Giulia that afternoon. All in a split second. A fixing of eyes. He found himself both bemused and jealous. It had happened so fast, he might even have imagined it…for his own future convenience, perhaps.

Whatever it was, whether it had happened or not, it marked the start of a gradual undoing between him and the mistress of Casa Stella. If a case of life taking care of itself, then so much the better. He knew they were treading water, the relationship going nowhere. However, he also knew he would always care deeply for her…They had shared so much, especially in terms of the unspoken word and for just over a year, had continued to save each other from their parallel fates of feeling 'different' from the rest. At the same time, it appeared that they had invested in nothing at all. There could be no future for them, a couple knowing only how to live out present time. He had realised from the start that she, like him really, was not capable of exclusive commitment or permanence. They were both separate beings and the same person, which they had recognised in the eyes of the other. Joint reflections in the glass of life.

Chapter 29
Big Unavoidable Once in a Lifetime Event

"So, what have you been up to, Doll? Haven't seen you around much recently," asked the ever-cheery Sean, the pub regular, who had first introduced Dorothy to James.

"I'll tell you, if you really want to know, but I don't think it will meet with your approval…"

"Upon my word, Doll. Never knew you had it in you, darlin' Aaaaahhh, a fancy man. Well, why not? Even at your age…" at which Dolly pretended to take a swipe at his head with a beer mat.

She shuffled a bit on her chair, tilted her head, adopting a rare somewhat faraway look, and declared:

"If you two are really interested then, I've been making preparations for that big unavoidable 'once in a lifetime' event." Taking her two companions a few moments of shared gaze to get what she meant.

Her words a weighty pebble thrown into a pit of silence.

James, having himself remained quiet up to that point, looked up from his own glass of thoughts and stared straight at her. Both he and Sean clinging on to a barrage of follow-up questions. Wasn't it a bit too early in the day for this kind of talk? What the hell had brought this on? Something to do with that mysterious menopause (the whispered word 'change', as it was called then), that turned late middle-aged women into monsters. It also begged the question that she might be gravely ill. However, her companions dutifully held back and let her have her say. A conversation stopper indeed. The two men by now sucked into the flow that followed oblivious as to what was going on around them. Dolly's explanation as follows:

"Yes, I started to get the idea when I was packing up the boxes and crates for my move back here. You know, wondering which things to throw away, which things to take with me…not so much in terms of the furniture. That was the easy bit. More like all the personal or private stuff that for some reason had accumulated in cupboards and drawers. So much of it undisturbed for more than twenty or thirty years. Notebooks, unfinished diaries, letters, cards, stray photos that had never made it into albums. Even a few ripped off postage stamps. In the end, I packed it all as it was. Sounds crazy, doesn't it? I was under no pressure to look through any of it. I could have just thrown the whole lot away, there and then. Wasn't the move all about starting afresh? The time wasn't right though and I somehow felt I would be able to handle things better at the new house. Once living my new life. So, I decided to spend half an hour a day sifting through each box or bundle. Sometimes it was nice, a bit like reliving half-forgotten pieces of your own existence. There was sadness too but I won't go into that now…Other times, it just didn't feel like my life at all. Someone else's details. Foreign. Awkward. As I said forgotten."

Dorothy broke off at that point, looking down at the floor, before feeling ready to continue her account.

"The most frightening thing about death, I discovered, apart from the fear of maybe having to remain in chronic pain for years beforehand, is that you feel totally out of control. Something that upon reaching a certain age we begin to sense, forever at the back of our minds. For people who are brave enough to entertain those thoughts, it becomes slightly more acceptable that…one moment we are here and the next…we are gone. Incredible."

"It made me want to leave some bits of everyday life behind…not just the normal stuff, the money and the house…to prove to the world, I suppose, that I really had once lived and breathed. That I hadn't gone completely. Even if I don't claim to have made much of a difference to the world at large. I also needed to put things right, as much as I am able. Like listening to that inner voice again and trying to make up with people that I'd somehow removed from my thoughts, after either letting them slip away, or even as a result of falling out with them. Wiping the slate clean. Not wanting to get into those situations again. Where acceptance or forgiveness has been an unthinkable option. I'm now ready to put that right."

"I suppose it's so much easier if you have faith in God and an afterlife. It must be such a comfort. I went to church for years. You know, Church of England we were and I used to enjoy it too. Ours was a pretty church, built in the middle ages. If I try hard enough, I can sometimes smell what it was like inside.

A mixture of damp corners and beeswax. I loved the polished brass, the hymns and harvest festival and on Mother's Day when the vicar allowed the children to hand out little posies of violets or primroses. I loved Christmas and the church fêtes, the colourful bunting and stalls crammed full of bric-a-brac."

"That's where it ended though. I now realise that as I grew up, mine was still a child's version of Christianity. Merely a series of stories, hymns and the Lord's Prayer, which I only realised a little while ago that I didn't fully understand. Words like 'hallowed' and 'trespasses'. Why were there so many words from a different age in a prayer that taught us how to live? Like a child, leaving the church each Sunday, certain just for a minute or two, that I could become a better person, but then real life taking over yet again. Giving those Sunday things no more thought whatsoever. When I tried to pray at home or listen more carefully to the sermons, I never progressed to believe that Christ truly had died for us. Died for our sins. To give us the chance of everlasting life. Or believe in the virgin birth. Even to believe that it was God in the first place, who had created the universe. You know all the supernatural stuff, where there is no real proof…I realised that I had no faith or understanding of any of that…and that it was somehow too late…"

Sean was by now beginning to twiddle his thumbs and shuffle his very long feet under the table. Feeling unusually hot and uncomfortable. What was happening to his fun-loving friend? Whatever it was, he didn't like it. James, on the other hand, having already formed the opinion that it all sounded a bit like the nesting instinct in reverse, and was about to tell her so, but decided that it was better to stay quiet. Both men realising that she needed to have her say…

"I've drawn up a will, of course…so that I know where my house and other possessions are going. The experts call it your 'estate'…sounds grand, doesn't it? I know exactly how much I have to live on, so provided I don't stray beyond those spending boundaries, I will be fine. Still haven't quite made up my mind about burial or cremation, but I've made plans for both in rough, so once I know what I want to do, I will just tear up the other sheet."

"And guess what, though I never knew I'd be doing such a thing, I've already chosen the church I want for the service, and drawn up a shortlist of hymns to sing and a couple of poems that could be read out. And as I was doing it, I suddenly got this overwhelming sensation of being at my own funeral. It was as if it was really happening, there and then, like I was there…well, I will be of course, but dead and in a box. So an unplanned rehearsal for being dead, I suppose, with me still a bit in control. Mind-blowing."

"The idea of death feels more acceptable now… I can't really explain it and have no idea how long that feeling will last. Of course, there's still much to do…whether or not to go for burial, as I said, and the other thing about who to leave those letters and diaries to, all those things that have no material value. There are my step-children I suppose…perhaps I should give them first refusal. It hurts me to think that they or anyone else will just bin them, without having read or gained from them or even enjoyed them in some way. I know nothing lasts forever. Perhaps in the end, it's all vanity. Yes, I'm pretty sure that's what it is. There the power ends…"

Dolly came to, out of her reverie, and looked up at Sean and James for a reaction. To see if their faces were offering up anything at all.

She let Sean go first. "Well, blow me down, Doll, didn't know you had it in you, there I've said it twice about you today. All that deep stuff. Meaning of life. Where we come from stuff and where we are going. All that worry and fuss about dying. Sorry, old girl, but I don't see it like that at all. Religion stinks if you ask me. Complicates everything. Screws everyone up. You said it yourself, here today and gone tomorrow we are. Somehow having to get through each day as best we can. Don't want to give it any more thought than that. Well, that's how it works for me. I'll leave it to the living to fix everything after I've gone. Good for them if they want to throw a little party to remember me by. Don't care too much one way or the other, really…but it's horses for courses, so they say. To each his own."

"One man's meat is another man's poison," took up James, slightly tongue in cheek. "Dolly, seriously though, you're not ill, are you? Is there something more to all this, that you're not telling us?"

"No," she let out a quick laugh. "Of course, not. When that happens, you two will be the first to know, I promise…will be easier to tell you two over a gin and tonic, in this here pub, than watching the fake faces of Reg's family trying to look heartbroken or even concerned. I'm certain of that."

"Well, that's a relief at least!" piped up Sean, almost back to his old self. "You had us worried there. The Abercorn Arms wouldn't be the same without you. Might have to find myself another drinking hole…Just one thing though, Doll girl. Don't get any ideas about leaving all those letters and diaries to me! Couldn't be doing with any of that. No offence like, but they really would go straight into the bin. But I'm pretty sure Jimmy Boy here would be ever so happy to be left them. Now that you're both a couple of fucking philosophers…what I have to put up with! Wasn't one enough?"

And so their conversation came back down to normal. Until into the pub strode…Father John. Dolly for some reason hoping he hadn't picked up on Sean's 'f' word! Whereas Sean couldn't have cared less.

"Hello, Father, over here!" called out James, as he pulled out a fourth chair from another table, "Do take a seat, these are my friends, you know the ones I was telling you about." Indicating each one in turn, he continued, "This is Dorothy or Dolly as we call her, and that rather louche looking one is Sean…"

"Well, thank you, James. I think I may have worked that out for myself…" which immediately caused Dolly and Sean to laugh out loud, partly because Father John had got one over their super intelligent friend, and partly because they sensed at once that Father John was going to be 'okay'. They could relax. Any personal prejudices against men of the cloth (not to mention Catholic priests) were temporarily at least, suspended.

Chapter 30
Immacolata

With new friendships growing, it was only a matter of time until James began to get closer to Tina (Immacolata). Also known as Immy to those outside of the family home. The two had in effect hit it off from the start.

She was the youngest of the De Martinos and he had always thought her the most engaging. She turned up to all the usual family events, went regularly to Mass, and never took sides against any family member. However, within all this, she somehow managed to stay true to herself. As regards the occasional heated argument (a few of which, James had already witnessed), it was usually Tina, who managed to restore calm or get the offended party to see reason…it was always she, who did her best to bring such disputes to an early close.

Such exchanges never taking place however when Giulia (not a De Martino) was in residence. Disagreements mainly having to do with the running of their delicatessen business, older sister Sandra's string of failed relationships…or Patrizia's lack of them. Voices raised. Half in loud quasi-English, half in an even louder Italian dialect, shoulders shrugging, eyes rolling, arms and hands flying…another language in itself.

Tina had therefore managed to carve out a life for herself without causing too much family backlash…her parents only occasionally having to let out a 'what is going to become of her?' type comment, with nodding hands arranged in prayer mode, and eyes raised heavenwards. The rampant social and sexual revolution whirling around outside, still unable to penetrate their sturdy walls. Things beginning to look up for Tina's parents though. Sandra had very recently found a nice Italian boy (therefore Catholic), from a 'good family'. Patrizia? Well, you can't have everything in this life. She might have to die an 'old maid', uttering through clenched teeth that always whispered word 'zitella', with her future role best marked out as that of a doting aunt. As for the youngest, well, that was anyone's guess.

Lorenzo and Serafina going on to have Carmen, Fabrizio and little Giulio, one after the other. De Martino blessings…

James and Tina came to share many lively chats of their own, and now that his intimate relationship with Giulia had fizzled out, he found himself spending much of his time with her niece. Had Tina guessed? Did she and the others know? Had it all been obvious from the start, in spite of their furtive behaviour? If so, nothing was said, nothing alluded to.

James was by now considering a permanent return to his own house. It had struck him that it was a good time to go, not quite able yet to refer to it as home, still 'the house', but that his convalescence at Casa Stella, if not exactly complete, had probably gone as far as it was able. There are things that we just have to learn to accommodate. Not everything finally dealt with or blown away.

He wanted to invite Tina round to get her opinion of it. To consider what he might do with the verging on empty rooms. A school holiday was imminent. It struck him that he had never thought to ask the same of Giulia, and she had never taken it upon herself to enquire. If he did eventually decide to leave, he was determined to return on a regular basis, especially to see Giulia, to turn up at the presbytery for a chat with Father John, and also once in a while…stop off to buy something at the De Martino delicatessen.

To continue seeing his friends at The Abercorn Arms. All these people and places were now part of his mental and emotional furniture. His wider family. As he saw it, a move would mean consolidating his progress, not a running away. Now with a life as full as he could have hoped. Once unimaginable. His sister, Harriet, and his nephews, although living in Oxfordshire, were in constant touch by phone and letter, they also having become fond of Tina. Harriet prompting her wilful brother 'not to let this one go' as it was obvious that they 'were made for each other'. A hesitant James tried to persuade his sister that she was on the wrong track completely, that he and Tina were simply very close friends, two people with common interests.

Apart from the murder of little Dominic, that terrible murder, whose silent black shadow never stopped haunting the family's consciousness, his own life at last seemed uncannily…doable after so many years of exile. For that, he was truly grateful. He felt more like other people for the very first time he could remember. Realising that perhaps some of the differences might have been of his own making…

Tina taught history at the local secondary school, and as James soon discovered, this left her precious little time to relax or socialise. With all the planning, marking, meetings and school trips to arrange, clubs to organise. Theirs did not start out as a romantic liaison in any case. They merely enjoyed each other's company, when free to do so, in an easy and unforced manner, generally sharing the same sense of humour and a similar taste in things like board games, music and TV programmes. Even films, with only a few exceptions. They both listened to U2, Queen, the Stones and the greatest of them all, Bob Dylan. James promising to introduce her more closely to classical music at some future date. She joked that he was trying to transform her into Giulia.

They swapped copies of Private Eye, and regularly commented on a range of articles from the Sunday newspapers. Perhaps Tina harboured more left-wing leanings, he thought, but broadly speaking, they agreed on most political issues. One evening totally astounded to discover that they had each gone to see a production of The Ragged-Trousered Philanthropists on stage at The Riverside Studios, a few years back and it could even have been on the same night. Considering her life and background, a little miracle in itself.

After sharing a cheap bottle of wine, James and Tina once sang, laughed, and postured their way through 'Come On Eileen' at a friend's party. Getting a standing ovation. This song becoming 'their' song in a funny, unsentimental kind of way. Once again, he having to make sure she was home by 11!

This state of affairs continued. When to move on? Should the pair even move on? James having already alerted Father John, as to how he felt about her, though a little nervous about speaking to Tina herself, or even the family. If the others had noticed anything, they had (unsurprisingly) stayed silent on the matter. Or did they talk about it when he wasn't around? So hard to know when and if to proceed. He remembered his 'old friend' the Prince of Denmark, and the usual dilemma. The curse of inaction. Would her parents be happy about the match? He realised he still didn't really understand how they thought and saw life.

Whenever he felt he was onto what made them tick, something would happen to show that there was still so much to uncover about the De Martino mentality. A very practical way of seeing the world…but with lots of anomalies. He assumed that they would be happy for their daughter to marry, especially because in this case, there would never be money problems, and that it was likely children would follow. The two crucial ingredients for making a good life. Also happy and relieved that there had been no signs of sexual behaviour between them. A daughter's age having little to do with it…

But was HE what they had in mind? Did HE fit their very exacting bill? They had always treated him fairly and with a detached kindness, as they might any guest, but now the situation would be different. Would they, in their heart of hearts, accept someone English, and an agnostic verging on atheism to boot! An idle dreamer with no job! Someone who had turned up at Giulia's house because of unresolved and deep-rooted psychological problems. From this perspective, his position was not looking favourable after all. James never certain about how much they did know or assume. There again, when it came to it, did he really care?

He realised that his thoughts had been straying too far and too fast in the direction of Tina's parents, and that perhaps he should be concentrating more on her, and her likely reaction. She had never flirted with him, nothing beyond affectionate, and the longer this impasse persisted, the more difficult it became to move on. It was incredible, he mused, that there had been no kiss, other than the customary 'one, two' on left and then right cheek, whenever they met or parted company. He thought he could read into her eyes, however. Almost certain he had detected that same quiver of emotions, albeit restrained, that he himself was feeling. Without an exchange of words on the subject, however, no matter how brief, he knew he couldn't be sure. If she weren't interested, why, as her parents might see it, was she playing with fire? Or from another angle, simply wasting precious time?

It was at this time that they heard the news that Denis's first child had been born, a baby girl called Daphne, about six months after the wedding. The master plan underway. D for Denis, which derived from Dionysus. Daphne also from the Greek, like Penelope, her mother…James's brain working overtime, whenever contemplating the life of his precious friend. As if still part of an ancient myth or saga.

The day had come when James knew he had to say something in a kind of do or die moment. He grabbed the moment, spoke of his love and asked Tina to marry him.

He had already prepared himself for both a yes or no answer, and had covered what his follow-up words would be in either situation. A 'yes', well that would be very good news and quite straightforward. He would take her to choose an engagement ring, followed by a meal in a suitably romantic setting or if she preferred, to watch a play in London's theatre-land. Then tell close family of their plans. He would accept a Catholic ceremony, and all that it entailed: religious instruction, classes, whatever was necessary. At least his friend Father John would take care of all that. Tina would be free to choose everything else, reception venue, honeymoon destination, number of bridesmaids and so on. Or she might prefer something altogether different. A small, more intimate wedding. He would happily leave all such matters to her.

Privately hoping that she would opt to live in his house facing the green, only 15 minutes away. That elegant house they, like Denis and Penelope before them, would turn into a vibrant family home.

A 'no' would be unsettling, but he would try to stay calm, and ask her for her reasons. Depending on the response, he might still muster enough courage to suggest that she needed a little more time to think about it, and that admittedly, he did kind of spring it on her! An 'I don't love you and know that I could never love you' would definitely be soul wrenching. Nowhere to take that…

However, Tina came back with something completely different. This time with the look and a tone of a Tina he simply didn't recognise.

Chapter 31
Dilemma

"Oh, James, you mean it, don't you? A proposal of marriage. Gosh, I didn't see that one coming."

The morning burst of unseasonal sunshine, already beginning to fade as she began to release herself from the moment…

"I think I have feelings for you too…though up until now, I was never certain that you felt the same."

Her facial expression and tone of voice beginning to harden.

"However, James, there's something I need to tell you, to explain why I can't marry you. Why we can't be properly together? I thought you'd already cottoned on and there would have been no point saying anything earlier; I had no idea that you were about to propose. I hope you don't think I've been misleading you…" Her eyes lit up again, but only slightly. Grateful for a few seconds respite. "Oh God, today of all days! Did you know, it's my birthday tomorrow…or maybe today; I was born at the stroke of midnight. Isn't that ironic?"

No answer. Tina obliged to continue.

"Even though looking back, I suppose it was obvious. Where things were heading. The two of us spending more and more time together. I just didn't think you were the marrying type…if I thought about it at all. I suppose knowing at the same time that we couldn't have gone on for much longer, without saying…or doing…something about it. Oh, it's so unfair the position you've put me in" …sounding as though it had nothing to do with her as if she was merely thinking aloud.

James was no longer able to stay quiet. Nothing she was saying made any sense. He insisted she hear him out first. Thinking he knew her motivation. She let him have his say. She could have predicted every word.

"Well, let's just go through each of the issues. All this must have to do with your family and their 'oh so sacred' traditions. OK, so I'm not Italian and not Catholic. Can't do much about the first one, I'm afraid…and probably not the second either. Then there's the question of my past mental state, which I cannot deny, or even guarantee that there aren't going to be future episodes. I get it. I've already given it a lot of thought. What I am certain of, what I can promise, is that I now know how to deal with all of it so much better. We can go into that properly later. During my time at Casa Stella…and thanks to a great extent to Giulia, your parents and your whole family in fact…my life has just become more stable and normalised. Being with you all has allowed me to let others in, let life in, that's it! Life. For the very first time. Like opening up a vast window. I couldn't do that before. Believing that I didn't want to, that I really didn't want to have to do with other people. That I had little or nothing in common with them."

"But now I have my sister and nephews back, and Denis and the others as well, and then there are my friends at the pub. Even Father John, he still looks out for me, and well Giulia, of course. OK, so I'm not what your parents would have wanted for you. I completely see it from their point of view, but given time, they will realise that they were wrong to be concerned. Of course, they are only trying to protect you…"

"They will come to see that I really do care for you. We have so much going for us…I have a house close by…a home I wanted the two of us to share. It's up to you whether you want to go on teaching or even do something else. You can go and see your parents as often as you like…not to mention the long-term financial security. See, all the things that are important to them. Things that make life better."

James's voice verging on angry now…

"They have no right to try and convince you otherwise. I thought you were stronger than that, Tina. Don't tell me they've arranged a marriage for you into the bargain, like from when you were 3 months old…but if it's nothing to do with that, more to do with…I don't know…past boyfriends, I really couldn't care less. Our life together starts now, in present tense."

"You are being ridiculous. You just don't have a clue, do you?" Tina cutting through his choice of words, ones that she would never have anticipated from him.

Then a little more in the way of tenderness filtering through the hissing brutality of her response.

"There again, why should you? You asked me to listen and I did, but I already knew you would be wasting your breath. You are right, of course…your last comment. If that's all I had to worry about, it would be next to nothing. I believe I do love you…and would marry you tomorrow, or even come and live with you if you had a problem with the marriage thing. I can't say better than that. My parents would just have to accept it or lose me in the bargain. Look, James, the situation is…if…if you and I were…were to become a real couple, there are things I would always have to keep from you. From the start. Forever. How can a deep and serious relationship survive that? You would ever be wondering and thinking the worst. Unable to trust me with things. I would feel disloyal and…and unhappy…from the outset. Going on as we are might be second best, but it's OK. Just as it is. This way, as close friends, you will be free from all the rest. Free to go when you need to…"

"Sorry, Tina," interjected James, "sorry, but I just don't know what you're talking about. What 'rest'? None of this is making any sense. What is it you have to hide from me? That you've had a thousand lovers, that you know you can't have children, that you've robbed a bank? I hope not for your sake, but none of that would make any difference to me, how I feel, will always feel about you. We are right together."

To which Tina replied softly, "I know it all sounds ludicrous. I am really trying…Could we just leave it for a couple of days? As in, do not refer to it at all. Let me get my head around what I am able to tell you, and the right words to use. I just want you to realise, that none of this is for me. I could easily have just stayed quiet. To remain in denial and get my own way. To ignore the consequences. Staying quiet, so that we can both have what we want, to be together. But it would be wrong. I have to do the right thing, even if it is the most painful thing in the world. It's to protect YOU…Come on, let's enjoy my few days of freedom. Freedom from the classroom, that is. It will be over soon enough."

James consented and quietly let the matter drop. Against his better nature and everything he was feeling. He agreed to give her the time she needed. Certain that she would stick to her word. The two soon finding themselves walking hand in hand…each oblivious to the quiet passing of time or their surroundings, things they might normally joke about or comment on…as they headed, instinctively, in the direction of James's house.

Once again, James choosing to stay quiet when, on arrival, he listened to her call her parents from the telephone in the hallway. To let them know that she was fine, that she would be back in a couple of hours, mentioning the name of a girlfriend. He would have wanted to tell her that he couldn't believe his ears. "Tina, you are 26 for heaven's sake…you live in London and it's the 1980s."

James, confident that he knew so much about their ways, was in truth, only just at the beginning of understanding how things functioned at Casa Stella. On this occasion, that a daughter's age didn't come into it. It was to do with ongoing respect. Respect towards your family. Respect for your elders. For the family home and its rules. And of course, what her parents didn't know couldn't hurt them. The lie protected them as well as Tina. It was back to square one! He had let off her off the hook, again.

It was also only hours away from her birthday and he guessed there would be preparations afoot at Casa Stella to celebrate the following day.

Tina, for her part, acknowledging that an earlier love, those stolen hours spent with the charming Nicholas Lydiard, was of a lesser kind. Not authentic after all. A delicious game, while it lasted. Secret, beautiful, but with an ugly twist, as he had a wife and children she was ignobly helping him to betray. They had created an illusion monster, which fed both egos…What would she do now though? As she had said, she needed to find the right words. To not speak in riddles. To tell James clearly as much as she could, in the simplest of ways, without really telling him anything at all, without allowing him to become caught up in something darkly awful. Something that didn't concern him. Because she knew that one day, paradoxically, he would hold it against her for telling him. About the dangers. About that other distant and shadowy world that she too had come to inhabit.

'That's it', she decided. She would seek some practical advice from her beloved aunt, Zia Giulia. She wanted to clear the air, to have the matter sorted, before returning to the classroom.

The next morning, James got up early. Imagining that he could see Tina's thick, wavy brown hair spread over the pillow, next to his. He had picked a few flowers from the little garden and placed them in a glass on the bedside table. Pretending that he could make out the slight movement of the bedclothes, as they rhythmically rose and fell, rose and fell. As though they had spent their first night together. Remembering at the same time, that today was her birthday.

Once back in the kitchen, his thoughts then turned to Giulia. Perhaps she was the link. Wondering about things that he had never bothered with in the past. Who was she exactly? It was very difficult to come up with any kind of answer. They had shared passion and intimacy on many occasions…but he still knew little more about her life other than what she had cared to disclose to him. Just like with him, her love of beautiful objects, whether sourced from the natural world or fine pieces, crafted by hand. Places, music, buildings, poetry, words. Her thirst for knowledge which he himself had begun to seek out from an early age. Why had she never married? Why did she go to such lengths to help others? To the extent of seeing everything through…when most of us might consider doing something significant, but that is where it ends. What was her real connection with the De Martinos? What was the nature of her friendship with Father John? Why had she left him on his own for a couple of days during their trip to Venice?

At the time, it really had felt like love. Love as an escape from life's torments. Intense and intoxicating…

Chapter 32
Aftermath

It was hardly surprising that in the weeks and months following little Dominic's death, everything at Casa Stella had felt different. In an instant. With every member of the family realising, each in their own way, that the life they had always known and shared could never properly return. Each sensing that the messages of comfort...based around that boring old chestnut, that time was a great healer...would for them, have severe limitations. A single human act had gouged out the heart of their home, leaving behind a permanent crater. The murder of an innocent reprehensible and unforgivable. All they had worked and lived for. Their little boy, Dominic, belonged to them all the first and much-loved grandchild. A birth that had hailed the continuity of family name, pride, self-containment...hope for the years to come. Their investment in future generations.

Something hitherto unexpressed had also died deep inside each of them. A rawness, which kept returning to gnaw away at their soul.

Casa Stella awash with police. An ongoing invasion of every room and corner of the house, punctuated by the ransacking of cupboards, wardrobes, cabinets, drawers, out of which spewed all their personal belongings. Insignificant items in the main, unless they happened to be yours. Even more painful for the De Martinos, so private and autonomous in character and behaviour. It felt like a siege. It felt like rape. Uniformed strangers trawling through piles of papers and letters. The taking of umpteen samples, fingerprints, photographs, followed by even more questions, questions, questions. Then all the same questions over again, worded slightly differently, day in day out. The answers hardly changing because no one knew anything, anything else that might be helpful. No one able to make sense of it during each restless night or in the cold light of day.

A murder with a message, though. The extermination of a baby. The whole family targeted and then, paradoxically, cast under suspicion.

Lorenzo, Serafina, Domenico, Carmela, Patrizia, Sandra, Immacolata and Giulia…

"What time was it again that you last saw the baby? Did you leave the house for any reason? How did he seem? Why was he staying overnight at Star House? Who else was present in the house? Were there any other visitors that day? Think. Think. Who exactly? Anyone lurking around the house? Anyone outside the family showing an interest in the child? Can you confirm that Dominic still had not learnt to walk? Could he crawl though? Had his father ever shown anger or violence towards him? Describe each family member, your neighbours. Have you any reason to suspect them? Would you say Serafina was a good mother? How was she coping with motherhood? She is quite young and far from home. Had the child ever disappeared before?"

Relentless. Exhausting. They had all come under the spotlight. Guilty before they could ever become innocent again.

"Can you explain (one more time) why Lorenzo De Martino, the child's father, was not at home? Why would anyone wish to murder a baby…Did your family have enemies? What do YOU think could have happened?"

They also questioned James, of course. He was the outsider and undoubtedly, for that reason, probably their prime suspect. Pale and pained, giving his own long, drawn-out account, deflated. There was also his medical history. The baby's death had brought about a profound effect upon him. He too had often seen the sweet little boy around the place. The police had discovered the journal containing the descriptions James had made of the family members. He had to explain that it was just a bit of fun…and no, he was not secretly in love with Serafina. He told them about the poetry of Alexander Pope, in order to back up his alibi, his interest in satire and how he had merely been trying to emulate the poet's style. They were definitely not impressed…or convinced.

"Where were you again the evening before the baby's disappearance?"

"As I said, I was taking the two boys Stefano and Matteo to the airport, because they were booked on a flight to Italy, travelling as 'unaccompanied minors'. I stayed there at the terminal with them until someone came from Passenger Handling to take them to the plane. Fortunately, it was leaving on time. They were the boys that Giulia had been looking after at Casa Stella, Star House, due to the earthquake in Italy last year. A real success story in the end.

The boys were returning to live with their mother. I then came straight back to the house, and the party was still in full flow. Giulia had organised it for the brothers. Some of their school friends and their families had come round earlier to say goodbye. Everything was fine. Apart from the sadness that the boys were going home. None of us thought they would ever return. We all came to like having them around...eventually."

Then shaking his head, and with a wry smile, he continued, "Apart from all the disruption they caused, we were going to miss them."

Then later in his lengthy account, "Yes, it was me who spotted Dominic's little body from the balcony at the top of the house, where my rooms are. It didn't make sense. I couldn't believe what I was seeing. In that awful, surreal moment, I tried to persuade myself that Giulia without telling me, must have bought a little statue or something, you know in the shape of an angel, a stone cherub for the garden, and that it must have fallen into the water..."

"And you, Mr Newhouse, can you explain to us once again, why you happened to be living at Star House, or Casa Stella, as you refer to it?"

"As you already know, it's a very long story...quite painful. Do I really have to go over it all again? Ok, one more time then. As I told you or one of your people on Wednesday, I've suffered from a sort of anxiety for most of my life, and for many years I just couldn't bring myself to talk about it. To do with a deep sense of feeling different from other people. I have no idea why this was, but I just got on with it really. Just accepted it. It wasn't always a problem. It's just who I am, what I was, am like. Never thought that anyone could do anything about it."

"Things got worse, though, much worse, when, I was at university...and I got the news that my parents had died. In a freak road accident, and my sister and I inherited a great deal of money and property, which neither of us knew anything about, that it even existed. It sounds bizarre, but it actually made the anxiety worse, probably I suppose, because I had never bothered to get to know my mother or my father properly. They were very disappointed with my choice of degree. I was suddenly wracked with guilt, feeling that I didn't deserve, you know, all this wealth, this good fortune after the bad. I soon had problems with how to manage my time, now knowing that I would never have to work for a living...or do anything at all. I felt left to my own devices. I tried to make plans, but nothing came of them."

"After spending years in and out of clinics and the like, it just got to the point that I wanted to seek some alternative help from someone totally removed…from the medical world. Maybe take a spiritual path for a while. But not in the sense of a cult or anything like that. The medication and therapy were all very well. To be fair, they had helped a lot. However, there is no actual cure. As I said, I just assumed I had been born with this condition. It was part of me. I was gradually recovering though…or let's say, in a much better position to spot and manage early symptoms. To nip things in the bud."

"That was all before meeting the De Martinos."

"It was by chance that I discovered Father John from St Raphael's. I just overheard someone mention his name, and even though I would never describe myself as religious…he, John the person…turned out to be just what I needed, regardless of what he did for a living. It was he, who first suggested I come to stay a while at Casa Stella. Strangely enough, he chose the De Martinos because theirs is a big and busy family and they would not have much time to bother about me. Genius. I was free, but…sort of…belonged at the same time, the way it is with Italians, I think. I could get involved, or not, whenever something was going on. There was never any pressure or expectation. To their absolute credit, they took me on without knowing much about me at all. All thanks to John."

"And surely to Miss Cristaldi, who is after all the owner of the property…" that day's interviewer suggested.

"Well, yes, of course, also to Giulia. It must sound stupid, naive even, but as a crazy idea, it's worked. I do as much as I can without anyone making a big deal out of it. I help Father John at the presbytery and I know he continues to watch out for me. Giulia suddenly had big plans for the garden and got me to help her with that too. Through her, I've managed to pick up quite a bit of Italian…"

"Let's stay with Giulia, Miss Cristaldi. Can you tell us a bit more about your…relationship with her? How do you get on with her? Is it a fair description to say, that you are her lodger and…as well as…gardener? She is very attractive."

"Yes, as you know already, we have until recently been lovers. Well, more than that really, much more. Hard to put into words, without cheapening it, making it sound run-of-the-mill. It's odd I know, but from the start, even before we properly spoke, it's like we could read each other, but without the need for words. We went on to discover that there was so much common ground, in spite of our different upbringings. Our love of nature, the arts, books, poetry… So hard to find people like that. It goes beyond intelligence. More to do with intense sensitivity. The others here don't know about us, by the way, and I ask you once again, not to say anything, more for Giulia…than for me."

"Thank you, Mr Newhouse. We are, of course, continuing to make all the necessary checks on everything you and the others have told us. Bearing that in mind, we must ask you one more question. Have you ever behaved violently? Towards others or even towards yourself? Have you ever experienced suicidal thoughts?"

"Absolutely not. I have been going over this a lot in my head. I was expecting you to ask me that. I also wanted to know for myself. My answer is…no way. Even if that is hard to accept, given my medical history. I can't think of ever dealing with problems using violence, not even as I was growing up. I got out of any potential fights using humour or deflection. All my struggles have always played out precisely inside my own head. I have never felt particularly aggressive towards others, even those I find unpleasant or tiresome. Neither have I ever lost hope to the extent that I wanted to finish it all. Even in my darkest moments, when all I wanted to do was sleep, I somehow never let go of the notion that life one day would be…well…alright again…"

The police inquiry was getting nowhere, in spite of their diligence, their constant presence and questioning at Star House. After they had gathered and sifted through all possible evidence, they found themselves back at square one. They had not been able to detect a possible motive to link any family member…or James…with the murder. No trace or whisper of past criminal activity involving any of them, not even a minor misdemeanour.

They now had to use their imagination, follow up wild hunches, and widen the net. To look outside of the family, to the local community and possibly beyond. Just where to start? Every so often, someone from the force returned to question them again, just to make sure they had not missed anything or check that their accounts still tallied. After months of working round the clock as well as dealing with local and media outrage, this was as far as they had come.

Mrs Serafina De Martino had put her baby son in his cot at about 9 pm and had gone to check on him a couple of times before going to bed herself. They were both staying overnight at Casa Stella, due to a family party taking place, and sharing a ground-floor guest room set aside for that purpose. When Serafina woke up the following morning, she discovered that her baby's cot was empty.

Within the hour, the wealthy lodger James Newhouse had looked down from his balcony on the second floor and discovered Dominic's little body floating face down on the surface of the pond. It turned out to be death by suffocation.

For Giulia, the investigation was also taking a heavy toll. Unlike James, however, she was not given to lengthy replies to police questions. She would never elaborate unless pressed. However, this was not merely a character trait. From a young age, she had both learnt and trained herself to remain on guard at all times. In this case, not because she knew anything more about Dominic's murder, but in order to protect someone she loved…her own father. A man in hiding, who she believed had ties with the criminal underworld. A man who could no longer live a normal life. She was not even certain how or when she had discovered this. It had little to do with anything he had actually told her. More with his mysterious business activities. Something unspoken she had absorbed over the years, as if by osmosis. It explained why, after taking her to live in England, when she was only ten years old, he had only been able to see her intermittently. Years later, meetings between them taking place in a range of secret locations.

She had only ever confided all this to one person, and that was…Father John.

Chapter 33
Preamble

The weather was mild and a park bench meant 'open air' and so neutral territory for James and Tina. In addition, there was a wide space stretching out around them. Each with no deadlines or other appointments that day, they could stay for as long (or not) as necessary.

Had either thought of looking skywards, they would have made out a continuous, near-perfect arrow line of aeroplanes, small, smaller, smallest, forming and reforming in the vast greyness above them, as each plane took off and came into land nearby. Much closer to the ground, noisy birds also came and went. Including an angry array of greedy starlings, perhaps to feed off something interesting lying in the short undergrowth. Forever screeching and squabbling, far more disruptive than any passing children cutting through the park on their way to school.

A public and private setting, therefore, enabling frank conversation and civilised behaviour. Normal life going on around them in the near distance. No one able to eavesdrop. Merely two young people sharing a bench. Set up for whatever might ensue.

James had turned up first, which allowed him to watch Tina come into view about ten minutes later. Her shape growing ever familiar as she drew nearer, filling him with a renewed shot of happiness. Regardless of what she was about to say. He had calmed down over the last day or two, putting aside any frustration he had felt about her declaration, that she was not able to marry him. Having given no intelligible reason. Inevitably less of a problem than she was making out. He was seeing another side to her though, a deeper side perhaps, set against the usual warm and fun-loving openness of her character. In fact, for a moment, he felt that he loved her even more, her taking things so seriously, evidently out of love for him. A kind of quaint, old-fashioned quality, something rare in people today, especially for someone as young as Tina. He had promised to let her have her say. She had asked for three days to gather her thoughts and 'select the right words…'

He made out that she was wearing a light blue dress, unusual for her as she nearly always wore jeans, and that she was carrying something bulky in a shoulder bag, which turned out to be something for them to eat…

"Hello, James, you got here early then. I hope I didn't keep you waiting too long. It's not cold though is it, thank goodness! I'm only a couple of minutes late I think."

She bent down to kiss him, as he slowly rose allowing her to sit down alongside him. "Love you," he said.

"Love you too," she managed to squeeze out, but clearly wanting to get on with the business of the day. James joked that he hoped that the chosen bench met with her approval, that he'd inspected them all and that it was obviously in better shape than the others. Tina noticed that it was also set apart, so it was unlikely that anyone would try to disturb them.

"Could I just make clear, Tina, before I hand the day's proceedings over to you…at great personal risk perhaps…" James now letting out a brief laugh. "That whatever you have to say, nothing will make me change my mind, my feelings will remain the same…you are the one, the only one I want and have ever wanted to spend the rest of my life with…"

He thought he caught sight of a tear or two welling up in her eyes, but she somehow managed to keep control of her emotions, not daring to comment on this premature declaration. She sat upright, for the most part staring straight ahead, but also occasionally turning towards James, in order to uncover his thoughts, keeping the palms of her hands on her knees. True to his word, he sat quietly and let her have her say. Her tone was formal and persuasive.

"I need to start at the beginning. Even though it will mean going back hundreds of years. The only way I know how to express myself. It might even seem that I am stating the obvious, but I've given things a lot of thought. I can assure you that I haven't come to waste your time…"

"Few bother to think about it, but it is a hard fact that no one can choose their parents, cannot choose the family they are born into…or even on which part of planet Earth they come to occupy. It's potluck from our first gulp of air. I was taught from an early age, that since it is our parents who give us life, which in turn is a gift from God, we must be ever respectful towards them. Honour thy father and thy mother. In spite of how they might treat us at any given time. Of course, no one is perfect…we are human beings after all and life itself can often turn out to be so difficult, unfair and cruel even. We can learn from so-called good parenting, just as we can from bad, and everything in between. The best we can hope for is that our parents love us and go on caring for us, go on wanting what they believe is the best for us, notwithstanding lack of time or know-how or financial situation, or absence of wider family support."

"In my own case, I am not a product of a random kind of parenting, but of a centuries-old, deep-rooted culture or tradition, which has grown out of my people's lifelong struggle just to survive. The majority of these having had to combat centuries of oppression. It has resulted in an ongoing quest, to make life appear worthwhile or meaningful in spite of all the hardship. Together with an unquestioned attachment to the beliefs and rituals of the Catholic Church. All this jostling alongside the stubborn remnants of ancient pagan superstition."

"People who leave their homes for a new life take all this with them. So much greater than the contents of their cardboard suitcases. It becomes even more important than before. A secure anchor. As 'stranieri', they feel vulnerable in their newly adopted homes, but eventually meet with others from their homeland and form local networks. People with the same ideas and beliefs. As they look around, they see examples of behaviour, family life in particular, that are at odds with the way they have always seen and read the world. There is the need to preserve their ways and customs because as far as they are concerned, they are the only things to guarantee a family's future. Coming from an age when change rarely happened or happened so slowly, nobody noticed. It's something more felt than talked about. Ingrained. A result of passed down, ancient wisdom. Pre-dating Christianity."

"If you start to take that from them, you take away their identity, their soul…"

"Historically, as I said, if you look at the place my parents are from and their social class, their life and that of their ancestors…you will see that it is made up of back-breaking hard work, often in unbearable heat, and always full of suffering and subjugation. You can read up on this for yourself. Men and women working the fields, digging, planting, sowing and harvesting. From early morning until the sun sets. Never a day off. I've heard stories of women squatting down to give birth in the fields, some for the umpteenth time, and getting back on their feet again as they continue to work. Babies strapped to their backs. Old before their time. Often dying of exhaustion. An exaggeration? Well, possibly…but there has to be more than a grain of truth in all this."

"My parents, Mamma and Papà…as you see, still working round the clock, in an England that has given them the freedom to live as they choose and they, of course, will always be grateful. Then again, in their case, fortune struck and Zia Giulia offered them a home at Casa Stella…"

"But nothing has changed within them. Nothing of England has penetrated. You know yourself how poor their spoken English is…it's as though they have chosen not to engage."

"It might be hard to accept, but all this is part of me…and a big part. I know I don't give that impression. Apart from dark eyes and pale olive skin, I totally pass as English. I was born here; educated here. I've gained a degree and teaching certificate. Very rarely having to refer to myself as Immacolata, my birth name. I have a foot in both camps. I understand both mentalities and am able to see the world from both perspectives. I admit I've often chosen to exploit my situation, at times almost leading a double life. I've told lies to my parents and kept secrets from them. Strangely helped by the name changes that evolved. Tina, at home and now with you, of course, but Immy to anyone outside of the family. Always to get my own way, when I knew asking permission would have been a waste of time. Yes, I probably continue to play the system to get the best of both worlds. To have the life and freedom others, English girls, in particular, take for granted. And yet they don't appear to have the unbroken family backing and support my situation allows me. It's also a privilege."

"To this day…my parents know nothing about my life at university. They never wanted me to go or see the point of studying, especially because I was a girl. I fought a long battle to convince them that it was a good thing. Without the ongoing help of my headmistress and Zia Giulia's support, I could never have gone. They don't see the need for higher education for their daughters or even for Lorenzo, come to think of it. They feared I would fall victim to harmful external influences. That I would lose my beliefs. That I might start smoking. Always saying that it wasn't me they didn't trust, but that of bad company, young men who would use all sorts of trickery to get me to sleep with them, even put 'something' in my drink…I never did find out what exactly…"

"But I always played my part, ringing them every week during term time. I went home regularly, whenever I said I would be returning. Hardly ever missing those big family events, Christmas, Easter, Holy Communions, Confirmations, and so on. I went to Italy with them every summer. I never got pregnant, so they could happily assume I wasn't having sex with anyone. In their heads, my virginity was still intact. Like this, no one could refer to me as a 'puttana', or 'zoccola', or 'troia' and the rest…so many names available, which all point to the same thing. A loose woman. Allowing the De Martinos to hold their heads high amongst other 'compaesani', keeping the name wholesome, the family beyond reproach. Perversely, in all this worldly wisdom of man's need to sin, they wouldn't even have considered that I might be using drugs. Their minds not having yet moved on to that…"

"Yes, it all smacks of hypocrisy on my part, double standards, I see that. But it comes out of respect. There you have it. That word again. There would have been no point trying to persuade my parents that the world was changing, that young people, and by now even back in Italy too, were finding alternative ways of thinking about or leading their lives. A total re-think of principles, once set in stone. For them, once abandoned, an unimaginable chaos would set in…"

This was still the preamble, James assumed. Was it merely the 'historian' in Tina that had provoked all of this…or was it really necessary for him to hear her out in order to accept what was coming next? Not just her life story, but also the history of her long-suffering ancestors? She had paused to sip some of the coffee she had brought with her, offering some to him as well, which he declined. He found it all very interesting, yes, but was little the wiser. It did seem to hinge on her parents. He had been right about that…

One new thought had struck him, however…just how huge the difference between the two of them was, in spite of them both having grown up in different parts of the same city. She was part of a seemingly unbroken line of deep-seated beliefs and traditions. He, on the other hand, had had nothing at all to cling onto or break free from as he was growing up. It appeared that his country had shaken off much of that kind of rigidity long beforehand. For his generation no longer had the urge to wave the national flag. He saw himself at the opposite end of a vast spectrum. A spare part in an indifferent society. After having to attend school, he had been relatively free to do whatever he pleased, take or leave any weakly given parental advice. With minimal community pressure. Mentally and even emotionally needing to rebel, but having little to rebel against, except for the distant, much earlier: tidy your room; get up or you will be late for school; don't forget to clean your teeth…and so on.

Chapter 34
The Whole Truth...

A white covered child's coffin furnished with white tassels, lined with white swansdown, side sheets and frilling...

Tina once again took up her lengthy account.

"Once in a while, out of all this hardship, a few strong-minded individuals rise up from the rest. It makes me think, like when I'm helping in the kitchen, of those two or three little gnocchi that are first to rise up in the boiling water. Why them? Position in a saucepan, greater airiness? Something about their shape?"

"A bit like with human beings. From an alien's perspective, we must all look more or less the same. Yet a few of us, acting perhaps upon a stroke of luck, begin to exploit a given situation. In the context of where my family is from, it often means having to operate outside of the law, which I know sounds totally unacceptable to English ears. I am merely outlining how things can happen. Not referring to anyone in particular. However, these men, for it always turns out to be men, begin to wield power over the other villagers who feel that someone is looking out for them, where the law or state has failed or is absent. They offer help and support...but ultimately, for the people, it soon results in yet another level of subjugation."

"There are those who might have difficulty paying back a loan, borrowed for a wedding, to buy a property or due to illness. Some might be looking for extra income even if it does mean operating on the black market. Others have problems with feuding neighbours, or with someone who won't see reason. A young man, who wants to marry and yet is unacceptable to the girl's family. The list goes on. Here is where an emerging 'uomo di rispetto', can begin to make a name for himself...begin to grow in wealth and stature, which for them is ultimately the same thing. He shows he can turn situations around and is therefore a welcome source of strength and support. A beacon of light in all the misery. No one wants to think, let alone talk, about how he manages to achieve these results. He is free…they leave him free…to build secret networks, using whatever is necessary…"

"Blackmail, threats, forgery, even violence if it comes to it. He is no Robin Hood. In spite of earlier ideals about overthrowing corrupt politicians, it is only a matter of time until he becomes just like them. In it for himself, always conscious that the risks are great. Those he helps find themselves forever in his clutches. Remember he is operating in a well-established climate of passivity, gratitude (genuine or not) and deference. Out of this therefore grows a culture of fear and silence…we call it 'omertà'…even amongst those who haven't yet requested his 'services'. The silence has always been there."

"Clearly everyone in the little town or 'paese' knows something about what's going on but if asked, no one has seen, heard or knows anything. Ever. All in a state of denial. Learned from childhood. A people removed and detached from the Police and the state, submerged below a layer of a silent, practically invisible power. As regards some of the teenage boys, there also runs in their veins a mawkish admiration for such individuals…Seen as men who have 'made it' in an impossibly unfair and hostile world."

"James, I realise you're being very patient and I thank you. Maybe you are wondering what all this has to do with me, with us. It must sound like light years away from how you live and think. The short answer would be, 'On the face of it, not much at all.'"

"This is the difficult bit for me now. I promised you a full explanation, and yet I am still aware…for the feeling never goes away…that the less you know about things the safer it is, the safer you are. That is why I'm painting pictures and not naming names."

Then as if thinking aloud, she added, unsure whether James had caught her words, "For me to speak up in this way is simply crazy. Why on earth didn't I just say that I didn't want to marry him…and be done with it?"

"That I'm now allowing myself to go against my family and the world they grew up in. You must be more mystified than ever. Trust me, that's all. It might be better for you to draw your own conclusions. There is so much I don't even know myself…everyone has always kept things locked away…and I fear I sometimes might merely be putting 'two and two together'. On the wrong path completely. As I was falling in love with you…the whole thing just took me over…"

"In the light of everything I've been saying, start to think, seriously, objectively, about certain people and events you are by now familiar with…that way you can make up your own mind."

"Let's start with Zia Giulia, and don't say anything…but yes, I do know…about the two of you. Once I had guessed…it was when I picked up on a shared glance between you…then everything just fell into place…but I promise, I really don't have a problem with it."

"She is, of course, still very beautiful. Intelligent and charming. She leaves a powerful mark on people…I've seen it play out before…and yet she is full of secrets. What do you really know about her? Her past? I imagine she has told you very little. Have you asked yourself how she came to be in England? As some kind of orphan apparently. How did she manage to acquire Casa Stella? She has never given us a proper explanation. Are we her blood family or not? We've always called her Zia Giulia…but is she really my mother's sister? They are close in age, but my mother seems so much older. They don't look alike either. Why then did she come and find us, invite us to go and live with her? Also, the private tuition, which is at best 'seasonal', is that really enough to finance her lifestyle, a lifestyle that allows her to come and go as she pleases…?"

"However, as you know, Zia Giulia is also kind and generous. She goes out of her way to help people…and on occasion, can even be unexpectedly light-hearted and funny. Then there is her friendship with Father John…her 'spiritual father' she refers to him as. Does he know more than the rest of us, because he's a priest? Don't forget that anything, ANYTHING, she might tell him in the confessional remains forever confidential. Now I feel guilty for unearthing all of this. Not only for putting it on you. I'm not accusing her of anything, but with Dominic's murder, I feel the danger."

"Naturally, my parents are also involved in whatever it is, but to what extent? I know my sisters have tried countless times to ask them about how they ended up in England. Why here? Who was it who helped them? To this day, their lips remain sealed. They even refuse to talk about their wedding, a marriage, which apparently took place after they had left Italy for good. I strongly suspect that Mamma was already pregnant with Patrizia, so that might have something to do with it. Sex outside of marriage considered sinful, shameful, where they come from."

"It's just so frustrating, especially for my sisters, who are really into, you know fashion magazines, hairstyles, wedding dresses, and so on. There don't seem to be any photos at all. To cut a long story short, all we know about our parents' early married life, is that times were very hard for them and that talking about it makes them edgy, uncomfortable. They clam up. All they've ever told us about their first years in England is contained in a handful of worn-out anecdotes, mainly to do with long hours at work and language-based misunderstandings."

"My brother Lorenzo is yet another mystery…for all sorts of reasons. As the only male child, though, 'un maschio', it's different for him…"

"I get what you must be thinking. That with all families, when you delve into them, can come across as a bit strange…full of skeletons in the wardrobe…oh no, you say cupboard…or is it closet? Oh, but that sounds American. I do that sometimes. Get sayings mixed up. One of my teachers called it language interference. I think it happens when I'm nervous. Look, I realise that I have spoken more about the gaps than anything specific, but when people don't want you to make certain discoveries, they make damned sure they never drop you any clues. Well, especially my family, who don't talk openly about anything."

"Perhaps once you have thought through, sifted through all of this, then we can talk again. Tell me how you see it. It's like then I haven't told you very much at all…that nothing new has come from me. Only stuff you have worked out for yourself."

James saw Tina floundering. For the very first time. No longer sitting in a composed manner on the bench, now more hunched, desperate hands flying, and sometimes even struggling to express herself. Where was the brave, confident and fun-loving girl, the only version she had hitherto let him know? Definitely absent that morning. He decided to speak out at last, quite harshly, in fact.

"I will tell you what I think now, Tina. That you are still not being truthful with me. Even if you don't know exactly what's going on, I'm certain there's much more stuff you've deliberately left out. I think you are afraid. You mentioned Dominic. That's what this is really all about, isn't it? A baby is murdered. An innocent baby boy! Not dead through illness. Not dead as the result of an accident. But murdered. It's an impossible notion. An unthinkable crime, with the police investigation, uncovering no possible motive or suspect. I was even the prime suspect for much of that time. Perhaps I am still. Your family continued to support me, however. Of course, I was grateful. I never once felt that they were pointing a finger at me. Strange in itself when you look at it objectively. Me the outsider. Me the so-called manic depressive."

"If the whole business didn't cause me to suffer yet another breakdown, it was purely down to the fact that I had nothing to do with it. You can't feel guilt when you know it wasn't you. Other people's suspicions are their problem, not mine. You tell me, just how that murder fits into what you've tried to cover up today? As I see it, there is only one possible explanation. Someone, somewhere, had or still has it in for the De Martinos in a big way. It's retribution. It's also symbolic; the killing of a baby means punishing and destroying a whole family. Even more so in a setup like yours, where silence and family ties are sacred…"

"So, this is the picture how I see it: a long time ago back in Italy, something really bad happened, with a couple of young people somehow involved. Maybe even unwittingly, who are are…encouraged…shall we say…to leave their little town, to start a new life abroad. This could have been because they knew too much about the event in question. Maybe the woman was also pregnant. It's like they were getting a second chance. The help they receive rests on a vow to stay silent. Then, who knows how this bit fits, but at some point, a ten-year-old girl finds herself caught up in the same story, and years later, by which time the couple has four children, she discovers a link between that family and herself, now all living in England."

"The family ends up moving in with her. She helps them even further. Thanks to some kind of generous loan agreement, they can now invest in a business, a delicatessen. They work hard and make a real success of it. Therefore, there comes a time when they are no longer financially dependent on her. However, for some reason, they continue to live at the house, when they could easily have bought a home of their own."

Then to lighten the mood, if only for a few seconds, he continued wistfully, "A bit like me really. I could or should have left Casa Stella long ago…"

From this point, a newly invigorated James begins to name names.

"Their son, Lorenzo, when still only about 20, marries a girl from Sicily. Serafina. Dominic is born within a year…and is suffocated before he has learnt to walk, with his little body placed in a newly created pond. Quite soon after that, your brother manages to buy a very expensive property a bit further out. In my opinion, far beyond the possibilities of an airline salary, and those extra hours he puts in at the delicatessen. I don't think your parents even pay him for that, do they? There's a prolonged period of mourning and intense police involvement…a kind of 'dark ages'. Only about a year later, do you, Patrizia, Sandra and your mother begin to discard those awful black clothes…and De

Martino life, on the surface at least, tries to return to some kind of normality. It's farcical. Like there's a massive cover-up going on. By remaining silent, you are all protecting the perpetrator!"

Chapter 35
DNA

Blade of sunray
Points to a new day –

Gifting us
A fresh attempt at life.
A greater stab at what
We think we learned
Under night's covers.

Scraping off yesterday's
Peelings, pondering
Tomorrow, with its sweet apple promises…
A wafer-thin, virgin layer
Of existence.

Fight the good fight,
Meet life head-on.
No regrets, just soldier on
Into the hazy realm
Of renewed opportunity.

Once again, James needed time to think. Without Tina present, or even anywhere close. All other thoughts submerged. He had finally landed in a different world…a world with a different mindset.

He had believed he knew her, the essential Tina. Had believed that he loved her. He probably still did. You can't just switch it off, can you? It's just that at that moment he couldn't feel a thing.

Theirs was not a love that had skated on erotic fantasy. More the stable old-fashioned kind. The kind of his parents and their generation. She was a nice-looking girl but exuding none of the icy sensuality, that had driven him wild about Giulia. Instead, this new relationship had had the makings of something solid, something that would last. Built on a warm recognition of shared views and a similar sense of humour. On normality. She had been open and easy. (After Giulia, a godsend).

The pair having started out as casual friends and, and only very slowly, had begun to spend more time together doing all sorts of things. Ordinary things. Going for walks in the park. An evening spent listening to a band in the pub. Loitering in the De Martino kitchen, as she introduced him to the less glamorous 'secrets' of Italian cooking, when to stir when to leave well alone. How to stop strands of 'fatta in casa' pasta from sticking together in the water. Things that you don't necessarily find in recipe books. Little snippets of culinary wisdom that she and her siblings had absorbed from childhood.

Theirs, an easy love that grew on both sides, with blissfully few complications. They still hadn't discussed parenthood…or even if they wanted children at all. There again, he had only just declared his love for her. He wondered whether Denis and his new lifestyle had held sway over him…some of their other friends had already married, one or two already fathers.

He felt torn. Realising now that Tina was sitting on a whole load of other stuff, like some kind of crazed hen, silently and yet manically protecting her poisoned eggs. It dawned on him that this is in truth how it had always been. She really did live according to those parallel lives, and had even referred to it, early on. Dropping it into other slices of conversation. He had missed it completely. Heard, even remembered, but never processed. Tina when at home with the family (and now with him), Immy when out in the free world! Tina, Immy, Immacolata in her own words…or worlds.

However, by living at Star House, he too was straddling both realities. Less than a week ago, he thought he had never felt happier, freer, more at peace than ever before.

Now no longer certain that this was what he wanted after all. He felt nauseous and wanted to kick himself for not cottoning on more quickly to the fact there was something 'not quite right' with the De Martinos. Tina was also part of that, no matter how many excuses he had found to ignore it. For the first time, he was forcing the total honesty card, having to admit that in effect he had been aware of it from the start, something strange lurking in the brickwork, like a resident ghost, even before Dominic's murder…but had chosen to disregard it. It was down to the fact that they had all unwittingly helped mend him, James, the lonely and melancholy Englishman, the once broken toy…and more importantly in the process, had never shown him pity or even much in the way of curiosity. Never tried to interfere or to appear to care one jot about his past or current mental state. In other words, giving him exactly what he needed. Acceptance and space, which in turn allowed him to accept himself.

Tina had fired the word danger. To James, it still sounded farfetched, too 007, so at that moment he had just let it go. Something he would have returned to at a future date perhaps…

He realised that Giulia had never drawn him into past or present De Martino 'goings-on'. Quite the opposite. So where did she sit in all this? Tina had named her first in her non-confession…had suggested that he try to learn more about her.

There never was going to be a shared future for him and Giulia. Their 'love' occupied present time only. His head now filling up with a long, slow-moving set of images of her, which ranged from Shakespeare's Dark Lady to Farquhar's Lady Bountiful…and every significant literary female in between. He had to acknowledge that there was still something of her skulking beneath his skin. Counterbalanced by the once honest face of her niece, Tina. He had willingly gone along with it all. Allowing himself to be sucked into the outer rings of their universe. He was a grown man and yet it had felt good in the way we remember, selectively, those happy days from childhood. Like sweet-tasting medicine, whose side effects (always written in very small print) we choose not to read.

He forced himself to reflect further and came up with a new more detached or 'scientific' picture.

To someone like James, a foreign tight-knit bilingual family such as the De Martinos, was always going to be captivating. An unusually large, multi-generational entity, whose members continued to present a solid and united front against the world. These were also 'real' people, who didn't need to play to any camera, people who liked to stay out of the limelight. Apart from Tina, not even particularly warm or friendly. In fact, for the most part, they kept themselves to themselves, at least until someone new showed that they wanted to join them. After which it was easy to become absorbed in their reality, to get swallowed up. Into what he now considered a black hole. He thought of those who had joined later on, of Serafina, and then the two brothers rescued from the devastation of the Irpinian earthquake, and then onto Father John. Also of the trusted Mrs Mogden, much more by now than just a charlady, having become a Catholic like them. Paradoxically, as individuals, it seemed that the De Martinos made no effort to be 'better than the rest'. No signs of competition. They were who they were. Simple people who attached great importance to sharing regular made-from-scratch meals around the table. A carrying on of the Last Supper.

Except perhaps for Giulia…always the exception, which proves the rule.

James had seen them in all their manifestations. Including some of their less admirable 'unwashed' moments (as he liked to think to them.) The early morning grumpiness. The banal chitchat and petty squabbles. Had noted that they rarely said please and thank you, which grated against the norms and sensibility of his own culture. How they just as rarely used the word sorry. He witnessed how they were able to send someone to hell one minute and then fling their arms around them the next. Dismissive of and indifferent to the fact they had a semi-permanent stranger houseguest, who might hold opinions as to what he was seeing and hearing. So what exactly was their appeal?

James went on to answer this question, born out of his own existential experiences. The adherence to structure; with feast days set against the ordinary ones. The hard work and diligence shown, regarding all domestic and work issues. The example set by the older members, who lived out the roles they had inherited. Never would there be room for any form of separation or divorce. It was for the unbroken unity, loyalty and shared support. Their authenticity. Things going on in the outside world having little claim on their own vision of how best to live. Something he had never before experienced, so hadn't thought existed outside of stage plays or the movies.

It could be mesmerising to behold. He knew that his own had not been a bad or unkind family. They too had led organised lives. Perhaps, more in the sense of neat and tidy. However, for James, it was now emerging that there had been no beating heart at its centre. Instead, a group of loosely connected people, linked only by a common surname, whom fate had randomly brought together.

His mother, with her faraway looks, which veiled past secrets and future longings, her head stuck somewhere in the stubborn clouds of an aristocratic past. The memory of the red lipstick, her armour to face each day, her head crowned by the hair that never moved. The housecoat and cotton gloves, shields against a dirty and disappointing world.

His father who had lived according to the quiet conventions of the day. Providing for the family, taking pride in quaint little rituals, such as tackling the daily crossword puzzle, cleaning his own shoes (the inflated importance of 'a bit of spit and polish') delivering up impromptu tap-dance routines, which always produced the same silly steps. Partaking in hobbies, such as gardening and singing in the church choir. Driving his beloved car out of the garage and then washing it every Saturday morning. Most of which, if James cared to think about it, took his father safely outside the confines of the house. There but not with. On the outside.

He and his sister Harriet unknowingly drifting apart as they got older. Until seemingly gone forever, their whispery conversations and shared bouts of boisterous tomfoolery.

James suddenly remembering the time he had found his father kissing (slobbering over, as he had then referred to it) that woman in the church vestry. Even the rock solid Raymond Newhouse had once felt the need for some illicit activity. To break free.

His a family therefore based on spare parts, which explained why he admired the fact that, with all their individual faults and shortcomings, the De Martinos collaborated as pure family force. Not dreamers as such, just carrying out acts based on old beliefs and well-tested ways of doing things. All travelling in the same direction. A bit like the Catholic Church itself, he decided. Always there, a colossal entity, rarely changing course, and if changing, happening at such a slow pace, you hardly noticed. Like Tina, if you were discreet and didn't bring problems home, you could get away with all sorts…

In Tina's family setup, there was no need for old people's homes. Something they considered abominable. Instead, together they took care of all the stages of human existence. The numbers were there, the willingness and past experience was there. Family love, hard work, gratitude and respect. The permanent sense of duty. Providing their own services. Together. Separated only by death. With the dead mentioned and prayed for during Sunday Mass. Publically named and never forgotten.

These rediscoveries, all of which making James feel sleepy, as he tried to deal with each interconnecting thought. Battering his brain; he no longer capable of deciding what to focus on. Then little Dominic sprang to mind. D for Dominic and for Death again, and then moving on to Denis and then DNA…

Vaguely remembering how in life, amazing things happen, things with both good and evil consequences. Due to the merging of beliefs, intelligence, tenacity, collaboration. Man's crucial need to go always further, higher. The importance of timing and of good fortune. He was tired but somehow managed to conjure up once again the thrill of the 1969 Moon landing, an event he still couldn't fully process, but which had somehow become glued to his psyche.

The discovery of DNA, again something he barely grasped but felt the power and weight of its implications.

James convinced that science wasn't the only way to understand the universe and man's place in it. One first had to aspire and to imagine…to go beyond. The science came later.

As his eyes grew heavy, his own daytime DNA doodles flashed into view. Never aware he was producing them, they would emerge during bouts of deep thought or being on the telephone. That poetic double helix. Sketched repeatedly on the cover of his notebook. Who cares that he didn't understand the science, which tried to frighten him with words from an alien language: Adenine, Thymine, Cytosine, Guanine. He was absorbing the beauty of its corkscrew swirls and curves. Its flow and continuity. Its microscopic reality. The vast amount of potent 'stuff' each trace of DNA contained. Connecting us back to our ancestors. It had been there all along, of course. Returning us to that unbroken line. No longer life's random orphans…

After which James slept solidly for the following ten hours.

Chapter 36
"Mirror, Mirror…"

It was already getting a little dark and Tina sat down at her dressing table, her face soon lost in the depths of its quaint oval mirror. A final rehearsal. It was as though the Mona Lisa herself was staring back. Then her mouth opened, the rest of her face remaining immobile.

"I should have known of course but strange forces are at work when you are falling in love. Huge parts of the brain appear to fold away. So many of its usual functions kept on hold. We only properly realise this later of course. Except when seeing it in others. I remember what it felt like with Nicholas. There again, nothing was going to come of that, so I never needed to talk about my family. It's different for my sisters…who sadly have little in the way of a curious nature. Not much imagination. They are there but don't see. Now when it comes to Lorenzo…As for me, there are many missing pieces. Sometimes I'm not even sure of the little I think I do know…"

"I am ashamed to say that if I do know more than I should, it's not because anyone in the family has ever tried to make me part of whatever that 'thing' is…well it's because, because…"

Tina could barely bring herself to confess, out loud, her own unpalatable truth across at the ever-darkening image in the mirror, which looked back at her in silent judgement, whenever she stopped talking. Such behaviour went against the grain. Against Tina's interpretation of the meaning of the word honourable. An attack on a person's privacy, altogether unsavoury. Louche.

"It was when I found out where Zia Giulia kept her diaries, and all those albums and scrapbooks. You can imagine the sort of thing. Going back years. The guilt I felt and still feel to an extent, at going behind her back. Not just once, but over and over. The drooling buzz of finding out about someone's early and then later life. In all its phases and stages. So much material to plough through, all beautifully presented, albeit the handwriting sometimes a bit spidery and on the small side, and the information not always accessible, as it seemed that she was writing in code. Codes that changed. Names of people and places abbreviated. Some impossible to research. So many things that she had never mentioned to us. Not lies as such, if I remember rightly, just lots of omissions. Everything was clearly set out and well organised. Page numbers, asterisks, dates, headings…and so many other little details. Interspersed with quirky doodles and arrowed diagrams, some with captions."

"Then that sudden changeover from Italian to English. Everything kept for her to reread. For her eyes only. I continued to return to it all, even making the odd note about something I thought I might not be able to remember or needed to check. Obviously, I didn't want her to find out what I was up to or equally important, miss out on what I hadn't yet seen or made sense of. I just couldn't stop. Like when someone is addicted to gambling…or maybe not…It was like getting to understand three people in one. Giulia, in the role of wise and responsible aunt. Giulia, the protagonist of a picaresque novel. Giulia, the human being."

"I never did mention it to Father John in the confessional. That her business had become my business. In any case, I convinced myself that it didn't seem to fit anywhere among the usual list of wrongdoings. No, that's silly, of course it did. It was that I was brazenly determined to keep at it. I discovered that when you get away with something the first couple of times, you have to make an even greater effort to cover your tracks in the future. How easy it is to become careless. On one occasion, I had to make a very quick exit… I can still remember my heart pumping, as it tried to break free from my body. It became both game and serious detective work. Exciting, exhilarating."

"There were times when I found what I read so mesmerising that I wonder whether I would even have noticed if she had entered the room. Fortunately, she was often 'away'. I don't know how she would have reacted if she had found out what I was up to…but such are the risks and dangers of recording the written word. When we commit private thoughts to paper. She must have known this too."

"Much later on, however, I discovered that I was going to be beneficiary of the diaries in any case. After all the sly digging and delving. Giulia told me that I was the only member of the family that she could entrust them to…I was the only one, she said, jokily, who could 'appreciate their historic, artistic and literary value' and so on. Unfortunately, this did not come with an invitation to have prior access. For that, I would still have to wait. At least I felt that a ton of guilt had already slipped from my shoulders. I persuaded myself, as we all might in such circumstances, that I had merely pre-empted the situation and speeded up the process. Been a little impatient. Giulia might live to be a hundred. It's not as if I was planning to reveal its contents to anyone or do anything with it. Well, only to you James perhaps…for her sake I have to be selective in what I reveal."

"From the moment I found out that it would all one day belong to me, the diaries suddenly disappeared from their usual 'home' and from then I've never set eyes on any of it. Neither has Zia Giulia since referred to it. I sometimes wonder if she had simply known all along about what I had been up to…"

"So this is what I discovered, the bare bones, pulled out over time of the pile of notes, anecdotes, poems and artwork, all her mental meanderings. The life of Giulia Cristaldi and what went on in her heart and head."

"The diary began when she was only seven years of age and therefore back in Italy. It starting out as a record of her daily existence. With little reference to the child Giulia's dreams or emotions. Each day mapped out, appearing much the same as the one before. Such are the lives of seven-year-olds, I suppose. Her lessons, sometimes what she ate and drank and names of the people she prayed for. The titles of books she was reading. Even then, each entry presented with great care and a childlike fervour to get things right. Not many crossings out either. Barely missing a day. As you probably know, she lived in an orphanage, run by nuns who also took care of all aspects of her well-being and education. That much of course she had already told us in the family."

"Each day beginning and ending with prayers and Mass attendance in the church or little chapel. I don't know why, but I somehow assumed there would follow instances of rule-breaking, severe punishments, or examples of rebellion. Incidents or problems with the 'horrible' (my word, not hers) nuns themselves."

"However, this wasn't the case. Giulia, the little girl, never came across as unduly sad nor resentful of the strict and monotonous regime, under which she and the others had to live. Nothing to compare it with, I suppose. Or angry for being an orphan in the first place. The first couple of diary-type notebooks therefore revealing little else. A couple of things in particular did strike me though…that she, unlike the others, was able to keep her hair very long, although she never explained why this was. Neither did she ever write much about her peers as friends. Perhaps close friendships were discouraged in such a place.

Also, and somewhat to my surprise, she began to write fondly of a couple of the teacher nuns."

"I gathered that she had always lived there…this being the only home and life she knew. A strange family setup."

"Apart from the odd lapse, she continued to make every effort with her writing, to make the lettering clear and the words correctly spelt. Making it so much easier for me to comprehend. In my mind's eye, I could see her seated at a little desk upon which she would regularly dip the scratchy nib of a fountain pen into a nearby inkwell. Regularly pushing back her long plaits if they dared come near her face. Dressed in a long white nightgown, with a weighty dictionary to hand. I tried hard to connect the seven or eight-year-old Giulia to the aunt I had grown up with and who was now approaching middle age…"

"Then a fair bit later came one entry, which broke with the previous pattern. It allowed me at last to see inside her heart and read something like…P came to see me today. The best day of my life. I wondered if she had mentioned a P before but I didn't think she had. It had been a surprise visit apparently. This entry turned out to have more to do with how she was feeling…some of the words written in capital letters…than how they had actually spent the day but I think they went out for a picnic, yes that's it. He took her somewhere not too far away by car. Just who was this P person, and how did he get permission to take her out of the convent? He must therefore have been some kind of relative. Perhaps a trusted uncle. Why in that case did she live in an orphanage? I also wondered of course what the P stood for…"

"She wrote down what he had given her that day, a book of fairy tales and an illustrated account of the life of Saint Cecilia. She promising P that she would treasure them forever, hardly wanting to open them, for fear of spoiling them in some way. Of course, I had already formed the impression that she was an unusual girl. Very serious and mature for her age. Confirmed a good few entries later, when she wrote about the day that a new teacher had happened to read a short French poem to them. She often referred back to it in her diaries, describing the profound effect that those magical sounds had had on her, describing the tingle she would get in the pit of her stomach before each French lesson. She made it sound more like the words of a woman about to encounter her lover, not that she could have known anything about that. She wrote that she loved the Italian language too. Only that in a different way, because it was already her own. Familiar."

"Over the remaining years in Italy, the entries showed that P continued to turn up, usually bearing gifts and taking her on outings. Any letters she wrote him, she would have to give, unsealed, to the Mother Superior, who would then pass them on. She also wrote about bits of remembered dreams, which she turned into little stories. About talking animals, or heroic rescues. Long journeys. Living on the Moon. Filling in the forgotten facts. Interspersed, on a more mundane level, with the names of who her partner had been during a PE lesson, or who was celebrating their saint's day, or which one of the girls had been unwell. Still no animosity towards any of her fellow pupils, but then again, no examples of closeness or complicity either. Yes, that was it. For Giulia, what appeared to matter to her were the adults: her teachers, especially the two younger nuns, the writers of books…and that man she called P."

"Naturally, it also surprised me that she rarely complained. Unusual in a child, who believed she was free to write anything she liked in private. Appearing to accept everything that was asked of her, undertaking all those irksome duties and rituals with little fuss or resentment."

Chapter 37
Comparisons

"It's odd and yet I've come to spot huge similarities between my aunt and James of all people. Yes, I know it sounds ridiculous. Completely different backgrounds and characters and of course gender. Quite an age difference as well. Then there is the subject of religious belief. Non-existent in his case, by his own admission. However, the more I think about it, the more I see the same person, the two of them merging."

"How they stand apart from everyone else. It's true, a lot to do with being free agents and having lots of money. Giulia works to keep busy, to make her life appear meaningful. Quite different from the kind of person you usually come across. They both know and feel they are different too. Each on a very personal quest. A kind of odyssey. To use something of their language. James is still searching. For him, it must have started out quite early on, when he became aware of just how scary life could be…how our lives dangle from a thread…and then realising that this wasn't the case for his peers, who by comparison appeared to thrive on the notion of risk and danger. He held different opinions from his classmates and members of his family. On a whole range of things. Not brave enough yet to speak out. Not really knowing or understanding what was going on inside his head. Not ready to accept that he was born that way…"

"Then there was the shared matter of a missing family member. James's older brother. He's told me all about it. A bit like Giulia finding an older sister years later. But I'm not supposed to talk about that. It really got to him in the end. Only later, to discover that it would be, not people, but things…things like music and books to provide a safe way out of his solitude and his misplaced sense of guilt. On top of all of that, feeling awkward and embarrassed about being James Newhouse."

"Whereas in Giulia's case, her whole life has been outside the normal run of things, so that is probably what has shaped her thoughts and behaviour. No traces of a mother. No family life as such. Always more in control of her feelings than James, I think. Her life built on a rigid structure. Then there was that gift-laden man she referred to as P in her early diaries. As he came and went in and out of her life. Piercing the cold monotony of sturdy walls and marble staircases, bringing colour, little bursts of joy into her life. A mere girl, brought up by a tough army of nuns, first in Italy and then in England, who somehow between them transformed her into this perfectly turned-out young woman. Erudite, well-mannered, charming. Someone who paid attention to posture, especially when seated. Knowing the importance of clean fingernails and tidy hair. Paradoxically all the requirements for an eighteenth-century courtesan, a geisha even. Yet soaked, like a 'baba au rhum', in rigid Catholicism. Helped along the way by Mother Nature…"

"However, it was much more than her looks. More to do with that cool exterior, which belies what might be going on inside. I wouldn't be surprised if she hasn't had a whole string of lovers…she is just so secretive. (I only got so far with the diaries). Giving little away. Nothing seems to come from it though. Like a trail of delightful love bubbles that are bound to burst, when over-stretched. God, I'm even beginning to sound like the two of them…"

"Just like James, Giulia was someone in search of beauty and poetry amongst the disappointments and mediocrity of everyday life, in her reading, her teaching, her travels, in her regular attendance at Mass. Emerging from an unusual childhood. In those early diaries, she wrote about P taking her to an ancient castle, somewhere high up a mountain. How she loved it there, sharing tiny bits of his life with him, feeling like a princess. She must have gone there a fair few times too, as she had much to record."

"How she loved reading her books in the room or 'chamber' set aside for her, and then in the morning as she would look down at the turquoise sea from high up. How she had chosen a favourite doll to leave behind on the canopied bed, as if wanting part of herself to remain. How she enjoyed going to visit the nearby village, where the people spoke a strange dialect, which she was trying to learn. Stating just how kind everyone was to her, especially when the villagers made her try local culinary delicacies, some created in her honour. Mentioning a young mother called Ninetta."

"Her heartache when she discovered that she had to go and live in England."

"I realise that I'm digressing. It must be her magic still working. With me, talking about and around Giulia rather than getting to the point...After sifting through her personal diaries I came to discover something of what's behind the family secrets."

"Well, even from the first time she mentioned him, what did become clear, was that P must have been her father...Padre, Papà in Italian. A man involved in very important work, that took him abroad a lot. That would explain why she couldn't live with him. A wealthy entrepreneur perhaps, a powerful politician or even an undercover agent? It had to be something of the sort, of that magnitude. Unfortunately, there were only ever vague clues and hints in her writing, nothing I could pinpoint. I got the impression that he hadn't explained much about his life to her either."

"She wrote that he always refused to speak about her mother (indicating at the very least that he knew her) something that upset and frustrated Giulia. He even once, in an effort to silence her on the subject, said that her name was Maria, but his daughter remained unconvinced, it being such an easy name to come up with and so had once again let the matter drop. Guessing (or wanting) that she had inherited her dark hair from him and green eyes from her. P's eyes were very dark, she had noted in the diary. A woman who might be called Maria, possibly with green eyes and probably no longer alive. All very sad. Not a huge amount to go on...if ever she did decide to track her down."

"It appears P wasn't able to see Giulia very often during the years she was in England, as a boarder at Fielding. She missed him terribly and referred to a particular photo she kept of him on her bedside table, which she would simply stare across at. He sent her beautiful gifts, which she treasured. Leather-bound books, expensive and elegant pens, an unusual signet ring, a grown-up watch and so on. One of the nuns would always let her know whenever he had contacted the school to make enquiries or to see how she was."

"With the passing years, and Giulia now a young woman, their meetings also became more and more clandestine. More complicated. Giulia often finding herself having to take multiple trains to secret locations, or sometimes such meetings even had to take place abroad. When she wrote about them, she never mentioned the names of places...or dates. Just referring to the encounters as if they had taken place at some point in the recent past. All these omissions were surely to protect him and his whereabouts, should the diaries fall into the wrong hands. She also referred to someone called G, who would regularly pick her up from an airport or train station…"

"Continuing to see P remained crucial to her (and no doubt to him also) sometimes causing her to feel sad and hopeless, but with each encounter leaving her with something beautiful as well: a promise, a poignant phrase from P's lips that she would faithfully reproduce in her diary, a precious anecdote, the mention of a next meeting. There was clearly a very strong…no, more than that…an unbreakable bond between them. Her writings allowing me to see a much more vulnerable Giulia, a side to her that is rarely on show at Casa Stella. Perhaps she wasn't forever flying off into the arms of her latest lover, after all. Perhaps it was P. The diaries never made it clear. Was he really her father? Was their relationship even more complicated?"

"Oh yes, of course. So hard to talk about everything in chronological order, when emotions begin to take over. I've got ahead of myself. One day, and to her great surprise, P told her that he had bought her a house. She was only about 20 then I think and when not abroad, the nuns let her stay on at the convent. She could hardly believe it. The thought of owning a property filled her with dread. Something she had never considered. Such a huge responsibility. However, it turned out to be a case of love at first sight, that encounter with an Edwardian building, as it loomed above her, her head quickly filling up with all sorts of ideas, as to what she wanted to do with it, how she wanted it to look. Yes, ever obedient, she would accept his latest gift. Yes, so that was, of course, Casa Stella."

"Come to think of it, where would any of us be now without it? In a curious way, it is what has brought us together, all of us. Even Father John, Mrs Mogden and more recently, James of course. We have all benefitted in some way. Either directly or by the people who live in it. In the early days merely serving to give Giulia a base… Years later providing her with a beautiful home, after that, a new start for my parents. Even after Dominic's tragic death she just couldn't bring herself to sell up…it's like yet another person in her life! In all our lives. Another member of the family to care for and cherish. A place of refuge."

"I know…I'm making little headway with this. It's Lorenzo I really need to talk about…but it's just so difficult."

"We didn't get on much as children; typical brother and sister, I suppose. I'm not saying that we fought or argued a lot. It was more a case of him hardly realising that I was there at all. Younger and there again…a mere girl. What could his life possibly have in common with mine? He, for the most part, was simply unaware of me, but I knew all about him! That he was vain…more the fault of other people…as they repeatedly told him from an early age how beautiful he was (ciccio bello!) as they playfully pinched his cheeks with two fingers and stroked his long loose curls…and this went on for years! Then there was the fact he was the only 'maschio'. Family members, especially his two older sisters, and visitors to the house simply drooled whenever they saw him. Then soon after we moved to Casa Stella I noticed just how much Giulia had also taken a shine to him. She probably thought no one had noticed, but I was able to absorb everything without even trying. A talent (or shortcoming) of mine, I suppose."

"She spent both time and money on him. Private tuition, piano lessons, trips to museums and so on. Nothing ever came of it though. All he wanted to do back then was play football and chase girls…or rather allow them to chase him. Aunt Giulia was…it seems ridiculous now…the very last person to realise this, even though the evidence was there in black and white. Eventually, she had to let him be, but not before a hundred or so last chances. It was then that she noticed me."

Chapter 38
Lorenzo De Martino

"It is true though that by the time I reached 16 or 17 things began to change and for the better. Lorenzo gradually becoming aware that he did have a younger sister after all. Sometimes deigning to take me out, you know to the cinema, shopping or a sixth-form disco. Always coming with heaps of advice and warnings as to how to behave in public. Whom not to trust (basically, no one). What not to do? Presenting the outside world as a scary place, full of people who wanted something from me. Thankfully, I didn't pay too much attention…well, you don't at that age. Occasionally, he would buy me something that I just happened to say I liked in a shop window. A bit later I left for university."

"We stayed in touch via the telephone, but I could tell he was never really interested in my degree course or in my new friends and like our parents, just didn't understand my wanting to go in the first place. In some small way, however, I think he was proud that I had put up such a hard fight to get there. More struck by my determination (so rare in a girl) than by recognising the pull of academia. He wasn't the type to grow close to anyone in any case…and well, our two older sisters simply lived in a world of their own…"

"This new closeness gave me the chance to get to know him a bit better, that is, learn a bit more about how his mind worked. Before that, he was simply my elder brother. Sometimes he would refer to a past incident, something that had passed me by. Mention a person who had angered him. The name of yet another girl he had grown bored with. A teacher who had spoken down to him. Never again. Oh, he would make sure it would never happen again. He would be ready for them all, in one way or another. It seemed important to him that I knew this, but I don't believe he ever saw me as a threat."

"As for the girls, I can hear him now, saying that girls were 'easily dealt with'. I used to hear him speak to them on the telephone, when they rang him in the evenings, his voice hard and cold. Speaking in clipped monosyllables. While I imagined how they must have felt as they pleaded or sobbed on the other end of the line. It never stopped them from calling though. I was ashamed that girls behaved in that way. Just so demeaning. Couldn't they see what he was like? You can't change people. Everyone knows that, surely. Accept his ways, or leave. Put up or shut up! His behaviour disgusted me, though. Even so, he was my brother…"

At which point she shuffled the chair forward, and placed her head in cupped hands, her elbows now pressed against the glass surface of the dressing table. And even when she raised it again, turned her face to one side, totally avoiding her image in the mirror now.

"To be honest, I didn't always understand what he was going on about but he wasn't given to clear explanations, or detail, or context. He also spoke very fast. Expecting me, I suppose, simply to follow and agree with him on a range of issues. Like our parents, talking of 'him' or 'her', 'this one' or 'that one', without bothering to name them. Presuming you knew what they were talking about. Like I could read his mind. Moving on from one subject to another, took me time to catch up. He seemed to know and use more Italian dialect than I did and would scatter these phrases amongst the English."

"He liked to talk big. He liked to show me how he always came out on top. Proud whenever his little bets or schemes came to fruition, ultimately to show that not even the 'powers that be', for want of a better expression, could ever get the better of him. All this set against an unwavering love for the family, but especially towards our parents. Forever showing this through hard work and total loyalty. Always there when needed. My big brother Lorenzo."

"As I said, we never talked about things in the family. Like when, admittedly a bit later, I happened to find out, that he did once go and thank my aunt for all the effort she had put in to prepare him for higher education. How he had always appreciated her trying to 'refine' him, to polish her 'diamante grezzo', but of course, it was never going to work…well, not in the way she had intended. However, he also told her he had in fact learnt a lot from spending hours at her side. Had learnt about patience, recognised her continued affection for him, and her resolve not to give up until the situation proved impossible. How she never spoke without purpose. Her self-respect, as well as that shown towards others. Her professionalism, given that she was also his aunt. None of this had been lost on him. He would take it forward and wanted her to know it."

"The trip to Sicily had clearly surprised, even alarmed, Giulia, however. Given all she had come to learn about the De Martinos, she still could not understand why Lorenzo had been so keen to take up the offer to go find himself a bride. He was still so young and as a 'maschio' (male child), didn't yet have any of the parental pressure to take a wife. As regards other women, she also imagined, that he would continue in his old ways because that's the way it was with men like him. Something they couldn't do without and in which they didn't see the harm, provided they continued to provide for their family and were fairly discreet of course. Starting long before their wives' looks were on the wane, their focus the home and children…because it had never stopped…"

"It would mean Lorenzo having to tread carefully, tell a few lies…but nothing her brother wasn't already capable of. To a certain extent, he had been living that life already. Satisfying his needs. Secret and personal. Absolutely no one else's business. So why give it up? In his favour, he would never abandon a future wife. She would be the mother of his children. The centre of family life, of hearth and home. The maker of meals. It hurt me to think about it but I somehow felt my father too fell into this category. If the opportunity came along. More passive than Lorenzo, and without his son's looks and hard charm…and yet…if something came his way. Oh, but this is all speculation…"

She shifted the stool once again to get a more comfortable position, noticing the pink patches on her face, where her hands had pressed into her cheeks. Looking up once again with her chin resting on her knuckles. She also tucked away some hair, which had come free from its clip.

"I don't know why I keep getting carried away like this. Well, as you know, Lorenzo found his bride. A beautiful girl from a remote Sicilian village. None of the 'trampy tarts' or 'damaged goods' as he referred to them here in England. Of course, that never stopped him from taking what was on offer. Girls flinging themselves at him. He needed someone who would take marriage seriously. A girl who supported the old, ingrained traditions. Someone who would trust in her husband's decisions for the well-being of the family. She would have to be young. He wanted to be a young father and saw no point in waiting."

"Not the lifestyle for me though. I have become too English. Things have moved on and when that happens, there can be no going back. Of course, I don't talk about this here at home…just no point. I merely do my best to show willing. That way everyone is happy. I don't know how I feel deep down though, living these parallel lives…I try not to think about it!"

"Anyway, as regards my brother, some of the entries speak of something else…and I never did find out what Giulia did about it or whether she found out more. By that time, she had removed all the diaries, possibly out of the house itself. It had something to do with P, but it also involved Lorenzo. She found it difficult to take in. A strong feeling that the two had somehow met up. When Lorenzo was supposed not to know anything about having a 'grandfather'. A slip of the tongue perhaps, or something Giulia had overheard or even misunderstood. Something that both alarmed and intrigued her. Why had P not confided in her about this? Writing that if this were the case, P would have made Lorenzo promise not to say anything. She knew his ways but wrote that she would have to follow it up. That it could change everything."

"I'm trying hard to remember her exact words. Let me start with what I do have clear in my mind. It first had to do with Giulia herself. A kind of would-be proposition, that P had felt obliged to make but at the same time, hoping against hope that she would decline it. Something about his 'empire'. Yes, his empire, that's the word he used. Sounds bizarre, doesn't it? He apologised for not having sorted things years beforehand, but that it had taken a long time to face the fact that he would not always be around, or at the very least, might one day become too ill or frail to continue. Giulia got the impression that he already had someone else in mind."

"That word…empire…what did he mean exactly? A business-type empire, no doubt, but then what was the nature of his business? Why was it shrouded in secrecy? Did Giulia go on to discover more? I never did find out. It's really quite frustrating…"

"So awful what happened to little Dominic…unthinkable, inexplicable. How have Lorenzo and Serafina coped with it all? The never-ending sense of loss and the drawn-out investigation, the niggling suspicion that they had to know more than they were revealing…and the long wait for an answer, for justice. But there can be no justice until the murderer is found. And even then, nothing, nothing can bring back our sweet little boy…"

Tina then turned her attention back to the stand-in mirror and an absent James.

"Oh, James, I wish you were here with me now, now that I'm finding a way to speak out. Even though it's in fits and starts. You naturally don't want to take all this on, as well as me. We will just have to admit defeat…It is here that you would pin me down though, and rightly so. Everything goes back to or stems from the murder. Even though we don't know who did it, it still begs the question why! What is my theory? That something happened, probably years and years ago. Someone somewhere has had it in for my family for a very long time, lying in wait for that optimum moment, when they could strike. Not ridding the world of their adversary, but delivering a life sentence of pain and heartache instead. The murder of an innocent, hugely symbolic…oh yes, so very…effective. Targeting a whole family, spanning different generations…the unbearable torture of a slow and seeping living death."

Chapter 39
A Brief Heart to Heart... With Himself

James began, "I've never breathed a word of this, not to Father John or even Dorothy, and it's obvious she hasn't either. How could she? By not saying anything, it is easier to behave as though nothing happened. A bit like a distant fuzzy dream. You become more and more detached from it. It was only once in any case. In my world, it would have been of very little significance...but in theirs? The fiends of hell would break loose."

"Hang on though...perhaps there is something else. Not even silence and a convenient amnesia can mask consequences, no matter how improbable. It wasn't until several months afterwards, that it struck me, in one fleeting moment, that...in theory at least...her unborn baby could have been mine. Ours. Why had I not considered the possibility, as soon as the news of her pregnancy had become public? Of course, being a man, I never sat down to work out dates and things...and then how could I possibly know? Ridiculous, a mere poisonous little thought that shoves you, momentarily, off guard. She had a new husband. Lorenzo, if I can apply that animal term, a true alpha male. As I said it was just the once. I'm pretty sure it wouldn't even have crossed her mind either. Well, that sounds a bit convenient, doesn't it? For me, I suppose. There again, what do I really know about the workings of the female mind...or body come to that?"

"It definitely wasn't planned. Nothing had led up to it. On either side. You know, just one of those times when fate takes over. The result of a series of trivial events, like speeded-up layers of sediment and then wow. The birth of a colossus. Yet it should have been yet another normal day. Just like all the others. Except...what was it that triggered it all? If I remember rightly, yes, that's it, I happened to mention to Carmela that I had to go and pick up my car from the garage down the road and she asked me to drop off a dish of her 'parmigiana' at Lorenzo's house on the way. I didn't even know what that was at the time. It so happened, so I was about to find out, that he was working at Terminal 2, there until about 11 pm."

"A repaired car, a delivery of homemade food, a convenient late shift and the carrying out of a simple favour. Forces all coming and pulling together."

"Well, as soon as Serafina happened to open the door, I could tell straight away that something was wrong, that she had been crying. Nevertheless, she welcomed me inside, a 'very Italian' trait I was fast becoming familiar with. Never leave a friend or relative on the doorstep. No matter how awful you look or might be feeling. No matter the state of your house. Instead, you are obliged to invite them in for a quick coffee. At the very least…"

"I remember that she was somehow even lovelier that day, in spite of the crumpled face and apron, the dishevelled hair and tear-smeared cheeks. Perhaps because of it, the tenderness of vulnerability. Always unaware of the effect her lovely face had on people. Transcending my own ingrained Englishness, I found myself scooping her up in my arms and not letting her go. Something she allowed and soon even welcomed. You just know. No struggle, phoney or otherwise."

"The scene reminded me of how I might have behaved years beforehand when Jenny had entered my room late at night in despair over Denis. Instead, I chose to let her be on the floorboards with my coat draped around her. I still remember feeling awkward and useless. Was it to do with my own friendship with Denis, or fear of rejection on her part, or even that ridiculous show of respectable phlegmatism we English do so well? Suppressed emotions and all that. The subjugation of the self. It just wouldn't have felt right, whatever the reason. Did this new turn of events now make me a man of action or simply a man no better than the rest, taking advantage of a given situation? It wasn't like that though. I would have known. Would have felt it. I can't say I felt guilt at the time and in a way still don't. Well, of course, for many people, there would have been the matter of going with someone else's wife, but that was never a big deal for me. Seeing the person, more than their situation or their role in society. Perhaps I should have…"

"Well, we stayed together for about two, maybe three hours. My car remaining yet another night at the repair shop. We never did afterwards refer to that shared time, as I said before, more dream than reality. It simply left a warm memory in its wake."

"I can't even begin to fathom that, biologically speaking, Dominic could have been mine…That I had fathered any child, let alone a little boy who ended up in an Italian family, whom some evil person had murdered. I was half tempted to go and look into his photo face…there are photos of him everywhere at the house…to see myself lurking anywhere behind those dark eyes or his expression. The results were inconclusive. He definitely resembled Serafina, even though Lorenzo claimed that he had looked exactly the same as a young child, and either way, no one in the family had ever thought to contradict him on the matter. And, of course, even Giulio now looks very much like Dominic too. Though this time, it definitely had nothing to do with me. All so confusing and yet reassuring…for me."

"Recently though, this got me thinking a lot about the discovery of DNA again and what might be possible in the future, as regards individual testing. To think that very soon it could be possible for ordinary people to find out about their biological origins. It's very unlikely I was the baby's father, but life does play its little tricks from time to time. Yet another reason I suppose for me to leave Casa Stella…and not marry Tina. Things are clearer now. I would feel stifled. I am much better…cured…would be far too big a word…but I already have a family: Harri and her boys. Yes, I have grown to love them. Love spending time with them. I believe they feel the same. I will talk to my sister. I'm due to see her in about ten days in any case. I am and have always been a free spirit."

Chapter 40
The Unburdening

Years later.

"Thank you for seeing me, John, and at such short notice. You are looking really well by the way. As for me, it's just that for the last few months I haven't been sleeping properly, I've lost quite a bit of weight and meals have become more of a challenge. I sometimes just forget…with Carmela and Domenico no longer with us…"

Giulia made her way from the hallway into her dear friend's study and sat down on the familiar armchair, re-arranging the cushions and draping her skirt over her knees. She then took a sip at the water he had just poured out for her. In spite of the passing years, he found her as lovely as ever, her sadness today somehow adding to her other-worldly appeal. The pain in those eyes impossible to ignore.

"John, listen, I've been sitting on something for…well, for a long time now…and can't let it go, no matter how hard I've tried and recently, there's been a kind of strange development. A coming together of things. Completely by chance in fact. It's about Dominic. It's not something you can do anything about but it's got to the point that I need to tell someone. I will simply burst or go insane if I keep what I know…or think I know…to myself for any longer. Once again, only to you, can I tell such things, in the confidence that my words will never…must never…leave this room. No, let me have my say. All will become clear. This time, it's not a confession exactly, so it's not the sacrament I require, but please if only for our friendship, I'm asking you to treat it as though it were."

John's crumpled face looked both puzzled and definitely more tense than when she had first entered the room. The by now elderly priest, only too aware, that outside of the confessional, he couldn't always stay quiet, depending on the gravity of the situation, as in a court of law, for example. She would have known that too. Therefore, he would have to sit this out, hoping that things were not so serious, as Giulia was making them appear, which then soon urged him to suggest to her, "Could you not make it part of your confession, and then as your confessor, I would be bound to absolute confidentiality?"

She agreed half-heartedly since she still liked to take the necessary time for a thorough examination of conscience in preparation for the sacrament, but it seemed like the only way around it. Giulia, unable to stay quiet any longer; he was once again offering her a chance to unburden herself. From the half-open door, her friend, the priest, called out to his secretary that he would not be available for the next twenty minutes or so and then got up to close it. In this way, it meant that she could stay put, without them having to transfer to the church next door. No time to change her mind. He put on his purple stole, which turned him there and then into the holy representative of Jesus Christ. Giulia made the sign of the cross and began in the usual way.

"Bless me, Father, for I have sinned. My last confession was three weeks ago."

"You are more than aware, that for a long time, I strongly believed…I think we both did…that Dominic's murder was somehow linked to the life my father led. Well, considering what I knew at the time, never the complete picture by any means even towards the end, anyone in my position would have thought the same. However, as much as I didn't want it to be the case, even prayed and willed it not to be so, for a long time in my head, that was the only explanation I could come up with. I must add though that I was never fully convinced, and not simply out of personal convenience or to let my father off the hook. Look, I will set out my reasons."

"I've been doing a bit of research on the subject of so-called crime families from southern Italy, and over the last few months must have read every newspaper article going of their activities, in both the English and Italian press. That doesn't mean I fully understand their goings-on, so I'm definitely no expert. I've even had to force myself sometimes to stop thinking about it…it was becoming a bit of an obsession and having negative effects on my mental health. Ok, sorry, I'm not here to waste your time. I will get to the point…"

"What I never came across, in any of their grizzly crimes…was the deliberate murder of a baby, the murder of a baby, a baby snatched from its cot and strangled. Yes, of course, there has been so much brutality: family feuds, vendettas, open gang warfare on city streets, kidnappings, and yes even of children and young people. However, never to my knowledge has this involved an infant, such as Dominic, an innocent baby boy, staying overnight at his grandparents' house…Also, I am not aware that there has ever been any kind of threat to the family here, everyone simply getting on with his or her own business."

"You may remember…yes, I think I told you…that a few months ago I went to stay with a friend in the south of France…"

"As regards what happened over there, if it's ok with you, I'm not going to give the names of people, places or dates, just because in my opinion, they are irrelevant in this matter. It's really to show you what I learned from this chance experience. How I was then able to piece things together. Well, one evening we happened to go to a little bar to meet with friends, well, friends of friends really, and as we walked in it became obvious that something was going on. That is, nothing was going on…even though it was pretty crowded. Near silence. None of the usual lively chatter. Instead, everyone's face turned towards the giant television screen, which if I remember rightly, was always on but that no one bothered to watch or even notice was there. It was not World Cup season either, or San Remo…oh, I will explain San Remo another time…"

"It took me a few minutes to realise myself what the reason was. It was a programme, in the form of an interview. An attractive woman, quietly spoken and very articulate, was giving her account of what she remembered of the day her little boy, aged 3, was found dead. Murdered in his bed with nearly twenty stab wounds. Any available evidence, which included her blood-spattered pyjama bottoms pointed to the fact that only she had been there. Only she could have carried out this horrific crime. The worst unthinkable crime of all. Infanticide…"

"During the programme, she said, repeatedly and always in a dignified manner, that all she wanted was to profess her innocence and mourn the death of her little boy, and that instead, she and her family were being hounded by the media. That the murder must have happened when she was taking her older son to the end of the road…as she did every morning, less than a few minutes in all…to wave goodbye to him on the school bus. She maintained that her younger son had been asleep, and had no recollection whatsoever of a multiple stabbing…"

"Within about a year and under house arrest, as the police investigations continued, she had even given birth to a third child, another little boy. A woman, who if we believe her story, had to deal (and so it would be for the rest of her life) with her little son's death and most probably face a long custodial sentence, forced to abandon her other children. Until then, she had been a highly respected woman, a loving wife and mother, with no history of violence towards herself or others, or symptoms of mental breakdown. Her husband stayed unwaveringly loyal to her throughout, adamant that she was incapable of such a monstrous act, and as I said, they had even brought another child into the world shortly afterwards."

"Needless to say, opinions in the bar that night and already across the country as a whole fluctuated. There were those who believed that it was impossible that a sweet and lovely mother could have carried out such an atrocity. It simply went against the grain. And then there were those, even more entrenched in their position who surmised that she was a brilliantly conniving actress, lying through her teeth, using her looks and playing to the camera to muster public sympathy. Concluding that she must have murdered her son in a fit of rage, having lost control. Everyone knows how trying children can be, especially that age, they said. How was it possible that in the space of a few minutes, a crazed person could have entered the house and murdered him, which was the only explanation she could put forward? They lived in a remote mountain area…and no one strange or unfamiliar had been spotted in the village around that time. Then there was an amorphous group who just couldn't fathom what they were seeing and hearing, their own opinions changing every few days."

"Well, John, Father I mean, I couldn't make any sense of it either but if someone had held a gun to my head to get an answer out of me, then I suppose I would have chosen to believe her. It also made me question whether it is possible to accuse someone of a crime, that they have no memory of…"

"Ok, now, I somehow need to fit this story into what happened that night…all those years ago…at Casa Stella. Let's suppose for one minute that the woman was telling the truth, as she felt it. That she had no notion or memory of the murder. Could that not also be the case for Serafina? That perhaps, both as mothers, otherwise kind and loving human beings, had murdered their little sons…possibly out of built-up exhaustion, sleep deprivation, I don't know…family pressure, frustration…but that they were then, to protect their sanity I suppose, able to totally block it out completely. Such a primaeval and violent attack, totally alien to their genteel upbringing and previous behaviour."

Father John attempted to make a comment for the first time during her account so far, but Giulia was ready for him.

"I know exactly what you are about to say, Father, but there is also something else, which goes back to the night of Dominic's murder…something I have never told you about. Or anyone, come to that. Silly of me, and of course in the eyes of the church, very wrong. At that time, and I don't think I've ever told you this, James Newhouse…you do remember him, don't you…and I were lovers, and on certain nights, I used to go up to his rooms at the top of the house for greater privacy. Well, sometime during the night in question, I happened to step out onto the balcony…I don't really know why…just to catch a glimpse of the night sky, I suppose. I suddenly became aware of some movement below in the garden…and I saw Serafina…it was definitely her…running back towards the house from the direction of the pond."

"I know, by itself, it doesn't prove anything but later I was so afraid of what I had seen. I tried to put it out of my mind, convincing myself that it was all part of a dream. You know, at night under a dark sky, when fantasy and reality seem to merge or overlap. I was also head over heels in love. So, over the following weeks, I somehow managed to shut it all away, it had never happened. Deciding that I hadn't left the bed after all…and never once considered involving James."

"Why would I? Always wanting to protect the family, and that means every member of the family…Little Dominic was dead in any case. There was no way of bringing him back."

"And before you ask, no I never did say anything to the police…"

Epilogue

At the Pearly Gates…

The distant sound of an impatient-looking man clearing his throat.

My name was…Lorenzo De Martino. No, I'm going to speak in the present, otherwise it's too confusing. I only died a few minutes ago. I think it was anyway. Even though my heart has stopped beating, life doesn't feel that different. Look, do I really have to do this? You guys up here must know all this stuff already, even better than me! Ok, if I really have to then. Aged 61. Born on the 7th December. In England. To Domenico and Carmela De Martino from Italy. Menicuccio and Carmelina. Can I see them soon? My two hardworking parents, who came to England with nothing and had a tough time of it, well at least in the early days. No money, little education, no proper family behind them, no one looking out for them. For years, they struggled and sacrificed themselves for us, their children. That's what they wanted though, even when things got easier. Even after buying the delicatessen.

I will never forget them. So, as I was saying, I'm really keen to meet up with them again. That's part of the deal, huh? You know the everlasting life bit…with Jesus dying for our sins. (Pause…as he nods his head. Then looking wistful.) Just so proud and grateful for every time they went out to work for us, every meal they put on the table. The clothes they put on our backs. A roof over our heads. How they passed on family traditions, their Catholic religion, their language, even though they left Italy when they were still so young. For keeping us together, whenever the outside world tried to get in to separate us. It wasn't easy. This is the air, I breathed in as a child.

It was their way of keeping the world at bay. The faceless authority figures and all those power hungry individuals, in it just for themselves, only pretending to serve the people. Don't you agree that if all families looked after themselves, the State would be redundant?

I can't stand those superior privileged types either, or so-called intellectuals with their fancy degrees and polite manners. How they look down on the rest of us and speak with plummy accents. Who cares we don't know which is the right fork to pick up! Who needs ten forks? Who cares that we didn't go to private schools! The old school tie, the old boy network. They are no better than the rest of us. In fact, they are worse. Parasites, leeches. Living off handed down privileges and inheritances. Like they are blaming us for being poor. Like it was a choice to be bottom of the pile…

Phew! Is it ok if I sit down for a few minutes? Under this olive tree. You can still hear me, yes? This dying business is more tiring than you'd think. Was hoping for a nice rest on arrival, haha. A cappuccino say or even something a bit stronger. But if this is how it has to be…

Oh, that's better. No, it's okay. I can lean my back against here. Now where was I? My two older sisters are Patrizia and Sandra. Both still alive, in their dotage. Then, there's a younger sister who we call Tina, but it's really Immacolata. I bet that name is right up your street up here! They all outlived their brother then. Not to mention my wife, Serafina. Mother to my children Carmen, Fabrizio, and Giulio. Two boys…and a girl. All alive and well, at least when I last peered down.

The more jokey tone coming and going in waves. Calming the waters.

Never forgetting my Zia Giulia, a very old lady now, with deep wrinkles and long silver hair…We all went to live with her at Casa Stella when I was about 12. So I barely remember life without her. I guess she'll be up here soon, expounding her own life to you. That is the right word, isn't it? Well, you know what I mean…I don't often use words like that. I think Zia's sitting on a whole load of secrets…Ok, so you know all of this, but you still need to hear it straight from her, right?

Just as well I've always believed in You. Believed that there was a place waiting for me called Heaven. Like from when I was a child. You're St Peter, aren't you? You don't look much like the one in that film 'Jesus of Nazareth'. But I don't suppose the real Jesus does either, with those blue eyes. There again, you probably don't have a cinema up here, and so don't know what I'm talking about. Can't wait to meet the great guy himself. You will point him out, won't you, like if it's not obvious. Anyway, all this should stand me in good stead. Give me a head start over those pathetic agnostics and atheists, who let's face it, can't be in with much of a chance. Well, yes, Peter…never did find out your surname…those keys you've got there did kind of give it away though.

Letting out yet another quick guffaw.

Some free advice for you while I'm still here…you don't want to make it too easy for all those morons lining up behind me. Yeah, well, I know you were a simple sort of fisherman guy. Okay to call you Pete? And come to think of it, I'm right in saying that you've got a bit of a temper, haven't you? Best I stay at a safe distance. Don't want my ear chopped off or anything else, come to that! You know what I mean, don't you? They call that sort of thing 'anger management issues' these days, so I hope nothing I say starts you off. Haha. Seriously though, it must be a bit embarrassing for so-called Christians not recognising you or expecting any of this. I'm thinking of all those who've come this way before me, whoever they are, who don't know what the hell is going on, and still don't know where they are heading! It just makes me crack up…

Look, as regards my own life, let me say it as it is. Ok, so I was born with a strong personality, and I've lived by principles that have stood the test of time. Back down there on earth, we're not really given the full picture, are we? Meaning people need to have a faith to cling onto. To never give up. It's all about survival, isn't it? That's our driving force. To stay alive for as long as possible and reproduce. To go forth and multiply. That's all anyone actually knows. Sounds a bit odd now that I'm dead…It all comes from what I was saying about my parents. I want to state here and now, that I'm someone who firmly believes in male and female. It was God, the Creator Himself, who made us like that. You only have to read Genesis or even better, take a look at our bodies…

Basically, not that I'm trying to teach you or anything, even you must know it all by now, but men are born to scatter their seed. Women to stay put, give birth and raise their young. It's all there even in the animal kingdom. When you try to mix all that up, things start to go wrong. Just look at Zia Giulia, as much as I love her. She, for some crazy reason, wouldn't follow nature's rules. Didn't marry, didn't have children. Poor old Giulia, she will even die alone. All that reading and study, ramming all that knowledge into her beautiful head. All that helping others, who would have been better off sorting out their own problems. What was the point? Crazy. Some peoples' brains have got way ahead of their bodies. It's really quite simple. How long have I got? Oh, ok. No problema.

I never talked about stuff like this when I was down there, but man to man Pete, if a woman shows me she wants to have sex and I fancy her, then I'm not going to say no now, am I? I don't suppose there is much of that sort of thing up here, pity. But I don't believe a man should ever beat his wife, or worse, walk out on her and the children. For whatever reason. It's always down to the man to sort things out, to look after the family. Keep his wife sweet. His responsibility. To be strong at all times. The worst day of my life? Well, you'd think it would be when Dominic was murdered. And yep, it was up till then. I could have murdered someone myself that morning, when they came to tell me. I could have strangled Serafina with my bare hands…for not looking after him…like a mother should.

Actually, there was worse to come. Around the time he was found dead in the pond, some people might call it a twist of fate, I found out from someone at the hospital that, biologically speaking, he wasn't my son after all. Something to do with incompatible blood groups. What? How could this be? I just couldn't believe it! I went to all the trouble of flying out to that poxy village in the middle of nowhere, Sicily of all places. To find a virgin to marry. A young girl, who had led a blameless life. To be told that Dominic was not biologically mine. Why did the nurse tell me? Look, can I go into that a bit later? You must know the reason why anyway. Yeah, alright, she was getting her own back, but what she said about the blood was true. I got it checked out. A second opinion so to speak.

Dominic, that child I had named after the 'buon'anima di mio padre', Domenico! Yes, may God rest his soul. I hope you've looked after them up here, by the way. Not kept them waiting or given them a hard time. They're my parents and deserve only the best. Well, it soon dawned on me that at least I didn't have to mourn any more. Well, not for a dead son, more for my reputation like. Wherever he came from, that baby was no longer mine. Nothing to do with me, no longer my business. Never had been of course. The shock of hearing the truth took away all the pain of loss and to an extent, the shock of the murder. In an instant. I still wasn't sure what to do. So many options, but I knew I was in no fit state to make a decision while I felt like that. Like still in a state of angry confusion. I first had to calm down in order to see the light, to see reason.

You know, as regards what to do about my wife, that unfaithful bitch. I soon decided, though, that to the outside world, and I mean to everyone who knew me, everything had to look the same, including how I behaved towards her. God that was hard. I may have married a beautiful whore but at the same time, I couldn't afford to let the world know that she had turned me…me of all people…into a 'cornuto' (cuckold)! I then realised I wouldn't have to do anything at all. Life itself would take care of that. All those reminders. Day after day! Every time she would look across at her future children. Every time she heard my mention of my father's name…

Every morning, she would wake up, reliving and remembering yet again that her son was dead. How she was also to blame. Not only allowed it to happen but because she had strayed been unfaithful, whether just the once or loads of times. There was no going back…she had to go on paying the price. No one could absolve her of her sins, not even Father John. Divine providence in reverse, she was getting her just desserts. An angry God from The Old Testament. The Lord giveth and the Lord taketh away. Perhaps she didn't even know, who the real father was. How sick is that! Had just been praying that he was mine after all. That her bastard son, a fake Dominic, would turn out to look just like me. At one point, I even thought the father might be James but every time I checked to see if there were any signs of a cover-up, there was just nothing. Nothing seemed to pass between them. He wasn't really the type and I had this feeling he was more into Zia Giulia, even though she was older…

A secret that Serafina would have to take to the grave. Even more torment as she had to go on paying the price for her debauchery. All I had to do was go on being the same. I made sure I had her watched though. She never did cotton on. Oh no, there were no more lovers after that. We would have more children and fast. Genuine De Martino children. I even let her choose the name of my first real son, Fabrizio. Probably made her feel even guiltier. A sign of weakness on my part? No way! The joke was on her and she just didn't get it. Fabrizio that character from the book that she used to go on about and take everywhere. Famous for saying something like, things have to change in order to remain the same…haha! Could have written that line myself!

Well, time to stretch my legs a bit now. That's ok, isn't it? As you know, there's quite a bit more to tell you. Just need a few minutes by myself. No worries, I won't stray far…

A little later, Lorenzo returned, continuing with the account of his life. He touched on everything from the football he was so passionate about (as a staunch Juventus and Italy fan) to the secret meetings with his grandfather (Nonno Pasquale), who had set him up in the antiques business. After saying that his grandson was unfortunately 'not cut out for' another project he had been considering for him. "His loss," Lorenzo had replied, with a shrug of his shoulders. No hard feelings though. From his days working at the airport to life at home with his sisters. From listing the names of all the women, that he'd had sex with (that is, all those he could remember) to descriptions of family meals and holidays. St Peter rarely interrupted (if only with a nod or a sigh) and Lorenzo was ever confident that he would soon be entering those shimmering Pearly Gates, that beckoned just a few metres away. To take up his rightful place in the Kingdom of Heaven.

He remembered that he had to explain why the nurse had told him the truth about Dominic's paternity, knowing Peter wasn't going to let him off:

Oh yes, I said I'd come back to that…

Well, I had been seeing this nurse, sorry, can't even remember her name now, behind Serafina's back of course. But she just wouldn't take no for an answer, when I said that it was over. That my heart just wasn't in it anymore. That my first son would soon be born, kind of sensing it would be a boy. To cut a long story short, she later turned up at Casa Stella with the news that he wasn't my son after all. She had seen the medical records. I sent her packing but she turned up at the delicatessen later that evening. Begging for forgiveness. That sort of thing. Pathetic. Well, after taking her one more time against the wall in the back room…a parting gift for old times' sake (yet another questionable joke), I got her to do one last thing for me. As soon as she got the chance, to change the blood group showing on those medical records. To something that matched my own. To do it properly, so that no one could tell…I pulled a few strings and then got her a job abroad. Canada.

This turned out to be one of my best decisions to date. You can guess why, can't you? Yeh, the murder.

If the police had found out that I wasn't the real father, I'd have been a suspect, accused of the boy's murder! Would you believe it?

With God always on my side. Ha ha ha…